Flawed Perfection

Beautifully Flawed Book One

CASSANDRA GIOVANNI

SHOW N'OT TELL PUBLISHING
CONNECTICUT USA

Show n'ot Tell Publishing

Connecticut, USA

This is a work of fiction. Names, characters, places, and incidents are products of the author's imagination. Any resemblance to actual persons, living or deceased, events or locations are wholly coincidental.

PUBLISHER'S CATALOGING-IN-PUBLICATION DATA:

Giovanni, Cassandra

Flawed Perfection

ISBN: 978-0692523155

Library of Congress Control Number: 2013921763

1. Romance—Fiction. 2. Friendship—Fiction. 3. Grieving—Fiction. 4. Love—Fiction. 5. Death—Fiction. 6. Massachusetts—Fiction. I. Title

Cover Art: Gio Design Studios © 2014

For the musician who stole my heart and healed my soul

Take me to the River
The River where I'll find my heart and soul
Take me to the River
And I'll finally be whole

• FADE BURN

Chapter 1

My eyes opened at the sound of someone throwing a rock against my bedroom window. I shot up in bed and looked around the pitch black room lit only by the hot pink comforter as the sound hit again. Mom had to take my night light today of all days when there wasn't even the moon outside. There it was again, and it was definitely a rock. I slipped out of bed and went to the window. Adam was hanging in the tree next to my window, and in his hand was a glowing jar.

I glanced over my shoulder at my closed bedroom door, my ears straining to see if Mom or Dad heard the sound of the rock. My heart hammered in my chest as I lifted the window making sure it didn't squeak.

"What the hell are you doing?" I asked, my voice a harsh whisper against the silence of the night.

"I heard your mom made you get rid of the night light," Adam replied, shoving the jar into my hands. I took it and narrowed my eyes at him as he swung in the window.

"Who told you that?" I asked with my cheeks burning. I was glad for the darkness for once—because Adam couldn't see how much his presence affected me.

"Bobby! Who else?"

"What a jerk!" I said. I watched as Adam shrugged and pulled two more jars from his backpack. "I couldn't fit them all in. I didn't realize how hard it was to climb a tree with one arm!"

"What's in these?" I asked as Adam set them on the ground, and the room began to dance with the light. Thankfully, my cheeks had returned to a natural hue, but as soon as his eyes rose I felt the burn rising, and I had to look away.

Adam was in my room in the middle of the night.

"Fireflies," he replied, and my eyes snapped back towards him watching as his thin lips turned into that crooked smile.

My jaw dropped as I took a step forward. "You put *what* in these?"

Adam's brow furrowed over his face.

"I spent an hour catching fireflies for you," he said, and I watched as his throat rose and fell as he swallowed. "Don't worry—I poked holes in the top."

He moved closer to me, so I could smell his cologne—the one I'd bought him for his sixteenth birthday a few days earlier. I tried to hide the deep breath I took of him as he moved my fingers across the metal top, so I could feel the holes he poked there. He smirked at me again with his fingers still over mine. I could feel the calluses from playing guitar; ones I'd felt a thousand times before as he leaned over me and tried his best to teach me how to strum.

"You know I'd never hurt your precious fairies, Riv."

I couldn't help but giggle. The heat rushed up to my face

again, and it only worsened when I realized not only was Adam in my room, he snuck in to save me from the dark.

"Thank you," I said. "But how can I keep them?"

Adam shrugged. "I did think of that *after* I'd caught them."

He reached into his backpack and pulled out a butterfly with what looked like liquid in its abdomen. He went to the outlet by the bed and plugged it in.

"It goes off in the morning—so your mom will just think it's one of those scenty things you chicks love so much." He looked over his shoulder before sitting on my bed. "The real issue is what to do with the fireflies now."

My eyes moved from his to the window he came through. "Let them go?"

I watched Adam's eyes flash over mine, and I knew he was coming up with some devilish plan—one I'd go along with, like always. I never could say no to him or his brother, Bobby, for that matter. He turned and grabbed a few of the stuffed animals from the chair by the bed and stuck them under the sheets, so it looked like there was a body.

"What are you thinking?" I asked, my breathing quickening as he came over and took the jars I wasn't holding and put them back in his bag. He then took the one I was holding and put it in the spot where the night light had been.

"It would've been a lot easier to carry the night light!" he said as he slipped it over his shoulders and ducked out the window.

I followed him and leaned out the window. "Adam!"

He sat on the limb below holding his hand out to me. "I

promise I won't let you fall," he said, and I couldn't deny the rush that streamed through my veins.

Adam would be the death of me. I followed suit and slid down onto the limb into his arms. They wrapped protectively around me, keeping me from falling, and my eyes wandered from his chest up to his brown eyes. They glowed under the light of the moon as he smiled down at me, and I could feel my pulse quickening.

"One section at a time, just follow my lead," he said, and before I could respond he was shimming down the tree.

I took a deep breath before proceeding, but when I was at the last limb, I looked down at him. I closed my eyes as the ground spun and my stomach twirled.

"Adam, it's too far!" I said as quietly as possible.

"I'll catch you!"

I pried my lids open as I shook my head and he nodded his.

"River!"

"Fine!" I replied as I closed my eyes and let go.

"See?" Adam said as his arms wrapped around my waist.

"Fine," I mumbled, unable to hide the smile that had crept onto my face from the adrenaline rush. His hand slipped easily into mine, and my heart faltered for a moment before my gaze locked on his.

"We should go to where I got them—the lake."

"What if we get caught?"

Adam raised his eyebrows. "Not going to happen, Riv."

"You'll get your new car taken away!"

"Bobby sneaks out all the time, and he never gets in trouble!" Adam said, and we both scoffed.

Bobby was the golden boy—he could do whatever he wanted. Adam was not—he was the boy all the girls wanted, including me—but he always had a wall around his heart.

"He's older than you," I replied.

"Two years, big whoop!"

I stared at him, my chest rising to my chin and he wriggled his eyebrows. There was no convincing him otherwise. Both Beckerson boys were stubborn, especially when it came to me—their best friend. I didn't want him to get in trouble again because of me, but that smile was melting me.

I looked up at the star-filled sky and nodded. "Let's get this over with!"

"Yes, Ma'am," Adam replied as he handed me the backpack and leaned forward so that I could jump on his back.

"Go, Adam!" I laughed as he ran forward. The worry faded as his arms tightened around my thighs.

TEN YEARS LATER

I yawned as I closed the laptop and blinked at the television clock – 10:00 PM – I hadn't even eaten yet. I began to stand, but dropped back down on the couch when I heard the giggle from across the hall; it was accompanied by a laugh I knew all too well, and the slam of the door. I opened my eyes and looked at the ceiling of my apartment. I should have been used to hearing Adam making other girls laugh like that by now, but I wasn't, and I knew I never would be.

I should have stopped caring years before. I should never have fallen in love with my best friend.

My hand flew to my chest as I jolted back to reality with the sound of the wood door vibrating as a fist knocked up against it. I took a deep breath to calm the now frantic beating of my heart before standing and slowly opening the door.

"Hey," Bobby said, his head leaning against the firm curve of his arm. "Can I spend the night here? I can't stand listening to his raucous lovemaking again."

"I was about to see if you wanted to split a pizza with cheesy breadsticks with me," I answered, signaling for him to come in.

I shut the door, and Bobby's frame towered over me, arms crossed, and his lips tipped downwards in displeasure. "What's wrong?"

I shook my head, and he reached out to put his hands on my hips. His eyes were tender as he lowered his head. "Pizza and cheesy breadsticks, Riv? I *know* something is wrong."

This close and my heart remained slow and steady as I stared up into his blue eyes. It reminded me it would be so much easier if I had fallen in love with the other brother; the one towering over me like he wanted to kiss me.

I pulled away and rolled my shoulders. "I'm fine."

"That's it, isn't it? You still love Adam?" Bobby asked as I walked over to the coffee table to grab my cell phone. I clenched my jaw as I stared at the space where he'd been standing. I admitted it years before, but from then on we only danced around the subject, mainly because I didn't want to talk about it with him.

I avoided the L-word like I always did, turning and smiling at him. "What do you want on your pizza?"

He narrowed his eyes. "You know my toppings."

"Hawaiian pizza it is."

That wasn't his toppings, but I knew he'd eat whatever I ordered without complaint.

He blinked at me several times before flopping on the couch. It groaned at his weight but somehow didn't fold. His hockey player frame didn't fit in much of the contemporary furniture in my place.

"Are you sure you want to sleep on the couch? Your body hangs off of it," I said as he stretched out and his legs stuck half-way over the edge.

A smirk came to his face as he put his arms behind his head with a thought I was sure I didn't want to know. "Where else would I sleep?" he asked.

"I suggest we *trade*. I'll take the couch, and you can take my bed," I answered with a nod across the room to my bedroom door.

"Alright, sounds good to me."

"Pervert," I said under my breath as I walked past him to go to grab him a beer from the fridge.

"It's not my fault you look like that," he said as I handed him the drink.

I ignored him and called to the order the pizza.

"Twenty minutes," I informed Bobby as he flipped to the hockey channel.

"So why are you alone on a Friday night?" Bobby asked as he knocked back the remainder of his beer and stood to grab another.

"You're going to wipe me out," I commented, avoiding the question as he closed the fridge.

He held up a can of soda. "One beer limit when I'm with you."

"At least someone follows my rules," I replied, smiling at him.

"You know it! I'll always follow your rules, Riv."

The commented was pointed, and I wondered why I couldn't love him back. I looked over his broad, muscular, hockey player frame, messy light brown hair and sky blue eyes. He was hot; there was no denying that, but when he touched me I didn't feel a spark. I only felt the tenderness of a friendship that began as children. Adam was so different than Bobby, yet I found myself constantly dating guys just like Bobby.

They were safe. They didn't make my heart race or my body flush with heat from just looking at me and smiling.

"So why are *you* alone on Friday night?" I asked.

Bobby grabbed my arm and pulled me up before moving me onto the couch beside him.

"I'm not alone. I'm with you," he replied, and his voice was a purr against my neck. His warm breath washed over my skin but did nothing to my insides.

I turned and smacked his chest. "Shut up!"

He winked at me before saying, "Careful, you don't want to break your hand on my pecs!"

"You and Adam are one in the same with your cockiness," I teased as I pulled my legs up to my chest.

"But different in so many ways," Bobby replied as his eyes washed over me again. The comment made me swallow.

"You're weird; you know that?" I replied as I locked my eyes on the television and pretended to be interested in it.

I was used to his half-hearted attempts at swooning me by now. He never directly came out and made any move. He just tried to nudge me gently in his favor, but the look in his eyes showed he knew it was a losing battle. There was a tease there, but it was flecked with sadness that showed in the twitch of his lips.

A knock came at the door, and our eyes unlocked from one another.

"Pizza!" Bobby cheered as he jumped up and went to the door. He pulled out his wallet just as I stood to go to my purse. He shook his head as he said, "This one's on me. I drink half the beer you buy anyway."

He opened the door and took the boxes of steaming food before handing the guy a twenty. A typical man nod was exchanged.

"Thanks, bro," the pizza guy said.

"Have a good one," Bobby replied with his voice deep.

I could never understand how both Adam and Bobby's voices changed when they talked to someone other than me. It deepened to a gruff, manly octave that, while I didn't understand it, I found attractive.

"You want another soda?" I asked as the smell wafted over me, and my stomach grumbled.

"Sure thing."

"I swear to God you must have the biggest bladder on the planet," I said as I handed him the can and sat down beside him.

"Don't forget my appetite. You only asked me over because you're only going to eat one piece, and you don't want this thing to go to waste."

"Technically, you invited yourself over."

"I thought you were coming to ask me anyway or were you looking for Adam?"

His lips were in a smile, but I could see the muscles in his arms tensing at his question.

I put my head on his shoulder. "No, I was looking for my teddy bear of a best friend."

I lifted my head at his still displeased look and frowned in question.

"Who's your better best friend, Adam or me?" Bobby asked, staring at me from the corner of his eyes.

"Come on Bobby! You know it's different with Adam."

He nodded in defeat. "Yeah, I know."

I knocked my shoulders against his. "Eat your pizza and shut up. Either way, your mom still hates me with the fire of a thousand burning suns."

Bobby smirked. "That she does, especially since you've got both of her boys tied in knots."

"Both of you?"

"Err...with having a best friend who's a chick. Screws up relationships like no tomorrow."

I narrowed my eyes at him, but he grabbed a piece of

pizza and took a bite. He smiled at me with his mouth full, and I conceded, taking a slice too. If Bobby knew Adam had feelings for me, he would've told me long ago, wouldn't he?

Chapter 2

It was like clockwork; the second I remembered how much Adam and Bobby's mom hated me, I would be roped into a block party, family party, or some other occasion that would remind me I was right. Their mom did despise my existence.

Even if the boys hadn't begged me to go, I'd still have to; after all, our families were practically one. We'd grown up almost every second of our lives with each other—our moms were best friends, and we even spent holidays at one another's houses. Getting out of a party like this was damned near impossible when my parents would want me to be at it, too. I could say no to them about as much as I could say no to the Beckerson boys.

The forty-five-minute drive had droned on in silence as I pouted over the idea in the backseat of Adam's VW.

Finally, I spoke up, "How did I get roped into this again?"

Adam looked over his shoulder at me and winked, sending a tingle up my spine. "I need your support. You know how it is."

"What does that mean?" Bobby asked, and I pushed my knee a little further into his back.

He knew what it meant.

"You're the favorite. River makes it easier to take their bullshit digs at me. I can't wait to hear what they say about my new job," Adam replied, and his voice showed the venom he rarely demonstrated towards Bobby.

"There's no favorite, man, that's all in your head," Bobby answered.

Adam looked over at me again, and I shrugged. The acknowledgment passed between us that there certainly was a favorite.

Adam's family held Bobby on a pedestal for his sports achievements, which eventually led to an injury that made it so he could never play hockey again. Still, as the hockey coach at the local high school he was a legend in everyone's eyes. From the backseat, the comparison between the two of them was almost laughable.

Bobby was in the seat in front of me, leaving me no room for my legs because he had to push the seat almost all the way back. His head was also only inches away from the ceiling of the small GLI.

Adam had a smaller frame; he looked like an average human in the car. Adam was nothing to laugh at, though; he still had muscles that would, and did, make any girl drool. It was just a difference in taste.

"At least your mom doesn't hate you," I said as I grimaced at the thought, sinking deeper into my seat.

"Mom doesn't hate you!" both Adam and Bobby said in unison.

"Sure," I said to myself. "That's not what you said the

other day Bobby—something about having a best friend as a chick messes up everything."

"Well, she doesn't. I was just teasing," Bobby said, glancing over and locking his blue eyes on mine.

"Yeah, she's just afraid you're going to lure Bobby into your sex trap," Adam teased.

"Shut up, man!" Bobby went to punch Adam, but I gripped his shoulder.

"I think if I wanted to lure him, I would've by now," I said.

If only I knew how. I shook the thought from my head as I felt Bobby's muscles relax underneath my touch. I patted his shoulder before I sat back in my seat.

"Here we are," Adam said as he parked the car on the curb behind the others.

It was the block-party for the neighborhood, and I knew despite my parents move outside of the area that they would be here, too. I really had no excuse to not come—besides I really didn't want to. I never enjoyed the anxiety of worrying about what would happen next, or what would be said next about Adam or me. We seemed to be easy targets.

Bobby jumped out of the car and headed up the road as soon as the car stopped while Adam and I lagged behind.

"I hate these things," Adam said, his hands still white on the steering wheel as he looked straight ahead.

I leaned over and put my chin on his shoulder.

"It won't be that bad. I'll be here with you," I reminded him.

Adam turned his head and kissed my cheek. "You

always save the day, Riv." His voice was soft, and it caught me off guard. I could feel the heat rushing up my neck to my face.

"I try to be superwoman," I replied, flustered, as I leaned back and struggled to open the door.

Adam chuckled, and I heard a click as he hit a button. "Superwoman can handle my crazy family but not a child safety lock."

I stuck my tongue out at him as he got out and then came around to help me with my door.

"It's not my fault your doors hate me," I said as he opened the door, and the summer air hit me full in the face.

Adam clicked the button on the remote locking the doors and slung his arm around my waist. I was suddenly glad for the warmth of the sun; it was an excuse for the flush that came over my face at his touch.

"My mom is going to have a heart attack when she sees you cut off all your hair," he said.

"She's going to say I look like a boy," I answered, hanging my head, so my asymmetrical bob titled, pushing my bangs into my face.

He dropped his arm, shaking his head as he stopped in front of me and tilted my chin back up, so my hair was no longer covering my face. "You don't look like a boy," he said as his eyes danced over my face.

"Thanks?" I said as I told myself to keep breathing.

I am still breathing, right?

I steadied my heartbeat with a smile before adding, "We

can take whatever she has to say together. She's going to hate my hair and hate your job."

Adam's eyes drifted from my eyes to my lips and then to my hair before he replied, "I love your hair and my job."

"Then there's nothing she can say to us, is there?" I replied.

He didn't mean anything by the comment. He was my best friend. He just was being a supportive best friend—he wasn't flirting with me, was he?

He tucked a strand of hair behind my ear. "Nothing."

God damn it! He was good at making me feel like I was the only woman in the world. This was the reason I was trapped in a never ending cycle of meaningless relationships. I didn't really want a relationship if it wasn't with Adam; in fact, having one had just become a defense mechanism for when Adam and I fought. Then again, basically the only time we fought was about each other's relationships.

"Ready?" I asked Adam, and he slipped his hand into mine in response, squeezing it before he dropped it to open the gate.

"What took you so long?" Bobby yelled, coming from across the yard with two beers and a wine cooler.

"For you," he said as he handed me the wine cooler.

Bobby scowled at Adam before giving him the other beer. "The parents are over yonder."

"Might as well get it over with," I muttered to Adam.

He winked at me, his hand suddenly soft on the small of my back.

"Together," he whispered, and his breath sent my heart racing.

"There's my girl!" Dad greeted, sweeping me into his arms as if I weighed nothing.

He planted a kiss on my forehead as he set me back on the ground. "It's been too long!"

"Dad, it's been three weeks," I replied, scuffing my foot against the ground with averted eyes.

"Three weeks too long!" Mom said as she pulled me into her arms. My body tensed beneath her; no matter how hard I tried I was never truly comfortable with her. She may have been my mom, but it was hard for me to be myself around her—or any of the people here except for Adam and Bobby. I pulled away and tucked my hair behind my ears, watching as Adam's dad greeted him with a nod.

"Son," his dad, Alec, said.

"Dad." Adam returned the coldness.

"Adam!" his mom squealed, yanking him into her arms.

I stifled my laugh as he crossed his eyes as if she were squeezing him to death.

"Hi Mom," he wheezed as he pulled away and tapped his chest.

I shook my head at him, and his smile dimpled his cheeks. His mom looked between the two of us, stopping at me with a glare. When her gaze returned to Adam, I mouthed, *hates me*.

Adam put one hand over his mouth and cupped his elbow with his hand to hide his amusement. He shook his head, *no*.

I nodded, and his raised eyebrows told me to stop.

"How's the marketing firm, River?" Adam's dad now addressed me.

I always felt awkward calling him by his name, but he would remind me he wasn't old enough to be a Mr. if I used the proper formality.

"It's great, Alec. I just pulled a few more Fortune 500 companies in with my branding plan," I explained.

"You're too smart," Alec said.

"For her own good," Adam's mom, Vickie, added under her breath.

Bobby had joined the group and shot her a look of displeasure.

She shrugged as if innocent.

"Lorie tells me you have a new job, Adam, is that right?" Dad jumped in to change the subject away from me, but only targeted the next weakest link instead.

"You got a job?" Alec's surprise showed not only in his tone but in his sudden movement towards Adam.

"Yeah," Adam replied, eyes averted as he rolled his sleeves up further.

"And?" Vickie pushed.

"I'm using my degree," he answered, and he looked up at me, his eyes darkening.

"Ha!" Alec said, head jerking back. "Doing what? Teaching fairies how to sing?"

I felt my fists clench at my side as I watched Adam's eyes moved from mine to glare at his dad. His voice was flat as he replied, "I'm teaching little kids how to play music at a private school. It pays well."

"It better for how shameful it is," Alec said.

This wasn't going to end well. Adam's face was red, and his jaw worked as he tried to come up with a response. Instead his hand went to the back of his neck and he swallowed, hurt flitting through his eyes as they met mine. My chest tightened as the pain built in the silence. I couldn't hold my tongue.

"How is it shameful?" I asked, turning to Alec with my sweaty palms pressed against my legs. My parent's eyes landed on me, protruding as they begged me silently to shut up. I stepped forward and looked up at Alec. "How?"

It was Alec's turn to fidget in his discomfort. "River, now you know I didn't mean it like that. It's just not—"

"As manly as Bobby's job teaching kids to do a sport that will eventually disable them, just like it did him?"

Adam was staring at me in shock, just like everyone else. I'd hit more than just Alec below the belt; I insulted Bobby too.

"What I mean is there is nothing wrong with Adam's choice of career. He changes kid's lives just like Bobby does."

Bobby's arms were crossed over his chest as he looked at me with a frown. He was thinking about what I'd said. He knew I was right.

"All I'm saying is I didn't expect my kid to become a teacher, especially not a music teacher," Alec said.

"What's wrong with him being a music teacher?" Vickie finally spoke up.

"Come on darling, did you really think Adam was going to waste our money on a degree to be a teacher? He could've done a girly sport like, you know, soccer or something, but instead he plays the guitar," Alec replied.

Vickie frowned but didn't say anything more to defend Adam.

"I'm still here," he said through clenched teeth before turning away.

"Have you ever watched him play?" I asked.

Alec's brows pulled together as Vickie looked down at her dress and smoothed an imaginary wrinkle.

"How many hockey games have you gone to?" I pushed, my nails biting into my palms as my body tensed.

"Every single one," Alec replied as he tilted his chin up.

I looked up at the sky, loosening my hands, so my palms faced up as I shook my head. "Think about that."

I stormed off after Adam. It only took me a matter of minutes to find him leaning against the hood of his white car, hands on his knees.

"Hey," I said, sitting down beside him as my pulse quieted.

"You know how often I wonder if I was born to the wrong family?" Adam asked, looking up at me.

I put my head on his shoulder. "I think you're perfect the way you are."

"I'll never really be a part of my family," he said as he hung his head.

I turned to face him, and he looked up, lips curved in a sad smile.

"Are you happy with who you are?"

Adam shrugged. "Yeah, but it doesn't change how they view me...I'm a failure because of my career choice, and I'm a failure because of what I look like. I'll always be in Bobby's shadow—" he let out a painful chuckle; "literally."

I shook my head, taking a step forward and wishing I could say something that would change the way he felt. "Stop—you're fine the way you are."

He raised an eyebrow as he twisted his watch around his wrist. "Who are you kidding? I have muscles because I'm not a big dude...Bobby's freaking Chippendales, and I'm Abercrombie and Fitch!"

"If that's what you're into."

Adam's eyebrow went up again. "Really, when was the last time you dated someone like me?"

I'd drop every single one of them for a chance to date Adam. I broke up with every single one of them *because* of Adam.

"Come on! As if you have any trouble getting girls! I've seen you with a different girl every week since you were six-teen."

His eyes went to his hands, and he picked at his cuticles. "Yeah, but not girls like—" he looked up at me and swal-lowed. "I don't know."

I couldn't seem to breathe as his eyes locked on mine. A part of me wanted to tell him how much I loved him, and how much seeing him like this, doubting himself, hurt—but

I just couldn't bring myself to do it. "Don't let them make you feel less worthy of their family—you're going to change kid's lives every day."

"With musical instruments?"

"I remember the first time I saw you teach a kid something on guitar...it was after one of your concerts at school. One of your friend's brothers was in awe of you. You taught him how to play a few chords...It was incredible. That's why when you told me about this job I thought it was perfect for you."

Adam leaned back with a smile—the one that always swept me off my feet.

"It's pretty impressive, isn't it?"

I nodded, and he wrapped his arms around me in a tight embrace. My senses filled with his cologne—still the one from when we were kids— before he pulled away, hands slipping down to the small of my back. "You're such an amazing girl...you know that? What would I do without you?"

I felt lightheaded as his head tilted down, forehead pressed against mine, and his warm breath washed over me.

The closeness was driving me insane, and my fingertips ached to brush across his jaw line. I clenched my fists to prevent the action before whispering back, "I'm sure you'd survive."

"I doubt that," he said, his voice deepening.

"Adam!" a girl called from across the street.

Adam pulled away from me, and his hand found the back of his neck.

"Oh, hi Amber," he said.

She jumped into his arms and kissed him while I stood back in shock, my body trembling with sudden jealousy.

Who the hell was this chick?

Adam managed to peel the well-endowed blonde off of him.

"Um...River this is my friend Amber."

Friend? I saw stars. *Friend?*

He coughed, his hand stuck in an awkward position in his hair.

"Right, friend. Amber. Nice," I said as I tried to control my temper. "Great choice."

I turned away and headed back to the party as the happiness disappeared as quickly as it had come. It was always like this; I felt something was changing, and then some bimbo would come into the picture, messing everything up—or just bringing me back to reality.

"Riv! River!" Adam called to my back.

"What's her problem?" Amber's high-pitched voice cut into me.

She was my problem and every other skank he dragged in at the wrong time. I was reading too much into it anyway, but this time, it *did* feel different—like whatever wall we'd built up around our relationship was coming down.

"Hey," Bobby called, his body slung over the white picket fence. "Why do you look so sullen?"

I shook my head. "Look, Bobby..."

"I'll be mad at you in the morning; right now you look like a Mack truck hit you." Bobby's eyes wandered to behind me, where I could hear Blondie's laughter mixing with Adam's deep voice—the one he used for everyone else. "Oh, right."

Bobby's face reddened as his nostrils flared. "On second thought—I'll stay pissed at you right now."

I was trapped as the tears began running down my face. Adam didn't love me, and Bobby did. Adam hurt me, I hurt Bobby. It was a vicious cycle I couldn't break. I didn't want to face the party with my mascara stained across my cheeks, and I couldn't move backwards with Adam and the giggle bitch behind me. Their voices were coming closer. I was screwed, either everyone saw my tears or Adam did.

"River, going in?" Adam asked as he and Amber came up beside me, and he opened the gate.

When he turned, his smile froze on his face.

"What did Bobby do?" he growled, his neck reddening.

"Nothing, he's mad for what I said to him. He has a right to be. Can you find my Dad and ask him if he can take me home?" I asked.

My hands formed fists at my side as more tears slipped freely from my eyes. I couldn't stop them now as the shock and irritation from the blowout with their parents, then Bobby and the high from Adam's attention mixed.

"How about I just bring you home? Bobby can find a ride," he said, and Amber huffed beside him.

"What about your date?" I asked, avoiding eye contact with her.

"Yeah, what about me?" Amber chimed in, hands on hips.

"You invited yourself, have fun." Adam ushered her away with his hand; his eyes still locked on my now hiccupping figure.

"What the fuck Adam? Is that any way to treat me?" Amber batted away his hand.

"My best friend is upset. You want me to have a party?" Adam asked as he turned to face her. I grit my teeth—another scene because of me. I didn't know why I came to these things when this was always what happened.

"For Heaven's sake," I said, pushing past him towards my parents.

"River, I can take you home!" he shouted at my back.

"Dad, drive me home?" I interrupted the conversation he and Alec were having.

Mom and Vickie glanced over at me. Vickie's smile widened at my face.

"Yeah," Dad answered looking down at me; "of course, dear."

"I'll be back in a little bit," he told Alec before wrapping his arm around my shoulders.

It was funny how he said a little bit when I lived an hour away without traffic.

"Are you okay?" Dad whispered in my ear as I wiped my face.

"You know how these things always get," I explained.

I saw Adam watching me out of the corner of my eye. Amber was hanging on him and kissing his neck as if nothing happened. He shrugged her away, and she pouted at him, but he ignored her, starting towards me. I shook my head stopping him, and his brows furrowed, wrinkling his forehead in a pained expression.

He knew better than to press the limits, though I doubted he understood why I was so upset.

Chapter 3

It was easy to avoid Adam for the next few days because he hadn't started work yet, so he was never up when I was. Bobby, on the other hand, was a different story. We went to work at the same time and usually made a point of walking each other down to the parking lot, but somehow he avoided me as much as I avoided him.

I knew I'd been wrong, and I had serious damage control to do. He was so many levels of pissed at me, and he had a right to be about at least one thing. I took a cheap shot at his job, but I knew more than anything it was the fact I defended Adam over him that ticked him off.

I made a point of getting ready early, but somehow still managed to miss Bobby. When I pulled into the lot after work, I sat waiting for Bobby's car to appear. When it did, I crept out of mine and waited for him to park and get out. When he did I raced across the lot, my heels clicking on the pavement and my pencil skirt threatening to come loose at the seams.

"Bobby! Don't you dare ignore me one more second!" I yelled.

He turned, eyes widening as I flung myself at him in what could only be called sexy work apparel.

"Now, this is the kind of apology I wanted!" He chuckled to himself as I came to a stop in front of him, gasping for breath.

"I'm sorry. You know I didn't mean it!" I said, grabbing his elbow for support.

"You're going to have blisters on your feet now," he replied, looking me over.

"And my silk blouse is going to be ruined with my sweat. Big deal," I said as I finally caught my breath and stood.

"You look beautiful," he began with a lopsided grin; "especially running towards me in *that*."

"I had to get your attention somehow, didn't I?"

He slipped his arm around me and pulled my chest into his. "Attention gotten."

I rolled my eyes at him as I pushed my hands into his chest. "If that wasn't a direct hit, I don't know what was."

"Hey, I had to try. You just flung yourself at me," he said with a playful nudge in my ribs.

I shook my head. "You know better."

"So, an apology?" he asked, running his hand through the length of his hair as we began to make our way up to the apartments.

"Look, you know I was only trying to defend Adam—"

"At my expense?"

"You know I didn't mean it as you took it, but that's the way your parents see things. They don't think Adam has accomplished anything because he's not the spitting image of you or your dad. You know it's true."

"It's not true, River! Adam just makes you think it is. He has you so wrapped around his finger—"

I turned, practically causing him to mow me down as I poked my finger in his chest."Do you think Adam's a failure?"

Bobby's strong jaw was taut. "No."

"Do your parents?"

"River—"

"No, answer the question, do they ever brag about Adam? Or is it always about you?" I demanded. When he didn't answer, I continued, "Think of how that makes Adam feel. He's been nothing but successful, but no matter what he does he's always in your shadow."

"He still has things I want that I can't have," he answered, his eyes burning into me.

I closed my eyes. Adam didn't want me – he wanted big-boobed blondes like Amber.

"This isn't about us," I said, opening my eyes and locking my gaze with his.

I felt Bobby's hand lift my chin. "I know it's not, but I always make it that way. It's hard for me not to."

I opened my eyes to see his lips turned downward as he shrugged. "I give up, Riv. I'm sorry."

"You don't think what we have is special? I do! I'm sorry it's not what you want, but you're my best friend—you both are."

He leaned down and kissed my forehead.

"I know; what other girls would let me crash on her couch and special order me hockey games?"

"Exactly, and who do you talk about your girl problems with?" I reminded him as he dropped my chin.

"Alright, you've got me. It *is* pretty awesome," he said.

"I'm making pasta tonight with meatballs from scratch. It'd be a lot easier if I could cook for two instead of one?"

Bobby's stomach growled its response.

Chapter 4

Not talking to Adam was killing me. I had Bobby to talk to, but there were some things I just didn't speak to him about—like work. He never understood, because his job was like play to him. He didn't understand why I did what I did because he didn't think anyone could love it. He thought it was boring and made a point of telling me that. He said the only benefit was the hot outfits he got to see me in. With Adam it was different, Bobby was my friend to hang out with and have fun; Adam was my serious friend, the one I shared in-depth conversations with. I hadn't had a serious conversation in three days.

I missed Adam. A lot. I was avoiding him because I didn't want to have to explain what about Amber arriving made me so upset. Logically, from Adam's perspective, there probably was nothing about the situation that *should* have upset me.

Besides the fact, I was utterly head over heels for him.

I shook the thought out of my head and concentrated on the sweat dripping down my forehead as I entered the most difficult part of the dance workout. I closed my eyes for a second, doing the moves to the music from heart as I let the rhythm sink into me. I heard my door swing open and assumed it was Bobby, so I kept dancing in my skimpy booty shorts and sports bra. It wasn't anything Bobby hadn't seen before. Bobby was my beach buddy.

When I opened my eyes, mid belly roll, I found a squeal escaping from my lips. Adam stood, arms crossed, one eyebrow up, and dimples deep in his cheeks with a smile.

"Wow, so that's what you do this early in the morning, hmm?" he asked as he headed towards the fridge.

He was shirtless still, in his cotton pajama bottoms with his hair mussed from sleeping. I tried to concentrate on something other than his lightly sculpted abdomen, and then when he turned the indents on his back where his hips caught my stare. I was going to die a happy woman with that imagery.

He turned milk carton in hand and flicked it open.

"Don't you dare!" I said, darting across the room at him.

He knew how much I hated it when he drank straight from the carton, but that didn't seem to matter to him. As I charged him, he grabbed me by my sweaty waist and twirled me, taking a big gulp.

"You asshole!" I said as he pushed me against the counter so I couldn't reach him. I was smiling, though, and he knew he won because I stopped struggling.

He wiped his upper lip before placing the carton down, hand still just below the band of my sports bra. His eyes wandered down to my low-rider workout shorts, hand lowering slowly. "How come you never told me about that?" he asked as he flipped his arm, placing it against the skin of my hip, so the tattoo on his forearm was directly next to mine.

"I swear to God it wasn't on purpose!" I said, voice almost inaudible as I watched his eyes widened.

My head felt too tight from the sudden pounding of blood. What must he be thinking? My breath caught in my throat, and it came out in a whoosh as he smiled up at me.

"No wonder Bobby flipped shit on me when he saw mine," he replied straightening. His eyes wandered back to my bare hips.

"Yeah, he came with me that day. He was upset already because I didn't choose the butterfly he liked. I saw this one and loved it instantly," I explained, watching as he reached forward and began to outline the stars with the tip of his finger. My skin was on fire with his touch, and I fought the urge to close my eyes and moan.

"I love the colors in yours," he said. His fingers stopped tracing the outline, and he took a step away from me.

He looked down at his tattoo, which happened to be the same set of nautical stars. The only difference was his were baby and navy blue while mine were lilac and dark purple.

He leaned back against the island that separated the kitchen and living room, elbows resting on the counter.

"Explain something?" he asked.

I nodded. "What?"

"Why didn't you tell me?"

"Honestly...I was embarrassed. I thought you might think I did it on purpose."

He looked up from his feet, eyes melting into mine. "I

can't tell you the rage that Bobby went into. He punched a hole in the wall! I thought he was just pissed I went and got it without him—that I'd do something like that without talking to him. He was jealous, though."

I shrugged, trying to act nonchalant even though my heart was beating out of control. "He doesn't like our relationship."

"I don't like your relationship with him either," he said, and my head jerked back in response.

"Why?"

It was his turn to shrug. "Sometimes I get jealous. You're more willing to do things with him than me, for example, you won't ever go to the beach with me...and I bet from that toned body you'd make a mean beach volleyball player. I could use another person on my team."

That toned body? I liked the way he said it. My whole body felt too hot. It was as if he enjoyed it.

I blushed, and unable to hold his gaze anymore, I looked away. "I'll make you a deal, next time you're going to go to the beach with the boys I'll go with you."

"Really?" Adam leaned forward, a wide grin coming across his face.

Breathe, River – breathe!

"Yeah," I said.

"This weekend it is." Adam looked at me and then to the time on the microwave. "Don't you need to get ready for work soon?"

"Shit!" I said as I turned and looked at the time. I would barely be able to take a shower.

"Sorry." He cringed, but the smirk stayed on his face as he took the milk and headed towards the door. "I need this for my cereal."

"You're such an ass!" I yelled as I went towards my bathroom.

"River?"

"Yes," I replied, turning with my hands at the bottom of my bra ready to lift it over my head.

Adam blinked twice, swallowed, and continued, "What are you doing tonight?"

"Nothing?"

"I need someone to help me pick out a new wardrobe for work. I have no clue what a teacher wears, or what it's supposed to look like. Would you mind coming to the mall tonight and helping?" He ran his teeth over his bottom lip as if I would say no.

"Sure, what time you picking me up?"

"How about we make it a date—I'll bring you out to dinner first, we can pick my clothes out and then catch a movie?"

My skin tingled as I repeated the word, "A date?"

He shrugged. "Not a date, date... you know what I meant."

Of course, I knew what he meant. I was just off in la-la land again.

"Yeah, like always."

He smiled at me, and I smiled back before turning into my bathroom and leaning my head back against the door.

What was wrong with me?

Chapter 5

I stood assessing myself in the mirror Adam bought me for my twenty-first birthday. It was a welcome to the apartment building gift after him and Bobby coerced me into moving across the hall from them. They had just moved in, and the day the location opened up they were dragging me to meet the owner of the building. It hadn't even been posted in the paper, and I already had the keys. Adam bought me the full-length mirror because the frosted flowers and butterflies reminded him of me. What the hell he was doing in the designer furniture store he found it in was beside me.

I ran my fingers over the butterfly with a smile as I looked at my outfit and took a deep breath. It wasn't a date, but I sure as hell wasn't going to look like it. I'd put on my best dark-wash skinny jeans, wedge booties, and a green sequin tank top that pulled the green out of my gray eyes.

Adam never knocked on the door, but I heard it swing open before he flopped on the sofa. I smiled to myself as I applied mascara and then stuck my head out of the bathroom door.

"Just invite yourself in," I said, and Adam looked up from his cell phone.

"Wow, you look beautiful as always," Adam said as his eyes went up and down my body. When they came up to my face, a chill ran down my spine.

Somehow I still managed to find my voice. "I figured I'd make you some good arm candy tonight. You ready?"

He nodded. "Crap, I'm lucky. It's a good thing I chose you to dress me."

"Yes," I nodded; "You do have good taste."

Adam placed his hand on the small of my back as we headed down the stairs. When we reached the front door, he held it for me, still smiling as he looked at me.

"What?" I asked, pressing my lips together to keep from smiling like an idiot. I could get used to him staring at me like that.

"Nothing. I'm just grateful you're willing to help me."

"I know it's a sore subject, but why didn't you ask Amber to help you?" I asked as we neared his white VW.

He looked over at me, and his lips pursed before he slid into the car and said, "I think it's more of a sore subject for you."

I rolled my tongue into my cheek and inhaled a long breath as I kept in the words I wanted to say.

"You really don't like her, huh?" he asked as he placed his arm around my seat, looking over his shoulder to back up the car.

"I don't like any of your girlfriends. You have bad taste," I said.

I could feel the warmth of his arm against the back of my bare neck, and despite how I tried to hang onto the feeling, it wicked away the anger I felt at him for the accusation. He left his arm there and sunk into the seat, steering with one hand.

"What's wrong with my taste in women?"

I grit my teeth before giving in and replying, "They're never good enough for you—you choose these high maintenance big boobed bitches, who don't respect you for anything but your sculpted body."

He shrugged, his lips tugging at the corner as he formulated his no doubt cocky response, "What's wrong with having women who worship my body?"

I sank deeper into the seat, and my eyes moved to the gray ceiling above me. "I should know better. I really should."

His arm slipped from behind the seat, and his hand went to my knee and squeezed. "If it makes you feel any better, I think you date a bunch of Cro-Magnon idiots."

"That's not my fault. Tara keeps setting me up with them," I said.

Adam kept his hand on my knee. "You're the one who continues to date them after the first failure of a date."

"A girl has needs," I answered, looking out of the corner of my eye and waiting for his reply. I wanted a rise out of him, and if he had any feelings for me that would certainly do it, right?

His nostrils flared as he thought over my response. "I'm

going to choose not to respond to that," he said through gritted teeth.

His brows arched hard over his eyes and his hand tightened on my leg. This was definitely a reaction, but I wasn't sure if it was because of the awkward statement or something else.

"Adam?" I asked.

His hand came off my knee, and he gripped the steering wheel with both hands. "You know what? I'm not going to leave it be. You deserve someone who worships you...knows your favorite color, your favorite fruit...that you're afraid of the dark—"

"Hey! You're not supposed to ever mention that!"

His eyes washed over my face before returning to the road. "You think I deserve better—I don't think I do, but I *know* you do."

"Well, until someone tells me they're going to worship me; I think we're stuck with Cro-Magnon, Tara's choice men."

Adam was thoughtful for a second before he shook his head. "So where would you like to go for dinner?"

"I could go for a big burger and some fries?"

"That's my girl!"

My tongue slipped over my lips as I glanced over at him. Another thing I loved hearing him say, even if I wanted it in an entirely different way than him. I cocked my head as I thought of the point of this 'date.' A smile came to my lips. "You're not going to be saying that when I put you in a sweater vest."

Adam's nose scrounged up, and he made a gagging noise. "Uh...sweater vest?"

I bobbed my head in an overly enthusiastic movement, and he gagged again.

"Why?" he asked.

"That's what hot teachers wear."

"Sweater vest and hot, don't usually go together in the looks department—maybe in the body heat department, but not in the sexy teacher department."

"Shows what you know!"

He looked over at me through his eyebrows. I was teasing him, but I was definitely going to force him into one so that I could get a picture.

~~~

"I'm not coming out there!" Adam yelled over the dressing room door.

I got my way and gave him a sweater vest to try on over a white button-up.

"I look like a frat brother for the geek squad!" he said.

"Yeah, yeah—get your butt out here!" I said from my seat. I'd picked several bathing suits out for our upcoming beach day and was sitting with them in my lap.

He opened the door, hand on top and leaned back, one eyebrow raised.

"Hey, baby, how you doin'?" He put on his sleaze-ball smile and winked at me before sauntering over.

He leaned down and tilted my chin with his index finger. "You know you want all this."

He stood signaling to his sweater vest.

"It turns you on, doesn't it?" he cooed, sticking his lips out in a pout.

I bit my cheek as I tried to hold back the laughter.

"Alright, alright...it looks bad...really bad."

In truth it didn't look *that* bad, the navy of the vest picked up his eyes, but it did nothing to show his A&F model shape.

"The other pants and button-ups looked good, though!" I said, watching as he leaned back against the wall, hand in chin.

"Yes, they did. Why you got this thing into your head, I have no clue. I just have the handful of regular vests you picked to try on. I'm sure they'll be just as awful."

I shook my head. "No, and don't forget to try on the ties I picked out to match."

I stood with my pile of bathing suits. "While you try on those vests I'm going to try on some of these."

Adam put his hands in his pocket and bounced on his toes. "I get to see at least one, right?"

I rolled my eyes as I entered one of the empty rooms, pausing as I closed the door. He was flirting, and I was flirting back. My heart pounded in my chest before I took a deep breath and settled in to try on the bathing suits.

I huffed after trying on several one pieces that just weren't sexy enough. I wasn't a fan of showing everything off, but nothing seemed to be fitting right.

"You okay in there?" Adam called over the door. "I'm waiting to show you my sexy teacher look."

I looked down at the pile of discarded bathing suits and

then looked up at the last one I picked out. It was one of the only two-pieces I picked up. The top was a twisted bandeau style, with a bit of push and the bottom had two gold hoops on either side right where my hip bone started. The mauve pink color was subtle, but that was about the only thing that didn't scream sexy.

"I'll be right out," I said over the door, my nerves getting the best of me as I shimmied into the top and bottom.

When I looked up, I knew it was a winner. It fit me in all the right spots, and the optional halter top would be good for volleyball. Right now, though, it was strapless for full on beach goddess status...or so I hoped.

I opened the door to find Adam leaning back against the wall looking down at his fingernails.

I coughed, and he looked up.

His body went rigid as he took a step towards me with his eyes wandering up the curves of my body. Mine wandered up his, concentrating on the way the vest showed the smallness of his waist, tugging perfectly at his muscular chest and broad shoulders.

He was the picture of a sexy teacher.

"Wow," he finally said, his hand going to the back of his neck to rub it. "You're not wearing that to the beach are you?"

I'd never been this bold with him before, but with him looking at me like that I couldn't help it. I wandered forward and placed my hand on his tie. "Why?"

He looked down at me, his hand slipping from behind his neck to my hip, thumb skimming over the tattoo there.

"I won't be able to keep my friends from tripping over their tongues."

I wrapped the tie around my finger, trying to look coy as I met his gaze, his lips only inches from mine. "How's your tongue doing?"

"Wow! River, you look smoking!" Bobby's voice boomed and broke us apart.

"What are you doing here?" I asked, eyes wide as he sauntered in, tripping over his feet.

He hiccupped before answering, "Had to check on my little brother; make sure he was behaving around my bestie."

Bobby slung his arm over my bare shoulders, and I almost collapsed under his weight as I tried to push him away.

"You're drunk," Adam said, his back facing away from us. He turned, and his eyes were cool as he looked at Bobby leaning against me.

"So?" Bobby retorted.

Adam was shaking with anger.

"Sit," I said, pushing Bobby down on the chair. "Wait here while Adam and I change."

Bobby's head lolled on his shoulders. "Not together I hope."

I heard Adam's dressing room door slam.

"What the *hell* has gotten into you?" I hissed as I leaned down into Bobby's face. His breath reeked of vodka, but I held firm in my anger.

"I see the way he's starting to look at you," Bobby mumbled, leaning up against the wall.

"What are you talking about?"

"I don't feel so well," he said, ignoring my question, eyes wide.

"How did you get here in the first place? Where were you?" I asked, still in his face.

"I was across the street," he began to answer, words slurring together; "I saw Adam's car, and I knew you must be here."

"You drove here!" I found myself yelling.

"So?"

"So? So? I'm going to kill you Robert Thomas Beckerson! Kill you!" I screamed in his face.

"River." Adam came out of the dressing room and reached for me. "Leave it be. He's going to lose his stomach any moment now."

His hands rested on my bare shoulders, and I felt my muscles relaxing. I shook my head as I looked down at Bobby. "I can't believe you'd be this stupid. I'm..." I swallowed hard, my teeth clenching as I tried to keep my voice from shaking. "I'm so fucking pissed at you."

Bobby shrugged. "Adam's going to chew me a new one too, who gives a shit?"

I looked over at Adam. His lips twitched as he looked down at his brother. "I'll take Jackass home. Can you drive my car back?" Adam asked.

"Yeah, I'll pay for our stuff and then head home," I replied.

Adam pulled out his debit card. "The bathing suit is on me, and don't you dare buy that sweater vest for me! Got it?"

I smirked at him, taking the card. "If you say so."

He leaned down, moving my hair out of my ear with his fingertips grazing my neck. The blood rushed to my head as his breath washed over my neck.

"The PIN is 1022," he whispered.

"That's my birthday," I replied.

He winked at me as he pulled his brother up and supported him, throwing the keys from his pocket at me.

"No sweater vest!" he said over his shoulder, his eyes smiling as much as his lips.

"Okay, okay," I replied as I shooed him with my hand.

I stood there for a good minute as I ran over the events in my head. The one that stopped me in my tracks was the PIN number—why had he chosen my birthday?

Then I felt the warmth spreading in my limbs as I remembered his thumb gently tracing the tattoo on my hip. Was he about to kiss me when Bobby arrived? I'd never know.

Bobby had impeccable timing.

Chapter 6

I couldn't sleep. I tossed and turned until six AM, and then decided it just wasn't worth it anymore. My mind kept wandering to Adam and then to Bobby drunk off his ass.

I'd seen Bobby drunk plenty of times, but the fact he got in his car and drove was driving me nuts. He was also beginning to drive me nuts with his obsession over Adam and I's relationship. I knew he was right; something was changing in the way Adam and I interacted, but it didn't mean anything. It didn't mean Adam would act on it, and I knew I didn't have the guts to. I pushed the thoughts out of my mind as I popped in the dance DVD and started punching the air, jumping up and down and swaying my hips. I just finished and plopped onto the couch with a bottle of water when the front door opened.

"Hey," Adam said, sticking his head inside. "Bobby's been puking his brains out for a good hour now."

"Serves him right," I said as I moved over on the couch and patted the space next to me.

Adam shut the door and came to sit beside me. "I'm sorry about last night—we didn't get to see that movie."

Just then a crack of thunder resounded through the building, and I found myself jumping into Adam's arms.

"Always were scared of loud noises, but I don't remember you being afraid of lightning storms. I remember sitting out on the porch watching them together," Adam said, his arms tight around my still sweaty waist.

I shook my head as I pulled away from him. "It was the sudden noise. I'm not scared of lightning— I still love it."

"I'm not loving it right now. It looks like our beach volleyball game is going to get rained out."

"I bet Bobby hates it too; just what a hangover needs, a thunderstorm," I said, trying to look sympathetic.

I ended up smirking instead.

"I bet he is, probably crawling around the apartment calling for me to make it stop," Adam replied.

He put his arm around the back of the couch, and his fingertips grazed my bare shoulders. My mouth watered as I leaned closer to him and my whole body tingled.

"Please don't make me go back in there," Adam said. His brows hung over his eyes as he stuck his thin lower lip out.

I laughed, leaning my head back, so his arm fit into the shape of my neck. I let my chin drift, so I was facing him. "I need to take a shower, but you're welcome to stay as long as you like."

He burst into a smile, and I tried to hide the deep breath it made me take.

"Alright, I'm showering. You know where the remote and the food are, help yourself," I said as I got up and headed to the bathroom.

By the time I finished drying my hair, I could hear Adam's voice echoing through the apartment, and the smell of bacon wafted through the air. I came out wrapped in a towel and leaned on the kitchen island. Adam stood at the stove, spatula in hand, nodding as he sang.

"I didn't know you could sing," I said, but his voice was so quiet, I could barely hear it.

He didn't respond but kept singing to himself. Beside him there was a pile of cooked bacon, and as he turned I could see the pancakes simmering in the pan.

"You should come over here more often," I said as I stood with hands on hips.

Adam's voice slowly drifted off as his eyes ran up my body. His jaw went slack before he turned back to the stove.

"Put some clothes on," he said, pointing the spatula over his shoulder in the general direction of my bedroom. "You're becoming more of a tease every day."

"I didn't think it was a tease unless it was something you wanted," I said coming forward and stopping next to him as I leaned against the counter.

Adam bit his lower lip as his eyes drifted over to me and then back to the pancakes. His voice cracked as he repeated, "Get some clothes on."

I narrowed my eyes at him before heading into the room to get dressed. I shut the door behind me and tipped my head back against it, my chest heaving. I was not crazy; Adam seemed to be genuinely attracted to me. I closed my eyes, letting a shaky breath out. He wasn't acting on it, though, and my hormones were all over the place.

"Get yourself together," I said to myself as I went to my closet and yanked a band t-shirt off a hanger before grabbing undergarments I knew would make Adam's face burn and a pair of jeans. When I returned to the kitchen, Adam was just flipping the pancakes over.

"Better?" I asked, hands on hips.

"Much," Adam said, looking over his shoulder at me in my jeans and t-shirt. "I love that band."

"Too bad I've never seen them," I said, taking a seat at one of the white plastic bar stools.

"Poser," he teased as he poured a glass of coffee, added sugar and creamer and handed it to me.

I took a sip and closed my eyes as the creamy taste washed over my tongue. "It's scary you know exactly how I get my coffee."

"It just shows I pay more attention than you think," Adam said as he took a sip out of his cup.

"I can't for the life of me understand how you'd know that, though." I shook my head at him as I took another deep sip.

He piled two plates with bacon and pancakes, balancing them as he grabbed the syrup from the fridge and came to sit next to me.

"You love mangos, but they make your lips itch...your favorite drink is black cherry seltzer water. Your favorite wine is Kangaroo Moscato. If you could eat anything, it would be fish and chips—a true New Englander. You hope fireflies are fairies that grant wishes; you're scared of the dark, and," Adam nodded down at my pancakes as I stared at him in shock; "You love your pancakes a little gooey in the middle, which is gross by the way."

I couldn't hold his gaze anymore, and I found myself staring at his hand holding his fork mid-air.

"You're incredible; you know that?" I finally whispered.

He leaned over and kissed the top of my head. "That's what friends are for, right?"

There was that word, but did friends act like this? I shook my head quickly to clear the thought.

"Thank you for making me breakfast. It makes up for the lack of movie." I chose to ignore the friend comment, and instead dug into my perfect pancakes— gooey in all the right places.

"We can still do the movies. Today will be the perfect day because I don't want to be anywhere near puke-face, and it's raining. What do you think? Or is that spending too much time with me?"

I took another sip of my coffee as if I had to think about it.

"I'm up for it, but I'm not sure how much more you can take without getting sick of *me*," I joked, but I knew I was self-conscious about it.

"I spent every hour of every summer at your side growing up. I've missed you, River," Adam answered, his hand finding my knee. "Sometimes being grown-up sucks."

I put my chin on my shoulder and looked up at him through my eyelashes. "I'm quite enjoying it right now."

He tried to keep the smile off his lips, but couldn't help the chuckle escaping him. "Me too, but we should probably leave before Bobby comes over here to have you babysit him."

"Good idea, he's such a baby when he doesn't feel well!" I replied, stuffing my last piece of bacon in my mouth and washing it down with the remainder of my coffee.

"Real ladylike," Adam joked as he picked up the plates and headed to the sink.

I swallowed as he turned and smirked at him. He nodded to the door, and I followed, grabbing my purse.

"I washed your new clothes," I said as he opened the door for me.

"Really?"

"I figured you'd wear them smelling like the department store—not the best impression for your first day of work. Plus, you don't know how to wash anything that isn't a t-shirt and jeans." I smirked over my shoulder as we headed down the stairs.

"This is true...you're spoiling me. Do you really want to have to do my laundry for the rest of your life? Because I might get addicted to it," Adam said as we reached the bottom of the stairs, and he grabbed an umbrella from the public collection.

I took a deep breath as he smiled at me in the way that sent my skin tingling. "I don't mind. It's better than having to go shopping with you every week because you've destroyed everything washing it wrong."

"Good, then you've been nominated to do my laundry for the rest of our lives. You know that means you can never live more than a few feet away from me, right?"

"As long as you make me breakfast every once in a while I can deal with it," I answered as he opened the door and popped open the umbrella.

Adam paused, looking over at me as the door shut behind us. "I'll make you breakfast for the rest of your life if you want me to."

My heart stopped beating, and all I could hear was his breathing and mine, in perfect rhythm with each other.

"I might get fat," I finally managed to say.

Instantly I wanted to smack myself. Couldn't I have said something else? Something that would have been, I don't know, as romantic as this whole thing felt? Instead, I said *I might get fat?*

Adam burst out laughing. "Not with how much you workout. Now," he said leaning down. "Hop on."

"Hop on?" I asked, crossing my arms.

He nodded, signaling to his back. "I don't want you to get your feet wet."

I looked up at overhang that was currently keeping us dry as my heart pounded in my ears.

Do it.

I looked down at him, and he wriggled his eyebrows. "Come on."

I hopped up, and Adam's hands slipped over my legs, causing a shiver to go up my spine. I wrapped my arms around his shoulders, and my breath hit his skin. I watched as goose bumps traveled from his neck down to beneath his soft cotton shirt.

"You just wanted me on top of you," I whispered into his ear.

Adam's body shook beneath me as he chuckled. "And you couldn't resist the temptation to wrap your legs around my body."

My jaw went slack at that, and I tried to think of some response or get my brain to move in any direction other than placing my lips against the vein pounding just inches away from my mouth. Before I could do either we were at the car, and Adam was setting my feet on the ground.

He reached around me, opening the door and winked as I sat in the car and he shut the door.

Chapter 7

When I graduated college I'd been lucky. Under some act of God, the internship I had during college turned permanent. The salary was a bit low for someone with a Bachelor's Degree, but it paid the bills, and I wasn't about to sit in my parent's basement and sulk because I wasn't making a 100K like I was promised. I wasn't even making half of that. I stared at the computer screen, puzzled for a moment that I ever believed that crock of shit. I sat back—at least I had a job, and one I loved to boot.

Life could be a lot worse.

"What you working on in there?" Jesse, my boss, interrupted.

I found myself looking over my shoulder at him as he entered my office. My desk faced the window and my back to the door because of the amount of people who always walked by and looked in. I could shut the door, but to the side of it was a wall of windows, so I could never escape from prying eyes unless I had my back facing the door. This way I also had a great view of the window. The only downside was I never knew when my boss was coming in, like now.

I looked at the two computer screens; one displaying the

company I was working on branding with signs, and the other showing the photo editing software I was working in.

"Just working on the ad campaign for Lovely Rags—that big high-end thrift shop we're working with," I explained as I pointed to the photographs.

"Nice, did those come from Joe?" he asked, leaning closer to look at them.

"Yeah," I answered, trying to keep my mouth shut.

The quality we were getting from our photographer had gone downhill substantially. I had bit my tongue because I didn't feel it was my place, but I knew the core values of the company weren't being met by this quality anymore. Our marketing firm edged itself in the marketplace by *not* using stock photography and by creating custom advertisements that no one else could give clients, along with our quantified measurements of the results of the campaigns amongst other advice. The product Joe was delivering was lackluster at best, so the advertisements reflected that.

Jesse shook his head as he came around to the front of my desk and took a seat.

"I have a proposition for you," he said as he tucked his chin in his hand.

"Yes?"

"Joe's quality is...lacking lately, but the matter has been taken out of my hands. He was supposed to show for a photo shoot for Sincere—that huge client with the pricey salons—he didn't show and neither did his models," Jesse explained, leaning forward with a smile that didn't match the situation.

"I need those photographs today to get the advertisements designed for the grand opening in two weeks! I have to get the ads to the printer, the files to the website developers—and the canvas company for the giclée prints!" I threw my hands up and sunk into my chair.

"Don't panic." He paused for effect, and I couldn't help the widening of my eyes as I waited for him to continue. "I do have a solution."

"And what's that?"

Jesse put his hands on my desk, and the smile he gave me was full of teeth almost as white as his shirt. "You took some classes on photography, right?"

I narrowed my eyes at him, turning my head slightly as I replied, "Yeah...I had some prints in a gallery."

Jesse leaned back in the chair, his hands forming a triangle in front of his face. "I have a credit card with your name on it begging for a camera to be purchased. I want *you* to be our photographer. Joe was overpriced anyway, and you deserve a raise. If all goes well—your nameplate," he said, pushing it with his hand; "will change drastically, along with your paycheck."

My head jerked back. "What?"

"You—Lead Brand Expert and Photographer."

"Me?"

Jesse stood and pulled a sapphire credit card from his suit, placing it on my desk with a wink. "It has a two thousand dollar limit, get whatever you need."

I stared at the shimmering card for a moment before picking it up and running my hands over the raised numbers and below them, my name. My "basket-weaving" classes as Dad called them would finally be paying off.

I picked up my phone with shaking hands and dialed the number of someone I knew could help me. "Hey, Bobby?"

Chapter 8

I stood outside the apartment, my lips in a deep frown as I crossed my arms and leaned back against the wall, wishing my stare could burn a hole in the door across the way.

Bobby blew me off. No one was home. I needed his help, and he knew it, yet he was nowhere in sight, and I couldn't get a hold of him.

Adam came up the stairs, and I couldn't help but be distracted by the way he looked as he loosened his tie. If I had my camera like I was supposed to, I would have snapped a shot. He was the perfect image of an A&F drool-pile-inducing model. My mind froze as his eyes slowly met mine, and a smile stretched across his face.

"Hey, Riv, why the extremely pissed look?" he asked, stopping in front of me with his hands in his trouser pockets.

I was trying to remember why I was mad. When I did, I took a deep breath and jammed my finger at the air over his shoulder.

"Your dumbass brother! I told him yesterday I needed his help; my job depended on it, and guess what? He's nowhere to be found," I explained, my voice low in its irritation. I held up my phone and waved it. "And apparently he lost his phone, too!"

He crossed his arms over his chest and gave a heavy nod. "New girlfriend will do that to a guy."

"New girlfriend?" I repeated.

Adam rolled his shoulders. "What was he supposed to help you with anyway?"

I leaned my head back against the wall, and Adam moved closer to me, his hands reaching for my waist, but then going back into his pockets. His eyes left mine and went to his shoes.

"My boss told me the photographer they hire for our advertisements, along with his models, had bailed on us. The quick fix was a credit card with my name on it and enough money to buy me a camera, and me finding a male model. Bobby was supposed to help me get a camera and be my model."

I closed my eyes as I rubbed my temples. "This was a tremendous opportunity. My work is looking at cutting down costs and wants me to do the photography and the advertising. It'd be amazing, and I'd get a raise."

"Alls not lost," Adam said, and I opened my eyes to look at him. Small blotches of red appeared on his cheeks as he continued, "If you wanted Abercrombie as opposed to, you know, Cro-Magnon-Muscle-Head, I could help?"

My jaw dropped. "You're serious?"

Adam gave me one of those faint-inducing sideways smiles as he nodded. "Of course, anything for you."

"I need to raid your closet first. I've got a location all set up for the shoot, and we need to get to an electronics store ASAP," I said.

Adam threw his hands up, still smiling. "Alright, Bossy Boss, lead the way!"

I tossed the clothes out of Adam's closet onto a pile on the bed. He sat there watching; leaned back with his button-up now half undone and his tie hanging so loose I didn't know why he still had it on—besides the fact he was aware that he looked gorgeous sitting like that.

"That should do it," I finally said, staring at the pile of pants and shirts with my hands on my hips.

"You sure we don't need to go to the mall and buy half the store?" Adam teased as he got up, threw off the tie and slipped the shirt off his shoulders with back muscles rippling.

"You don't need to be half-naked until the photo shoot," I said as I distracted myself by grabbing a bag off a hanger and starting to fold the clothes and put them inside. If I kept staring at him, I might melt—or worse make a move on him.

"This isn't like a boxer-brief company, is it?" Adam asked as he slipped on a v-neck t-shirt.

"Really?" I asked, rolling my eyes so that I wouldn't be staring at him. "Don't you think if it was for clothing or something like that *they'd* provide the clothes?"

He looked up at the ceiling and moved his head side to side. "I suppose you're right."

"Logic, it's always astounding," I joked as I headed towards the door.

"What's it for anyways?"

"A high-end hair salon," I replied as Adam took the bag from me and slung it over his shoulder.

"Wouldn't they want to, you know, do my hair?" he asked, his brows shadowing his eyes.

I looked up at his head of hair, perfectly styled in its light brown, hand-run-through-once-glory. It fit him perfectly.

"That's the illogical part. I just need some shots of a hot guy."

Adam definitely had that covered.

"Wouldn't they want some of a girl, too?"

The blood drained from my face, and my jaw went slack. "Maybe..."

Adam put his arm around my waist and lowered his lips to my ear. "Good thing we have you to model for me, huh?"

I pushed him away as my body gave an involuntary shudder of pleasure. "You? You're going to take pictures of me?"

Adam pushed his lips out in a cocky gesture before narrowing his eyes at me. "I've taken some gorgeous pictures of you before."

"You have?"

We were at his front door, but he held one finger up for me to wait a minute as he disappeared back into his bedroom. He came out with a picture frame and handed it to me.

My breath went out in a whoosh as I looked at a photograph of me backlit by the setting sun, head in my hand as I laughed. I was stunned he had a picture of me like this, framed in his bedroom.

"When...when did you take that?" I asked, looking up at him as my body flushed.

He was standing only inches away from me, and his hand went up to tuck a strand of hair behind my ear. His palm stayed against my cheek as his thumb stroked my chin. "I have more pictures of you than I can count...but this is one of my favorites. I took it at the family dinner you dragged me to for your dad's birthday," he explained.

Adam's eyes washed over my face, and the heat of his hand holding my face made me dizzy. Adam's eyes moved to my lips, and he swallowed.

"River," he began.

The door burst open; throwing me into Adam's arms and making us tumble over the side table onto the couch.

Adam attempted in vain to grab hold of me to keep me from crashing to the floor, but I still slipped through his arms, my head slamming against the coffee table. When I finally hit the floor, all I could do was moan and sob against the fright, and the pain reverberating through my skull.

"Shit!" Bobby yelled as I curled up in a ball on the floor in shock.

Adam pulled me into his arms and rocked me back and forth, yelling at Bobby, "What the fuck is wrong with you lately?"

"I knew I was late—I was rushing!" Bobby explained, his hunkering frame filling my view as he leaned down. "I'm sorry Riv, I really am!"

I shook my head, feeling the warm liquid dripping from the corner of my eye and down the side of my face.

"I—I...I think I'm bleeding," I managed to hiccup, my head pounding.

Adam pulled me to face him, gently touching my temple. "Come on, let's go to the bathroom. I'll get you cleaned up."

"I can help—" Bobby started to say.

"You've done enough!" Adam said, leading me away and shaking his hand at his brother to stay put.

I lifted my hand to my forehead, and Adam grabbed it.

"No, don't. You'll pass out if you see the blood," Adam said as he guided me into the bathroom.

He sat me on the toilet and grabbed a wash cloth, dampening it with warm water before touching it to my temple.

"When did you need those pictures by?" he asked.

I tried not to cry at the thought.

"Yesterday really—tomorrow at the latest. I know he's your brother, but he's got a head like a god damned brick."

Adam gave me a weak grin as he grabbed a butterfly bandage from the medicine cabinet. He rubbed a small amount of antibiotic ointment on my injury before placing the bandage over it. Adam kneeled in front of me and took my face in both his hands, wiping my tears away with his thumbs.

"Are you okay?" he asked, his voice a whisper.

"My head is pounding like I just slammed it into a metal pole," I replied, the pain forgotten at the sweetness of his treatment. It reminded me of the moment only minutes ago before I was slammed into the ground—where Adam was close to kissing me, or so I thought.

"I tried to catch you, but it happened so quickly—and you're so tiny, you just slipped right through my hands."

I put my hands on his wrists as his own remained cupping my face. "It's okay."

"Excedrin?"

"Please."

"Do you still want to do the photo shoot?"

"I don't really have a choice, but I'm not sure how you're going to work in this." I moved my head, so the injury was in his full view.

Adam used his hand to tilt my face in the opposite direction. "This side is still perfect."

I shook my head at him as my heartbeat calmed and picked back up at his gaze.

"Thank you," I finally said.

"I'll always take care of you, Riv," Adam said with a wink as he stood.

He held out his hand. "Let's get you that medicine and go get this shoot over with."

When we walked out of the bathroom, Bobby was sitting on the couch with head in his hands. He heard our footsteps and turned, putting his hand on the back of the couch.

"I'm so sorry, but we can still do the shoot if you want," Bobby said.

"You've done enough," I snapped, grabbing the bag containing Adam's clothes.

"Adam!" Bobby growled as he stood.

"I offered to help when you didn't show," Adam said as he opened the door for me.

"Adam!" he repeated his voice a lower tone.

His eyes were threatening. He didn't want Adam to go with me.

"You fucked up Bobby. I'm just cleaning up your mess. She's my best friend, too."

As I looked between them, I sensed a sibling rivalry I never felt before. Even with their parent's blatant favoritism Adam and Bobby had a good relationship. Adam always took it in stride, venting to me, while Bobby ignored it and bitched to me about Adam's obsession over it. Now as they stood staring one another down, I somehow felt I was stuck in the middle of it; as if *I* was the reason for it.

"Some other time, Bobby," I said, continuing out the door in my anxiety to ease the sudden tension in the room.

"What was that about?" I asked as we began to walk down the stairs.

I heard something shatter above us, and I knew Bobby had thrown something.

"He's a bit more jealous than usual...of us. He doesn't like the table being turned on him," Adam said. "That and my parents invited me to dinner without him."

"What?" I asked in shock as he held the door for me.

"Yeah, and I'm sure that has something to do with what you said last time...they asked me to bring my guitar."

"Wow!"

Adam nodded as he clicked the remote for his car to unlock. It beeped, and I got in before responding.

"Wow!" I repeated.

"Guess who's coming with me?"

I shook my head, and he nodded before heading out of the parking lot.

"It's this weekend, so after our volleyball tournament, we can see my parents."

"You're an ass!"

"Is that any way to treat the guy who saved you?"

"You still owe me after this—a photo shoot is nothing compared to a night with your parents."

"You'll get to see me play guitar. You always enjoy that."

"This is true," I said, squinting a bit at the streetlights but still smiling.

"We'll stop here," Adam said, nodding towards the pharmacy on the corner. I squinted as I remembered I had medicine in my apartment. In the fog of pain, I forgot. I went to take my seat belt off, but Adam put his hand over mine. "I'll take care of it, just stay here and rest your head. You're going to need to be able to take those shots of my hotness."

I looked up at the ceiling of the car and rolled my eyes.

"That's more like it," he replied with a chuckle.

Chapter 9

The last thing I needed was another reason to dream about Adam, but he sure gave me that at the photo shoot. I lay in my bed as I came out of the dream with the clear awareness of how my chest was rising and falling rapidly, matching the pace of my heart. I squeezed my eyes shut as my fingers found my lips.

I was screwed. If I kept having dreams like that, there was no way I would ever come out of the la-la land Adam created for me. It didn't help that he'd made the photo shoot so amazing—that he'd convinced me there should be couples shots, and he held me so gently against him with his eyes melting into me.

God, his eyes.

I swallowed and rolled my face into my pillow, screaming into it in frustration just as a knock came on the door. As I turned over in bed, I pulled the cotton sheets with me and grabbed for my glasses.

"Coming!" I grumbled as I looked at the time—eight o'clock.

I decided to sleep in because I would get enough of a

workout at the beach, and I needed my beauty sleep to deal with Vickie and Alec for dinner.

"What?" I asked as I yanked the door open. At this hour, it could only be one of the Beckerson boys, and they knew better than to wake me up.

Adam stood there in a white t-shirt and black swimming trunks with an oversized cooler at his feet. His eyes rose up to my disheveled hair before coming back down. He pulled his lips into his mouth to keep from smiling before asking, "Forget something?"

"I was sleeping in—what time do you get to the beach at?" I replied through a yawn, ushering him in the door with my hand.

"How is *that* comfortable to sleep in?" Adam asked as he looked at my plunging v-neck tank top and booty shorts. "Don't you get a wedgie?"

I blinked at him several times as an embarrassed tingle crept up my spine and to my face. "I knew you'd be waking me up early, so I wanted to give you something to stare at."

Adam bit his lip and cocked his head. "I like that answer."

And I liked the way he was staring, but I shouldn't be thinking about that now. I threw my hands up at him as I walked towards my bedroom. "Explain to me why you're here so early?"

He flopped on the couch, grabbing the remote as he answered, "We're driving to the Cape. It's like two hours away."

I turned as I reached my bedroom door. "We couldn't go to the lake?"

Adam's brows lowered over his eyes, cheeks dimpling as his lips rose up. "Really, Riv?"

I heaved an exaggerated sigh as I went into my bedroom. "Give me thirty minutes."

"If you say so," Adam called back. His tone was sarcastic, but he knew well enough that I never took that long to get ready. He never actually complained, although he always teased me about getting dolled up for a 'fashion show.' When I came back into the room twenty minutes later, Adam was spread out on the couch watching music videos on the TV.

"Wow, it's a miracle," Adam said as he looked down at his watch, then back up at me. "Less than thirty minutes!"

I rolled my eyes at him and hit one of his bare feet. "Let's get going."

"Way to be a bossy boss," Adam said as he jumped off the couch and slipped his flip flops on. "It's going to be a long ride if you're going to be in a bad mood."

"I'm not in a bad mood," I snapped back, and Adam raised his eyebrows, mocking me.

"Not a morning person today then?"

"Since when are *you* a morning person?" I asked as I nudged him in the ribs.

"I went to bed early," he answered, looking down at me.

"Oh, so no girls last night?" I joked, but I was thinking about it and the dream I had. I shook my head as if it would rid me of either of the thoughts.

It didn't.

"It's not an every night thing, Riv."

Just every *other* night. I raised one eyebrow at him, and he elbowed me in response.

"What about you? Bobby still trying?" Adam asked as he opened the door. When I looked into his face, it was blank, as if he was trying to conceal some emotion he was feeling.

I shrugged as I walked out into the warm sunlight. "When will he ever stop?"

Adam chuckled to himself. "Still not giving in?"

"He's like a brother to me—and I'm not just saying that. It's true...I just don't see him like that," I said as I opened the passenger door to his car and watched him close his trunk.

Adam's hands stayed on his trunk, and his eyes hovered over it before moving up to mine. "What about me? Am I like a brother to you?"

I tried not to react to the question, but I knew my face turned red. Not with the dreams I was having...I shook the thought away before answering, "You're just Adam to me."

Adam's eyes shifted back and forth over my face, and his jaw tightened before he moved to the driver's side door. He looked over the roof at me.

"Let me guess what that means—the boy next door who has a different girl every night. The player," his voice was hard as he said the words.

"That's not what I think of you."

I slid into the car, and then he followed, jamming the key into the ignition with a bit too much force.

"You're one of my best friends. You keep the image of

the player...but I don't honestly feel like you're playing any-one but yourself," I said.

"What do you mean by that?" Adam asked.

His hand was on the shifter, but he didn't put the car into gear.

"You don't let anyone in."

He looked up. "I let you in."

"But I'm me."

"You're special."

His gaze bore into me, and my eyes flickered to his lips. The air seemed to freeze as we leaned towards one another, and I wanted badly to kiss him. I let my eyes wander over his five o'clock shadow to his strong chin and then back to my lap.

"If you say so," I said, eyes now averted. "Drive—you don't want to hit beach traffic, do you?"

~~~

By the time we reached the beach our conversation had trailed back to normal, smooth talk about things like work, music and family.

Adam stepped out of the car and tilted his face up to the sun.

"I love this," he said, and his head dropped, eyes meeting mine. "And I love that you're finally here with me."

I bit my lip, containing my smile.

"That's because you want to win for once," I replied.

Adam grunted as he lifted the cooler filled with drinks,

snacks, and lunch. "Damn, right, but I'll have you know I'm already pretty diesel at this."

I blinked at him a few times, and his eyes widened at me.

"What?" he asked.

"Pretty diesel?" I repeated, unable to control the laugh that resulted from his phrasing.

"Yes, I'm diesel!"

"Diesel? That is not a way that I'd describe you, man," a guy with a beard in desperate need of trim said as he came up to us.

"Mark!" Adam greeted, placing the cooler down and grabbing his hand and tapping him on the back with the other. "You know we're going to crush you."

"And who is this?" Mark asked, and when I expected his eyes to trail down my body they didn't. They stayed respectfully on my face.

"I'm River," I said as I took in his chunky frame and lopsided grin.

"So this is *the* River," Mark said looking at Adam.

Adam's eyes drifted off into the distance as he returned the nod.

"Well, Joe's going to be on my team as usual, and we've got a few stragglers that we gathered up," Mark explained. He seemed to know Adam was uncomfortable, but I didn't feel he changed the subject to ease the tension. Instead, his rubbing of his hands showed he was ready for the game to start.

"You ready to go?" Adam asked as he slipped his t-shirt over his head.

I let my eyes drift over his bare chest and slight six pack. The definition was just enough, showing he wasn't completely obsessed with himself, but he cared enough to make every girl drool. Adam caught me staring and ran his teeth over his lower lip before raising his eyebrows.

Two could play that game. I shimmied off my shorts and tank top and put my hands on my hips.

"I'm ready to go," I said, watching as Adam's eyes drifted over me. A shudder ran through my body as his eyes lingered on the tattoo at my hip before his gaze came up to mine. His lips tilted ever so slightly as he grabbed the cooler from next to me and then nudged his shoulders into mine. "Let's kick some ass!" he said.

My jaw slackened as I realized whatever the lingering gaze meant, I was still just one of the guys.

"If you think so," Mark said as he led us onto the court. "This is your side, and I'm going over here to kick *your* asses." He ducked his head to go under the net and headed towards the back to serve the ball.

"Which one is Joe?" I asked, leaning over to Adam.

He pointed to a kid with the head of shaggy blond hair, and a frame similar to his own, except there was no muscle tone at all.

"He's pretty reserved, but you should see him play guitar. He makes me look like an amateur," Adam said.

I raised an eyebrow. "That's possible?"

"Think Eric Clapton," he said.

I shrugged. I knew who Eric Clapton was, but I couldn't recall his playing.

"You guys ready to be crushed?" Adam hollered across the net as he moved to the right of me.

Chapter 10

We got home from the beach in enough time for me to shower and relax a bit before going to the dreaded dinner with Adam's parents. I sat on my balcony watching the sunset with my head tilted, so the sun washed over my face. I knew why Adam decided to drag me along—they were less likely to dig into him if I was there. Then again, if they did, I was there for him to run away with.

I smiled at the thought, closing my eyes. As kids we always ran away together; to the lake, to the creek behind my house, to the tree house we hid in the woods—anywhere where it could just be him and I. Things were easier then, not complicated by feelings I knew I had but wasn't sure he did.

"You ready?" Adam asked, breaking my thoughts and causing me to open my eyes slowly. He hung half out the window with a grin on his face.

"Are you?" I asked.

Adam shook his head as he cracked his knuckles. "What do you think?"

"I'm looking forward to watching you play tonight," I

said as I climbed back through the window, grabbing my purse and following him out to the living room.

"At least that makes one person," he said as he slung his guitar case over his shoulder and grabbed his mini-amp.

"What one did you bring today?" I asked, tapping on the black mesh fabric.

"The purple bass you got me," he answered with a wink. "Dad should love that shit. He'll probably believe I'm gay for real."

I stared at him before we started down the stairs. "If he lived across the hall from you, he'd know there's no way in *hell* you're gay."

"What's that suppose to mean?"

I forced a fake, high-pitch giggle out and twirled an imaginary lock of long hair around my finger.

"Oh, Adam!" I purred, suddenly bold as I put my hand on his shoulder and leaned in to nip his neck. "Tell me how you're going to take all my clothes off!"

Adam's body went rigid in response to my playful tease, and he coughed.

"Crap, Riv...did you really just bite me?" his voice was gravel as I jumped off the last step and turned to face him, hands on hips.

"Why? Did you like it?"

His eyes stayed locked on mine as his Adam's apple moved up and down.

"They never ask how I'm going to take their clothes off," he finally replied with his mouth playfully pursed at me, daring me to respond.

I was all in this game.

I raised an eyebrow before leaning up on my toes and placing my hands on his shoulders. My lips hovered inches over his as I seductively purred, "Oh, Adam—I can't wait to rip your clothes off!"

A smile spread across his thin lips, and he took a deep breath, nostrils flaring.

"That's more like it," he growled back at me, taking the last step and running his hand from my right hip across my stomach as he walked past me.

I literally stopped breathing as his touched seared not only my skin but my mind, making it impossible to formulate any reasonable response.

"You coming?" Adam called, and from the breeze coming over my shoulder and blowing my thin cotton shirt, I knew he was at the door waiting for me.

I looked like an idiot, for what, the millionth time this month? I squeezed my eyes shut before turning with a smile. I was definitely at the losing end of whatever game we somehow started.

"So you have any idea what you're playing for them tonight?" I asked as we fell into step with one another.

Adam opened the back door to his car, placing the amp on the floor and laying the bass guitar gently across the seats.

"Not a freaking clue," he answered, shrugging as he slid into the driver's seat. "Any requests?"

I shook my head.

"Maybe Mom will have one," he said before turning to back out.

"Maybe." I wasn't sure what she liked or if he knew how to play it. I honestly didn't know much about Vicki besides she was Adam's Mom, Mom's best friend and someone who hated my existence.

"So I haven't seen any cavemen lingering around your apartment lately, did you finally tell Tara you could make your own choices about men?" Adam asked as he fiddled with some settings subconsciously on his steering wheel. He knew Tara was one of my only girl friends, and she was responsible for virtually every date I went on. But he didn't know the reason she was always setting me up was because she was trying to get me over *him*.

I ignored the question. If he could take a cheap shot, so could I. "I noticed Amber wasn't lingering around waiting to throw her panties at you."

Adam squinted at the road ahead, tapping his thumbs against the steering wheel as he answered, "Yeah, after the party, she kind of...dumped me."

I threw my hands up in mock shock. "Oh, my goodness! Is this the first time the great and wonderful womanizer Adam has been dumped?"

Adam pressed his lips together as he glanced over at me. "You'd be surprised."

"Really?" I asked, and this time, I was serious.

I always thought he broke things off with the many girls he dated.

"They give up on me quickly," he replied.

"So what's the reason?"

His stare was straight ahead, and I watched as his hands tightened on the steering wheel before he gave a painful chuckle. "You know, the usual shit—I can't commit."

"I could've told you that."

"Why do you always end up breaking it off with the Bobby-Look-a-Likes?" He turned the question on me, and I sunk deeper into the seat.

Him. It was all because of Adam.

"You know, the usual shit—I can't commit," I said.

Adam shook his head, looking slightly puzzled with his furrowed brow. "I would think it was the other way around. Really? You, not wanting to commit?"

"I guess I'm just waiting for the right person."

Our eyes locked on one another for a moment that made my stomach flip flop. Screw butterflies, I had a whole circus rioting inside of me.

"I guess I don't think there's a right person for me," he responded, and his gaze finally pulled from mine and back to the road.

Me. I'm perfect for you.

There it was again – the annoying little voice in my head saying I should tell Adam how I felt. The butterfly circus in my stomach flitted up to my brain, and somehow turned it back on. I glanced over at Adam with his hands tight against the steering wheel. He was stressed. This wasn't the time to add a nonchalant, *by the way I've loved you our whole lives*. I sank deeper into the seat, letting my gaze go out the window. Not that there would ever be a time to tell him that. We drove the rest of the way in silence, and we stayed that way as we pulled up the driveway to the darkened house.

"It doesn't look like anyone's home," I said as we both got out of the car.

Adam's lips flatten into a thin line, and I watched as his ears flushed. He didn't respond as he stalked up to the steps and tried the door. His fist rammed into the wood when the knob didn't turn.

He turned and threw his hands up, looking at the sky as he came back down the walkway.

"Adam," I said, stepping forward and reaching out for him. He shrugged my hand off and grabbed his bass from the back of the car.

I followed him as he continued in his silent rage across the backyard and down a path we had taken many times as children.

"Adam," I tried again, but he didn't respond and instead only quickened his pace.

When I finally caught up Adam was sitting on the rock next to the lake that we swam at thousands of times as children. I took a deep breath; so we were running away again. I watched as he laid his purple bass in his lap, and when he looked up his eyes were sad.

He began to sing—something I'd never heard him do before. I was shocked by the gritty but flawless voice that came out of his mouth. I shook my head in wonder as I found my legs curling beneath me. My hands rested on the soft carpet of grass as my fingers entwined in it.

I knew the song, and I had to take a deep breath as the

words of Five Finger Death Punch sunk in. It was painful to watch and hear him singing that song; to know that was how he felt in this very moment, and so many times over. A break came in the singing and he looked away from me and down to the strings as he slapped them with his thumb. I knew he didn't need to look away. He knew the song by heart, and his voice came again, clear, strong— angry. Just like the singer from the band, he dragged out the *alone* until it ended in a growling scream. His shoulders collapsed under the pressure of the words, and his knuckles turned white from holding the guitar neck too hard.

I knew he was crying.

I stood slowly and pulled his head to my stomach, running my hands through his hair to comfort him. He didn't respond to my touch at first, but then as I continued to run my hands through his hair, he caved, wrapping his arms around my waist as his back wracked with a silent sob.

"I'll never be enough, River, never enough for them," he finally said, his voice cracking.

He pulled away from me with one arm still around my waist, fingers tangled in my back belt loop while the other wiped his face.

"Why do you always try to be enough for them?" I asked.

He was more than enough for them, but they were too blind to see it.

He shook his head as his chest rose with a deep breath before his red eyes met mine. "Don't you always try to be the enough for someone else?"

The truth in his words silenced me. I'd always tried to be

enough for them too—to prove I could be enough for *him*. It just never seemed to work.

"I don't know what you mean," I finally said.

His eyes fluttered as his tongue ran over his parched lips. He stood, free hand moving the bass guitar behind him, one arm still around me, before letting his fingers run up my arms as he leaned his lips to my ear.

"You'll always be too good for me," he whispered, sending an electric shock up my spine.

He knew. He'd always known.

His lips traced my jawbone and my body stiffened against his touch before his lips found mine.

My hands rushed into his hair, tangling in it as his arms pulled me tightly against his body. His tongue traced over my lips and into my mouth as his hands slid down and pulled my hips to his own. I lost my breath at the motion, and he pulled away breathing heavily.

"Holy shit," Adam gasped. "If I'd known kissing you'd be like that, I'd have done it a long time ago."

I still had my eyes shut as I tried to catch my breath. I waited so long for this moment, but something about it just didn't feel right. He was too emotional, and he acted based on that and nothing else.

"You'll regret this in the morning," I said as I let my lashes lift. The smirk on his face faded into a confused frown.

I couldn't believe what I was saying.

"What do you mean?" he asked, his hands still holding me firmly to him.

I pulled away; my breathing ragged with emotion as I shook my head. "You're only doing this because you're upset," I replied.

It was the only explanation if he'd always known. Why was now any different than before?

"River, you don't get it!" Adam said, and his brows shadowed his eyes now.

"Adam, leave it be...you know you don't want me," I replied, turning and walking back up the path.

The tears sprung from my eyes. I knew Adam too well. He was emotional because of his parents. That was it, and I was there for him, like I always was, but this time it had been too much for him.

"Wait! How am I going to get home if you take my car?" Adam called me, and I knew from his tone he was upset.

"Sorry, come on. Let's go," I answered without looking back.

By the time we got back to the car I calmed the beating of my heart, but the heat of his lips against mine haunted me. We drove back in silence, and walked up the stairs to our apartments in much the same fashion. My mind wouldn't stop reeling as I raced from thought to thought.

Him. Me. Kissing.

"Hey," Adam said, grabbing my wrist as I turned to my door.

"Yeah?" I turned to face him, fake smile on my face.

He cocked his head at me; his forehead furrowed with lines of worry. "You going to be okay?"

No.

I nodded, and he leaned in, pressing his lips against my forehead.

"Good," he said.

I opened the door with his eyes burning into my back. I shut it and pressed the back of my head into the wood, sinking to the floor. Tears poured down my cheeks as my body racked against the wood with my sobs. I knew he was still there, just beyond the threshold, but I didn't hold back. After a moment I heard his footsteps move across the hall-way and then fade away.

Chapter 11

The next morning I collected myself enough to crawl out of bed, shower and shove more makeup than necessary on my face.

I looked like hell. The blood vessels under my eyes had popped like they usually did when I sobbed, but it had been a long time since I'd cried like that. When I looked at the clock, I had more than enough time to make breakfast and a pot of coffee, but I just didn't feel like it.

I needed a Starbucks™. I grabbed my purse and headed out the door.

"Power suit?" Bobby said, making me jump as I locked my door.

"Sure," I replied as I turned to face him and headed down the stairs.

"Wait up, Jesus! What's wrong with you?"

"You know where your parents were last night?" I asked as my ears began to pound.

"Sure, they were at the hockey game."

I turned, jabbing my finger in his eye-level chest. I had enough of everyone's games, and Bobby had just confirmed my intuition. It was going to be bad for him, which was fine with me because it was half his fault anyway. He'd known where Adam was going and still didn't say anything to remind their parents.

"What?" I asked, my voice pitched and shook with anger.

He threw his hands up, stepping back and asking, "Whoa there! What the fuck did I do?"

"Let me get this straight. Your parents were at a *hockey* game?" The words were toned with my angry Boston accent and Bobby cringed.

He knew what the accent meant. Trouble.

"I think I'm missing something?" he asked.

"Oh, bullshit!" I said as I stepped forward, looking up at him. "You know exactly where they were supposed to be!"

Bobby's chest rose and fell with the flaring of his nostrils. "And why the fuck do you have all that makeup on?"

"That's none of your business," I said through clenched teeth.

He grabbed my chin in his hands. "You were crying."

I pulled away from him, shoving my hands against him. "Don't you dare change the subject! You knew where your parents were supposed to be, yet you still made them forget their obligations to their *other* son—or have you forgotten that *he* exists just like them!"

Bobby pushed past me, and I had to grab the rail to keep from falling.

"We all know for God-damned sure that *you* could never forget about him!" he shot back over his shoulder.

I watched him leave out the door and slammed the back

of my head against the wood-paneled wall as the tunnel vision set in.

"River?" Adam's voice came from the landing above.

I ran my hands through my hair as I started back down the stairs.

"I'm not strong enough for this," I said to myself.

"Don't walk away from me!" Adam called to my back, and I could hear his feet take the steps two at a time.

"Listen," he began, pausing as we reached the bottom floor at the same time, and he jumped in front of me to block my exit.

I looked down at him as he rubbed his forehead with his hand.

"We can forget about last night, but you don't have to fight all my battles for me. There's no reason for you to get mad at Bobby because of me."

"You heard that?" I asked, and in an instant, I was mortified by my actions.

He shrugged. "I appreciate it, but when I got home, they were there celebrating with him. I've been strong about it for years. Last night was just a weak moment."

My heart stopped. Then I was right. It was just a moment of weakness, and nothing to think about. Yet I couldn't stop thinking about it—his hands on my hips, body hard against mine.

I blinked hard. "Okay."

Nothing was okay, but I couldn't think of anything else to say.

"I'll walk you to your car?" he asked, but I shook my head.

"I'm on the other side of the lot from your car."

His brow furrowed, and I knew why—my assigned parking was next to him.

"I'll see you later then?" His eyes searched mine.

"Sure."

Not if I could avoid it.

Chapter 12

When I got to work, I buried myself in finalizing the pictures for the grand opening of the Sincere salon. The only issue was the fact the pictures were romantic. I closed my eyes as I flicked past the ones of Adam and me. We looked like we were in love, and it just reminded me I certainly was. I found my fingers on my lips as my mind wandered to that kiss.

I imagined it in my head since I was twelve—since the day, I realized boys weren't just someone to play hockey with. I peeled my eyes back open and let them wander to the photographs of Adam, then myself and back to the ones he swore were needed to balance everything. I took a deep breath to steady my thudding heart as I thought of how long it had taken to figure out the timing setting on the camera to get the shots just right. We'd laughed as we struggled to reach each other's arms before the timer was up. Those pictures didn't work for the shoot, but in my mind, they were the best.

They captured the happiness that Adam made me feel 99.9% of the time. The only time I was miserable was like now, when I couldn't get the thought of *what if* out of my head; when I couldn't stop thinking about the lush feeling of his lips against mine.

"Now, that!" Jesse's voice boomed over my shoulder as I adjusted the contrast on a picture of Adam. "*That's* perfect!"

I jumped, my face flushing with the thought. I took a breath to settle myself before looking over at him leaning against the doorframe with arms crossed as he beamed.

"I love that," he said before striding into the room to take a closer look.

"Really?" I asked as I turned in my chair to face him.

"You have to use it. The clients will love it," he said with a nod.

"You're the boss," I answered. "You want to see the other ones I chose?"

"Of course!"

I clicked through the files.

"I like them. Go back to the one of you and the hot dude you're in love with," he said, and my finger hovered over the mouse. I didn't want to go back to it. I never wanted to see it again; to feel the emotions I felt in those moments.

Finally, I managed to force my finger down to click back. "I'm not in love with him."

"And he's not in love with you either," Jesse said as his eyes widened at me.

"As far as I know he's not."

Jesse stared at me a moment before he shook his head and pointed to the photo. "Can you revert this back to color, and then dim the color, so it looks a bit vintage?"

I did as he instructed, and he straightened his back.

"Perfect, now send them to the printer so we can get the files for the grand opening."

He began to head out the door but then turned.

"Oh, and by the way, your new name plate will be coming in soon."

I shook my head in question.

"Lead Brand Expert *and* Photographer," he said.

I opened my mouth, but nothing came out.

"Ten percent raise will be in your next pay check, au revoir!"

He left me sitting there in shock. I turned back to the screen with my hand over my mouth as I stared at the picture Jesse loved so much.

Adam had his forehead pressed to mine, and our eyes were closed as my hands entwined in his over his heart.

It screamed love, so why was it breaking my heart?

Chapter 13

I knew I had to be strong, but when Jesse sauntered into my office waving two tickets to the grand opening of Sincere, I wanted to launch myself out the window. I'd been there for the delivery of the marketing materials including three oversized prints of Adam and me, but I'd left just as the interior designer began to rip the brown paper off of them.

I didn't want to see them again...or ever.

"You going?" Tara asked, nodding to the tickets on my desk as she flopped in the chair.

I looked up at her and sighed. "I don't really want to."

"Come on! It's going to be so cool—we never get to go to these things."

I nudged them towards her and grabbed the keys to my desk.

"You go then," I said as I locked up.

She shook her head. "I have class."

"That's a bitch," I replied, scooping up the tickets and shoving them in my purse.

"Besides, Jesse would totally be pissed if I showed instead of you," she said, cocking her head. "You deserve to go. There could be *famous* people there!"

I stood and grabbed my leather jacket off the coat rack. "This is Boston, not LA."

"There's still plenty of famous people here—doesn't Martha Stewart live somewhere around here?"

I blinked at her a few times; one arm stuck in my jacket as I stared at her. "I think that's Connecticut."

Tara rolled her shoulders. "Whatevs."

"Get out of my office!" I ordered as I slipped the remainder of the jacket on.

"You're such a b-i-t-c-h," Tara teased as she walked out in front of me.

"Watch it," I said, nodding to the plaque on my door. "I'm big time now."

"Make sure you wear something sexy to that thing; you could meet Adam Levine there." Tara winked, and I looked at the ceiling.

The only Adam I wanted was the one holding me like he loved me in the photographs that would taunt me tonight.

Chapter 14

I looked in the mirror and heaved a sigh before slipping into my snakeskin pumps. I decided to go with a dash of mascara, red lipstick and a teal one-strap dress that flowed off of my hips. I took one last look; I might have looked pretty, but I felt like hell.

I closed the door to the apartment, clutch in hand, to hear a whistle behind me.

"Wowza!" Bobby said, and as I turned he leaned against his door, arms crossed, eyes wide. "Where are you going looking like that?"

"I've got another invite if you can stick a button-up and a tie on," I said as I pulled the two tickets out.

"I'll be out in five minutes," he replied as I let my shoulders slump.

I wouldn't have to endure this alone.

When he came back out, he'd fluffed his hair, sprayed on some cologne and was wearing a white button-up ready to bust at the shoulder seams with a skinny blue tie that played off the color of his eyes.

"How do I look?" he asked, sauntering over to me and holding out his arm.

"Like good arm candy," I said as I slipped my arm comfortably into his massive one.

"Ditto on that one, Madame. So what is this thing we got all dolled up for?"

I cringed as I said, "The grand opening of the salon."

"The one I gave you a nice black eye for?" Bobby asked, his body tensing.

"You can still back out."

"Nope, I screwed up enough on that one. I'll support you for this portion of it."

"Thanks," I said, resting my head on his arm as we walked down the stairs. It was moments like this with Bobby that I loved. He made everything hard easier with his smile and ability to make a joke about everything. I breathed in, sighing. This wouldn't be so bad with him by my side to support me.

"Of course," he replied, his voice quiet. "You seem like you don't want to go."

I took a deep breath to compose myself, and he pulled away to open the door. His eyes searched mine as I walked by him.

"It's not that," I managed to say.

I looked up, and Bobby cleared his throat, eyebrows drew together.

"Fine, I'm not really looking forward to it," I admitted.

"And why is that?" Bobby asked, taking his keys from his pocket and unlocking his over-sized truck.

I jumped up into my seat and waited for him to slide into the driver's side. As he turned the key in the ignition he looked at me, eyes blinking in expectation of my answer. My jaw slackened, and I felt sweat building on my brow. The images flashed in my mind, and I wondered if this was a bad idea. How would he react to those pictures? I swallowed as I looked straight ahead and tried to think of an excuse. "I've never seen my photography on display like that."

Bobby reached out and squeezed my thigh. "It's going to be great!"

"If you say so." I looked down at my hands in my lap before changing the subject. "Tell me about this new girl-friend of yours?"

"Her name is Jackie—she's a teacher at the high school," Bobby answered, his eyes straight ahead and unenthusiastic.

"And?"

"And what?"

"It doesn't seem like you're thrilled," I said.

His lips pursed, and he scrounged his nose up. "She's a control freak."

"Exact opposite of one teacher we know," I joked.

Bobby's face soured at the mention of Adam. "Yeah, Adam's something else."

"You guys fighting again?"

Bobby snorted. "Like we ever stopped?"

"Why are you all of a sudden at war with each other?" I asked.

Bobby didn't answer; instead, he continued to stare straight ahead with shoulders hunched and face hard.

"I guess I'm not going to get an answer?"

Bobby slowed as he hit the traffic for the event. "Is that it up there?" he asked, nodding towards a brightly lit building with a red carpet visible.

I narrowed my eyes at him but didn't push it. He wasn't going to answer me.

"I'd say so," I replied.

Bobby snuck into the last open space, which was actually two. He put the truck in park before hopping out and coming around to open my door. He held his hand out for me, and I jumped down into his arms. The moment felt awkward as his hands slipped up my sides and to my bare back. It felt wrong, especially when he was looking down at me as if I was everything. I smiled and pulled away as naturally as I could, but he let his fingers slide through mine. It was like he was reminding me about his feelings, and it left me feeling empty.

"You couldn't get an average sized vehicle?" I decided to ignore it and playfully nudged him in the ribs.

"I'm not average sized," he answered, and his lips pursed out in a suggestive way.

I closed my eyes, shaking my head before I straightened the dress.

"Let's get this over with," I said.

"It won't be that bad," Bobby assured me, his hand guiding me on the small of my back.

As soon as we entered the dimly lit room, we were greeted by servers with food, which Bobby was happy to devour. I shook my head *no* as I glanced around the room, taking in the plush red leather barber chairs lining the black and white walls. People were lounging in them like sofa chairs as they laughed with their faces painted in the lights from the DJ. The room reverberated with the bass from the pop music he was playing. I scrounged my nose, never a fan of mainstream music, and let my eyes wander further into the room to the back wall.

There they were—the three large canvas photographs I'd taken. They looked amazing backlit against the black wall.

I squeezed my eyes shut and looked away.

"River!" Jesse called out, coming towards me out of the crowd. "They look amazing don't they?"

I nodded, feeling lightheaded as my gaze wandered back to them and the biggest photo in the middle—Adam and me.

"It's more than just a display of your photography," Bobby growled in my ear.

He pulled away from me and crossed his arms, eyebrow twitching as he looked at the photograph of me laughing at something Adam had said as he snapped the picture. I watched as his jaw clenched at the one of Adam standing with his shirt unbuttoned, hands in his pockets as he looked off into the distance. It was my favorite picture of him, and I could see Bobby hated everything about it.

"Who's this?" Jesse asked as he came closer to us.

"Cool it," I hissed under my breath to Bobby, who looked like his head was about to pop off.

"This is my friend Bobby—Bobby, meet my boss, Jesse."

"Ah! You were supposed to be the original model for the shoot, right?" Jesse asked, shaking Bobby's hand.

"Yeah, regretting that a lot right now," Bobby managed to say, his voice rough.

Jesse looked at me, and I mouthed the words *sorry*. Jesse shrugged before turning back to Bobby.

"Amazing photographs, though, huh?"

"Yeah, that's my kid brother there," Bobby said leaning back on his heels and crossing his arms.

Jesse tilted his head, his eyes moving from Bobby to the photographs, then back to Bobby, landing on the bulging muscles in his biceps. "Uh," he said, clearing his throat as his eyes moved back to Bobby's face. "Who would know; you don't look anything alike."

"I guess it's a matter of taste," Bobby replied, and I reached behind his back and pinched him. He nodded to the photograph. "That's more Riv's speed."

Jesse's lips lifted in the corner twitching before he nodded towards the crowd. "I should mingle, you two enjoy yourselves!"

I wanted to be pissed at Bobby for his behavior, but I dragged him here not even thinking of how this would affect him. I was only worried about how I felt. I shook my head at him before going closer to the artwork. As I stood looking up at them, the feeling in my stomach worsened. It was obvious I loved Adam.

God, it *so* obvious, especially in those photographs.

"Now I get it," Bobby said with his tone even as he stood behind me.

"What?" I asked. I didn't bother to turn. I couldn't face

him when I felt like this. I knew it would be written all over my face.

"It wasn't about your photographs being on display. It was about your feelings being on display."

I turned to face him. He always knew— just like Adam obviously had. What suddenly changed? I needed to know. Had Adam told him about the kiss, or admitted that he did have feelings for me?

I locked eyes with him as I asked, "Why are you suddenly hell bent on destroying Adam?"

Bobby's eyes darted across my face, then up to the pictures and finally down to his hands. "Listen Riv; the Beckerson boys share one common flaw—*you*."

"You're fighting over me?" I asked, and I felt my eyes blinking too fast for them to focus.

Bobby's eyes rose to mine, and he stepped forward. "It's not much of a fight is it?"

"Adam doesn't have feelings for me," I said, my chest rising as I became frantic at the thought.

Maybe if Bobby was acting this way, Adam *did* have feelings for me.

"Keep telling yourself that," Bobby answered, shaking his head. "That's what he keeps telling himself...but I see the way he looks at you—the way he's always looked at you. It's the same way you look at him, and it kills me, Riv, it really does."

I put my hands on my temples as a wave of lightheadedness washed over me. When I spoke, my voice quaked. "Our whole lives and you tell me this now?"

The room felt as if it was getting smaller around me, and all I could do was focus on Bobby as his chest heaved with the same anger.

"I'm not going to lie to you." Bobby's eyes met mine with venom. "I don't want him to admit it. I want him never to see the way you love him."

"What?" I asked, and the room around us blurred. My focus was on him and nothing else.

"I want you to myself. You've known it *our* whole lives, too—so don't act so innocent."

I could feel the heat rising in my cheeks. I had known our whole lives, but I never kept anything away from him. He knew I loved Adam, yet he lied to keep me to himself.

"You know I don't feel that way," I replied, and I knew hot tears were building in my eyes.

"I could make you, though." Bobby's voice cracked as he reached for my face. His large hand cupped my chin—soft, warm, and loving but no feelings besides loving friendship rose inside me.

"No," I said. "You can't change it."

He leaned his head down towards me, his lips hovering over mine. "Let me try."

I turned my head just as his lips would have met mine, and he cursed. My stomach rolled as the emotions washed over me. Anger, sadness, and embarrassment weren't a good mix.

"Damn it, River!" he said, his head dropping back as his fists fell to his side.

I swallowed, my eyes crushing shut. "Take me home."

"Whatever," he said, turning and heading towards the door.

I wrapped my arms tightly around myself as I looked around the room. Luckily, it was so busy and crowded that no one seemed to have noticed our little spat. I followed Bobby out and looked over my shoulder one more time at the photographs.

Did Adam love me?

When I got to the truck Bobby already had it in gear, and before I had even shut the door, he was pulling out into the traffic. He drove erratically in his irritation, and I closed my eyes as my head began to pound.

Somehow we managed to make it to the apartment in one piece. Bobby didn't utter a word to me as he stormed away.

I used the elevator for the first time in years. I just didn't have the strength to walk anymore. When I got to my apartment, I kicked off my shoes and flopped on the couch to look up at the ceiling.

I couldn't let myself believe the kiss Adam, and I shared meant as much to him as it had me. If I did, there would be no turning back, and Bobby saw that in those pictures.

I was losing grip on everything, and worst of all, I was hurting everyone I loved.

Chapter 15

Bobby's revelation about Adam only made it harder to talk to him. It was easier to avoid Adam altogether, but I couldn't help but glance at him as I got into my car, or as I closed the door of my apartment before he could speak. His eyes were always sad, begging me to stop and talk to him, but I never did. Bobby, on the other hand, was too busy with the reappearance of the girlfriend he didn't like. But instead of moping around alone I broke down and invited Tara over. Tara was one of my only girlfriends, but between work and hanging out with the boys I never really found too much time for her.

I had been avoiding her for the mere fact I knew she would try to fix me up with someone as a solution to the Adam problem. She had a caring nature which always inspired her to hook me up with one of her current boyfriend's friends. It also didn't help she had a major crush on Bobby, and telling her he had a girlfriend would motivate her even more to create a ridiculous double date. It was just a matter of when more than if.

We stood out on the balcony with wine coolers chatting about work when I heard giggling below. We stopped talking, and I watched as Adam came to the entrance with a girl piggybacked on him. I knew my body had frozen with drink half-way up to my mouth as I watched. It confirmed the kiss meant nothing, but sent nausea rolling in my stomach.

Adam's eyes drifted from the path in front of him up to the balcony, and the smile plastered on his face disappeared as we stared at one another. I looked back up at Tara as I tried to keep the anger and hurt down. Her chin tucked into her neck as she looked at me. She'd seen the glance Adam, and I exchanged, and her wrinkled brow signaled she was suspicious.

"Wait a second; did something happen between you two?" she asked.

"Why would you say that?" I replied much too quick.

She narrowed her eyes at me as she loosened her pointer finger from her bottle and pointed to me and the space where Adam had been. "That was awkward, and you look like someone took a hockey stick to your stomach more than the usual amount when you see him with someone else."

"Well, Bobby has a new girlfriend!" I managed to say.

She looked up at the sky and blew her hair from her eyes. "So, I have a crush on Bobby...it's not like you and Adam."

I rubbed my face with my free hand. "Nothing happened."

Tara broke out into one of those smiles I hated—one that let me know she had an evil plan.

"Great! I have a new boy toy, and he has a friend who's

dying to meet you," she said, and her eyes begged me to deny her the pleasure.

"Wonderful, when did you set it up?"

I knew she had done it without asking.

"Tonight?" she asked, tilting her head and fluttering her lashes.

"Great," I answered, dragging out the word.

~~~

Tara knew I wasn't very amused as she layered on my eye makeup with a pout in an attempt to change the way I felt. She pulled a lipstick from her purse, slowly pushing the stick out and revealing its bright red color.

"Pucker," she said, and when I did, she applied the makeup. She stepped back and put her hands on her hips. "Could you act a little more enthusiastic?"

I looked down at the little black dress she chose from my closet. It was ruched on one side and just above my chest the material turned to lace.

"At least I look hot," I answered.

"Andy won't be able to say no, even if you do act like you have a stick up your ass all night," Tara said as she shoved the makeup drawer in my vanity shut. "But I'll be pissed at you if you do."

"Tara," I began as I stood. "Let me remind you; you dragged me into this like you always do."

She rolled her eyes as she left the bathroom, swaying her curvy hips on the way out. She chose a red dress that hugged her frame in all the right places. I should have known when she came up with a bag she planned something more than just hanging out all day.

"I'll be tolerable," I said just as a knock came on the door.

"I thought we were meeting them there?" I asked as I headed to answer it.

Tara shrugged. "We are."

I opened the door to see Adam standing there with his head hanging.

"We need to," Adam began as he looked up. He paused when he saw my outfit then continued in a barely audible voice; "talk."

Tara popped up over my shoulder, dangling my red stilettos. "Sorry, River and I have a double date we need to get to."

Adam's jaw clenched, and he nodded. For the second time that night I wanted to flip my hand back and slap her.

"I can see that. You both look beautiful," he said, his eyes never leaving my face as he gave a weak smile before turning with his hands clenched.

"We can talk later if you want," I said to his back.

When he reached the door, he paused with his hand on the door. His upper lip arched up as he thought of his response.

"No, on second thought I don't think it's necessary any-more. Have a good time," he answered, his eyes on his hand as he turned the knob.

Tara nudged me with the shoes again as I stared at the now closed door. What had he meant by *necessary anymore*?

I wanted to knock the door down to ask him what he

was talking about—to demand he felt the same about me as I did him. To save me from the infernal Hell Tara was about to put me through; to save me from myself. I couldn't, though. Instead, I turned and took the shoes Tara was shoving in my face.

"We'll be late if we don't get going," Tara reminded me.

I slipped the shoes on before answering her, "Can you drive? I'm not feeling that well all of a sudden."

"Andy will fix it," Tara said as she grabbed her keys and slipped her shoes on.

"Doubtful," I said to myself as I followed her out the door.

Chapter 16

I sat in the car staring out the window trying to figure out a way to force Adam to tell me what he wanted to talk about. His face flashed in my mind, and I knew from the thin line of his lips and the fog in his eyes he would never tell me. It was a look the Beckerson boys shared, and it was one that always sent my stomach on a roller coaster. It meant they were hurt and wouldn't tell me why. But with Bobby I always knew what it meant—Adam was another thing. I never knew what that broken look meant when he gave it to me. My mind drifted from Adam to Bobby and back again as Tara sat huffing at my silence. Halfway to the restaurant I couldn't take it anymore.

"What's wrong?" I finally asked.

Tara's eyes formed narrow slits as she glanced at me and then back at the road before asking, "Are you going to mope like this the whole time?"

"I told you I wasn't really up to this tonight," I said.

It was true I told her that, but I hadn't told her why. My lips burned with the reminder of the kiss. It didn't matter why; I should be acting like such a bitch.

"I'm trying to help you get over Adam," Tara sighed.

I glanced over at her, and her lips were pulled down. She really was trying, but she always was.

I managed to smile, and I nudged her. "After years of trying you're still up to that trick?"

She smirked over at me. "I'll win eventually."

"And why are you so set on me getting over Adam?" I asked.

She shrugged, hands drumming on the windowsill to the song on the radio. "Don't get me wrong—if he finally realized how perfect you are for each other I'd be okay with it...I just want to make sure he wouldn't treat you like everyone else he's dated. He's a player."

"I know. I've known him my whole life."

"Don't get mad at me, please. I know you know him better than anyone else—"

"I do."

"Right, so do you really want to wreck your friendship if it doesn't work out?"

I looked down at my hands. I didn't, but we couldn't go on like. I needed to forget that kiss and what it meant to me but obviously not to Adam. I just wasn't sure it was possible. How could something I dreamed about for years turn out to screw everything up so badly?

"I think it's already getting there," I replied.

"Was that what that was about back there?" she asked as she put her hand on my leg and squeezed.

My voice was weak as I replied, "I think I'm losing both of them."

Tara glanced over at me again, and that evil returned to

her eyes. I knew something dirty was about to come out of her mouth."You can't lose Bobby; then I'll never have my fantasy come true!"

"That'd be a tragedy!"

"Here we are," she said as she patted my leg one more time before parking.

"Is that them?" I asked.

I pointed to the two Bobby-bodied boys standing at the door of the restaurant.

She nodded. "Hot, right?"

All I could hear was Adam saying *Cro-Magnon.*

Chapter 17

Somehow I managed to make it through that first dinner with Andy. I giggled on cue, fluttered my eyelashes just like Tara wanted, and she was even convinced I liked him. When he asked me on another date I smiled and nodded, only to flop my head into my pillow and scream when I got home. Tara hounded me the next day at work about how she was *so* right about him. For her sake, I decided to give him another shot, but I wasn't going to look like the hotness he'd seen on the first date. I was going to look utterly normal and see how he felt about that.

I slipped on a casual outfit with minimal makeup before grabbing my leather jacket as I answered the door.

"Hey lady," Andy said, his head in the arch of his over-sized arms. I hadn't thought it was possible for a human to be bigger than Bobby, but Andy was definitely up for the challenge. He had to be on roids.

"You look great!" he said as his eyes wandered over my body, pausing at each curve. I had a feeling he thought the visual appraisal was a compliment. It just felt skivvy to me.

"Thanks," I replied, cursing myself for putting on a tight t-shirt as he pulled me into a quick hug and left his arm around my shoulders as I shut the door, and we walked to the stairs.

"I'm surprised this place doesn't have an elevator," he said as we began to descend.

I waited for the two seconds it took to reach the bottom of the first set of stairs and nodded directly in front of me to the big silver doors.

"We do."

God. He. Is. Stupid.

He gave me a crooked grin. "I guess I was just so excited to see you that I rushed up the stairs instead."

Gag me. I smiled because I knew I should play along; try to make this work.

"It looks like a few stairs wouldn't hurt you," I said. I looked up at him and fluttered my eyelashes.

"Yeah, it's not like I don't work out or anything," he replied as he flexed his arm around my neck for effect.

I took the bait as we headed down the final flight of stairs, trying desperately not to act like a total bitch and shrug his arm off me. "How often do you workout?"

Andy scratched his head. I wondered what was so difficult about the question; maybe he was trying to figure out what would impress me.

Adam's voice echoed in my head *Cro-Magnon.*

"Cardio in the morning, weight lifting in the evening," Andy said with a big smile.

He thought it would impress me. The fact he used a word as big as *evening* was the real shocker. I stifled a bitchy giggle.

"Sounds like that takes up a lot of your time," I said as he held the door for me.

His face dropped as he considered what I said before he perked up again. "It's worth it, don't you think?"

His arm slipped around my waist this time, under the leather jacket, and his jaw slackened as his eyes went wide. "You workout too!"

"What makes you say that?" I asked as I tried to retain the twitch in my face.

He squeezed my side with his oversized paddle-for-a-hand. "Tight abs."

Tara's voice rang in my head—*Try, River!*

"Aerobic dance five times a week. I give myself a break on the weekends," I said as he pulled out the remote key to his car. I tried not to gawk at the circle with three slashes.

The lights on a white Mercedes up ahead flashed. My steps staggered as my mouth opened and closed with no words coming out.

No way.

"You like it?" he asked, wiggling his eyebrows.

It wasn't just any hunk of junk old Mercedes; it was a new CL- Class Coupe; all sleek lines and dollar symbols. I stopped midstride as I stared at the shiny white exterior and already visible red leather.

"What the *hell* do you do for a living?" I managed to ask.

"Eh, it's not that pricey," Andy replied, shifting foot to foot uncomfortably.

Bullshit. I turned to face him and crossed my arms.

"I'm a car girl," I began as I tilted my chin over my shoulder. "You're talking about a hundred twenty thousand dollars right there."

Andy's green eyes locked on mine. "Car salesmen."

Now that made sense.

"So it's not yours?" I asked.

He looked at the sky, cracking his neck in a way that made me cringe. His eyes met mine again, and he smirked all cheese and nausea. "Nah, I'm just that good."

Oh. No, he didn't.

I blinked hard a few times before answering, "I guess so."

My eyes moved back to the car, and that bitter-bitch giggle erupted from my lips again, but this time I couldn't hide the tone.

"You're laughing at me!" Andy took the cue to pull me into his arms in a playful gesture. He took the opportunity to kiss me lightly on the neck.

"So you're a total bullshitter?" I asked as he loosened his grip around me and opened the door.

He was being a gentleman. Wow. Maybe I should give him a chance. I might get a nice Audi TT out of it.

"You know it, honey!" he said, walking around the car and somehow managed to fit his frame inside.

"It's a bit small for you, don't you think?" I asked. His head was barely an inch from the ceiling, and the seat was pushed all the way back.

Andy laughed and tilted his chin towards Bobby getting out of his truck. "You expected something like that?"

"I guess so," I replied.

"Not all big guys are the same," Andy said as we drove past Bobby.

Bobby's gaze rose at the flashy car, and I slipped further down into the seat, covering my face with my hand.

The rich tool next to me was right. Bobby had a brain compared to him.

Chapter 18

There was one thing about Andy that was amusing, his complete inability to do anything besides bullshit. The guy's ego was almost as big as him, which was so extreme it was almost funny. He also seemed pretty enamored with me. He bought me flowers on our third date, chocolates on our fourth, and a bottle of wine for this date. I felt like a complete masochist because I suffered through five whole dates and half a bottle of the nastiest red wine I ever tasted. I tried to tell myself I liked him, but every part of my body reeled with how wrong he felt. I hated the clumsiness of his big body hovering over mine. There was nothing dainty or standard sized about Andy, and I wasn't sure I wanted to learn *just* what else wasn't normal sized on him. He certainly wanted to show me from the way he sucked on my neck in a way that made me bite my lip in annoyance. I swore if he gave me a hickey he had another thing coming.

He practically busted the buttons off of my shirt as he fumbled with them before pushing the top over my shoulders and down my arms with a groan. I was un-amused, and I sure as hell wasn't turned on by his groping. I should have been. There was nothing wrong with Andy—tall, dark, handsome and chiseled. Hell, my waist was practically the size of one of his arms, but it was everything I didn't find attractive. He continued to nuzzle between my breasts, and I pretended to like it by letting my nails dig into the flesh of his back.

He was gasping for breath now as he fiddled with his belt and my heart pounded in my chest. I needed this to stop.

The wood of the front door reverberated with a knock, and I looked at the ceiling.

Thank God.

Andy tried to pin me down, his moist breath hitting my neck and making me cringe. "They can wait."

"Coming!" I yelled.

He huffed and moved away as I buttoned my shirt haphazardly and rushed to answer the door. I yanked it open with too much force, afraid that whoever was there hadn't heard me and might have left. Adam stood there, head against his upper arm, pouting at me.

"Was I interrupting something?" he asked, straightening up and looking over my shoulder.

"Yea—" Andy began.

"Not at all," I cut him off, using my hand to pull Adam in the door. "Come on in!"

Andy stood zipping his jeans and pulling his shirt back on. "Err...can I take a shower?"

I raised an eyebrow at him my voice flat as I said, "You don't need one."

I watched his throat as he swallowed. "Umm...I guess I'll get going then. See you later."

Andy shook his head at me as he went out the door, slamming it behind him.

"Wow," Adam said, whistling. "You're one cold-hearted bitch."

"I wasn't going to have him whacking off in my shower," I snapped as Adam took a seat at the island, and I grabbed a glass of water.

I really hated myself right now.

I swished it around my mouth and spat it in the sink with Adam watching, but as I looked up, I choked. There was something dangerously gorgeous on Adam's face that hadn't been there the last time we talked.

Adam smirked. "What?"

"What?" I asked, forgetting my previous anger. I placed the glass in the sink and pointed at his lip. "Is that?"

He pulled the lip ring into his mouth with his teeth and let it out slowly. Now, that—that turned me on. The lip ring fit him perfectly. In fact, I'd never seen a lip ring that appealed to me before his. They always seemed too big for the scrawny kids' faces, and too overkill for the big tough guys.

"You like it?"

My face flushed as my mind went places it shouldn't be; to places where that lip ring shouldn't be. Somehow I managed to form a reasonable response, "How did you get that with your job?"

"The little kids love it! The administration thinks it looks like I have a fish hook in my face, but they said they'd deal with it until it's healed enough that I can take it out during the day," he explained, standing and coming around the counter. "Lucky thing I'm such a good teacher. They couldn't get too mad at me."

"Right," I said as I rolled my eyes so that I didn't have to look at him.

"So what was that all about?" Adam asked, nodding to my neck.

"He didn't!" I covered the area he was staring at.

Adam nodded, and I couldn't help the growl that came out of my mouth. "I'm going to fucking kill him!"

Adam's eyes widened at my swearing. "Whoa, now! No need for indecency..." his eyes moved over my half-buttoned shirt; "though, I guess you already crossed that line."

I glanced down, and you could clearly see my red bra through it.

"Adam, don't test me!" I said, but I didn't cover myself.

I wanted him to see what he was missing. I wanted his mind to go where mine went and most of all, I wanted to see the reaction on his face.

"So is he satisfying your *needs*?" Adam pushed further, a scowl on his face despite his playful tone.

"Do I look satisfied?" I asked, crossing my arms, so my cleavage practically busted out.

Adam's eyes drifted for a moment, causing my heartbeat to pick up. It was working. They came back up to my face. "Then why are you dating him?"

I found myself shaking my head at him as I opened and closed my mouth with no answer. I didn't have a clue other than Tara had said I should try to move on. I couldn't, though. Andy didn't turn me on half-naked and climbing all over me. Adam turned me on just by looking at me.

I was a freaking mess.

"Commitment-phobe, remember?" I finally managed to answer as I played with the hem of my shirt.

"Right, me too. I dumped Clara; she was a freak," he said as he opened the fridge.

"You hungry?" I asked as I watched him.

"I could go for some chicken parm?" Adam said, a concealed smile coming to his face.

"I don't have the ingredients to make that," I replied as my stomach growled. "I totally would, though."

Adam held out his hand for me. "Dinner's on me then—I'll pay if you cook?"

I slid my hand into his and let him lead me to the door. Now I had butterflies, and he was just holding my hand. It was that simple with him, but so damn complicated at the same time.

Why did he have to make me feel so good?

"Sounds like a deal," I said.

"Oh, wait." Adam stopped and signaled to my shirt with the tilt of his head.

I dropped his hand and began to unbutton it before flaring it open to straighten the layout before I began to rebutton it. When I looked up, Adam was staring at my body, face red and eyes wide.

"What? It's not like you've never seen me in a bathing suit before," I said as I reached over him and grabbed my purse.

I was acting calm, but suddenly it felt like the room had risen ten degrees, and it only got worse as his hand reached for my waist and steadied me as I lost balance.

His breath was warm on my neck, causing pleasure goose bumps to travel down it and over my chest as he replied, "There's a big difference between red lace and pink spandex."

I leaned back and cocked my head at him. "What? You have a thing for lace?"

He shook his head before going out the door, saying under his breath, "I think on you I might."

I tried to hold back the smile that came to my face. I waited ten years for that kiss. What were a few more months waiting for him if the attraction was obviously already there? My mind slipped to Bobby's words as Adam moved his hand back into mine and smiled. Maybe Adam just needed time to realize it.

Chapter 19

When I rolled over in bed the next morning, the last thing I thought I would see was a text from Andy on my phone.

We need to talk. Is it okay if I pick you up for coffee at 10 from your work?

I let a breath out as I stared at the ceiling. I could break it off with him face to face then. I squeezed my eyes shut praying maybe that was what he wanted to do anyway.

Sure. I replied before getting out of bed to put on my workout clothes. At least I could burn off some anxiety about the situation. Halfway through my workout Bobby opened the front door.

"Hey," he said with a smile made of half teeth, half lips and completely awkward. There was no doubt this was going to be an interesting conversation.

"Come in," I said, grabbing the remote and shutting the TV off before flopping on the couch.

Bobby stared down at me, rocking on the balls of his feet as if he didn't know what to do with himself. That was unusual in and of itself. Bobby never lacked confidence in what he said. I patted the seat next to me as I pulled my feet to my chest.

"You look nervous," I said as he finally took a seat.

"I'm just confused," he managed to say.

"About?"

"I don't want to fight, but I want to call you out," he answered, leaning forward and clasping his hands together.

He cut his sandy blond hair back, but his five o'clock shadow was looking more and more like a permanent fixture on his face. I leaned back before letting my eyes drift down to his as he looked at me over his shoulder.

"Andy," I said.

"I don't think he's your type," Bobby replied with his eyes locked on mine. He was right, but I couldn't face telling him that.

I stood and ran my hands through my hair before turning to him. "At least you and Adam agree on one thing."

"You don't need to get back at *both* of us by dating someone like that," he said, and his body tensed as he waited for my reaction.

"What's so bad about him?"

"All money; no brains."

I smirked at the comment. "Yeah, you're probably right about that."

"Why are you dating him? Physically he's the exact opposite of what you like—I should know. You've never been into me, and I'm not even as huge as him."

"Tara set us up," I explained with my hands on my hips.

"That makes sense. He's totally *her* type," he said. "I just don't want to see you settle because Adam's still playing the field."

My breath caught in my throat. It was as if he was saying Adam might come to his senses, and he wasn't acting completely nuts about the thought. I sat back down, and he finally relaxed, leaning back and putting his arm around the back of the couch.

"What are you saying?" I asked.

"I'm saying you've waited what, ten years so far?"

"You hate the idea of Adam and me."

Bobby burst into a full smile. This one wasn't awkward, but it was diabolical paired with the twinkle in his eyes. "You have no idea how much I despise the idea, and I have no idea how I'd react—it wouldn't be pleasant."

I leaned back, my head dropping on his arm as I looked at the ceiling and then let pressed my chin on my shoulder, so I was looking at him. "Thanks for the warning."

"I do want you to be happy, River. I fully believe I could be the guy to do it for you if you'd let me," Bobby's eyes locked on mine before he continued; "but I'm not going to force that on you."

My eyes drifted away as I carefully measured my response. I had to decide between being truthful and being nice.

"Really? Because sometimes it feels like you are—like you flipping out at me at the grand opening, for example."

Bobby's broad chest rose, making the fabric of his shirt pull tight. "Yeah...I told you it wouldn't be pleasant. That's just me *thinking* about the possibility Adam could have you."

Silence fell over us, and I looked down at my shoes, playing with the laces before I glanced up at him. I took in his strong jaw line, haunting blue eyes and full lips. Gorgeous but nothing. I felt nothing.

It had been years since I said it, but I needed him to hear the words now and see in my eyes that I meant it. "Bobby, I love Adam."

"And I love you, River."

I looked down at my hands. "Will things always be this twisted?" I asked.

Bobby pulled me into his arms, kissing my head.

"I'm afraid so, but maybe if you became a fatty, I'd be less attracted to you," Bobby replied.

I yanked away from him and thumped him on the chest. I knew not to hit too hard for fear of seriously hurting myself. "You're an ass; you know that?"

He winked at me. "A cute ass, don't you think?"

I rolled my eyes, and he stood, wagging his butt as he made his way to the door.

"Cute, huh?" he asked again as he slipped out the door.

I picked up one of my decorative pillows and chucked it at him just as he shut it behind him. I couldn't help the smile on my face. The Beckerson boys had equal shares of my heart. One half was reserved for loving Bobby as my best friend, and the other half was silently reserved for Adam. I rubbed my neck. If only he would take me up on it.

Chapter 20

I wasn't looking forward to seeing Andy, and I quickly came to the realization that this wasn't the breakup coffee date when he walked into my office to place a soft kiss on my cheek before tucking his hand in my own. I tried not to grimace as he led me out of my office and down the hall towards the exit. As I walked past Jesse's office, his brows furrowed at the hunkering man with his hand in mine. I shrugged, and he laughed before spinning in his chair to face away from me. Jesse thought I was nuts, and I was beginning to believe he was right.

"So," Andy began as we walked across the street to the Starbucks™. "I thought we needed to talk."

"Sure," I said.

He glanced over at me, green eyes seeming puzzled by my nonchalant reaction. Andy held the door open for me, and we stood in the line without speaking. Once our coffees were ready, we walked to a seat in the corner of the shop and sat across from one another.

"What's up?" I asked.

Andy tapped his fingers on the side of the paper cup before taking a deep breath and smiling. "I feel like the other night you were uncomfortable with how quickly things were going."

I blinked a few times at his observation before nodding. He reached across the table and took my hands in his. This was definitely not going the way I wanted it to.

"I didn't mean to be too forceful," he said, his eyes drifting away before coming back to mine. "You're kind of hard to resist is all."

I choked on the coffee I had just taken a sip of. He'd gone from sweet to sleazy in a matter of seconds. I shouldn't have really been surprised, but his gentlemanly observation coupled with his cheap pickup line was a startling combination. I couldn't even muster the bitchy giggle I mastered for him. Instead, I replied, "Thanks?"

He sighed, another surprise, he seemed to sense my dissatisfied tone—maybe he wasn't *that* bad.

"All I'm saying is I'm sorry I was pushy. I get I was way out of line. We can take our time...I really like you, River," he finally said.

I concealed my confused expression by taking a sip of my coffee. As if I had to think about it. No.

"Sure," I said.

I was a complete marshmallow, and I knew I'd regret it. Andy broke into a huge smile as he took my face in his hands and kissed me. It was light, sweet, completely unanticipated, and it...kind of left me breathless—or stunned. I wasn't sure which one it was.

When he pulled away I swore, I saw Adam's white GLI speeding away, and everything inside of me screamed. I felt like vomiting as Andy launched into a conversation about the new line of Mercedes that was coming out next year.

Why had Adam been at my work in the middle of the day? I tried to pay attention to Andy's ramblings, but in the end, my mind remained on one person...Adam.

Always, Adam.

Chapter 21

Bobby warned me when Adam showed up a few days later with yet another girlfriend. The whole thing really was my fault, or so I told myself. Adam had seen Andy and me together when he thought we broken up, and he went out and found himself another big boobed bimbo. At least that's what I was blaming it on. Andy's sweetness had worn off, and he'd gone back to being pushy and egotistical after only a handful more dates—apparently his 'waiting' meant three dates. Still, I was glad I hadn't had the heart to break it off with Andy when I saw Adam with *her*. I knew the second I saw her I was going to hate her with every inch of my being.

Everything about her made my skin crawl.

"River, this is my..." Adam began when we met in the hallway of the apartment building.

"Girlfriend," the chick finished, sticking her hand out. "Monica."

I was completely caught off guard by the girl, and only just managed to choke out a *Nice to meet you* as I stared down at her petite, barely five-foot frame, and the fakest set of breasts I'd ever seen.

Her almond-shaped eyes matched the blackness of her

sheet of straight hair. She was the exact opposite of me in every way, including her milky white skin. The red lipstick she managed to smear across Adam's lips only washed her out and sent my imagination into a tailspin. His lips on hers made me want to yank her hair out. I hated her more than his typical girlfriends—maybe it was because before when I looked at Adam's lips, I only *imagined* them against mine, and now I didn't need to imagine it...only remember.

"Are you going to come to the party tonight?" she asked, fluttering her eyelashes at me and pulling me out of my self-recrimination.

"Bobby told me about it last night—Andy thought it'd be a good idea," I said with a shrug. I watched as Adam cringed at Andy's name.

That's right, buddy, cringe.

"Andy?" she asked, cocking her head and twirling a silken piece of her midnight hair.

"My boyfriend," I replied.

I watched as the twirling stopped and her smile vanished. She must have thought I was single and mopping over her recent acquirement of Adam.

"That's so nifty! Bobby's bringing Jackie, too," Monica said.

I looked at Adam and mouthed the word *nifty*. Adam tilted on his heels and scratched his ear.

"I thought Bobby broke up with Jackie?" I asked, watching as Adam's face turned red.

"Well, they are totes back together. Jackie and I work together," Monica said.

Her lingo was ridiculous, and I had to bite my lip to keep from laughing at her.

She narrowed her eyes at me and tilted her head. "You know what? Jackie kind of looks a lot like you...except she's blonde."

I watched as Adam blinked his eyes in shock.

"Doesn't she?" Monica asked him.

"Yeah," Adam began, rubbing his scruff; "a bit."

"Any who—can't wait to meet your Andy."

I couldn't bite my tongue. "I don't own him."

She shrugged at me as her lips tugged up. She seemed to know that idea irked me. She turned to Adam and smiled, sugar sweet. "Ready to go, Boo?"

Adam swallowed, and his eyes were hard and vacant.

He did not like being called that.

"Sure." He still answered to it, though.

Chapter 22

When Andy came to my door and swept me into an overzealous kiss, I suddenly felt myself looking forward to the party. It meant we were in public, and he couldn't get too far with his frantic groping.

Adam greeted Andy and me at the door, and before I could respond Andy scooted straight to the beer cooler. I stood next to Adam taking in the room, and my eyes easily found Monica.

"Don't make that face," Adam said as he handed me a red cup.

"What face?" I tried to act innocent. It wasn't like I could ever hide anything from him, especially when it came to my facial expressions.

"It would mean a lot to me if you *attempted* to like at least one of my girlfriends," Adam said, his hand on the small of my back as he guided me into the room.

I looked down at him as he dropped onto the couch.

"Really? You think I'll ever like someone who uses the word nifty? I honestly didn't believe that you'd ever like any-one who used that word either, *Boo*," I shot back as I sat next to him and took a sip of the bitter tasting liquid in the cup.

Adam leaned forward and flicked a hair away from my eyes with his finger. "That's not very nice, Riv."

I narrowed my eyes at him. "You're selling out."

Adam's arms flung out across the top of the couch as he fell back, bursting into cynical laughter. "And you're not?"

I didn't answer, and our eyes met, cutting off his laughter.

"I'm going to get myself another drink," Adam said as he stood in sudden discomfort.

I watched him walking away; back muscles tensed under the thin cotton of his shirt, and I wondered if he would come back to sit with me. I wouldn't blame him if he didn't. I glanced around the room, but Andy had disappeared into the throng of moving bodies. As my eyes drifted, they landed on Monica. She stood next to a girl who looked much like me, with a bit more junk and too much bleach in her hair. They were both scantily clad in skinny jeans with more holes than fabric and barely there tank tops that their oversized busts threatened to burst out of. I closed my eyes and swallowed back another swig of the nasty stuff Adam had given me. I didn't know why he handed me a beer when he was aware that I hated them.

A cough made me open my eyes just as I finished the last of the liquid in the cup. Adam's gaze bore into me as he handed me a hard apple cider.

"I figured this would wash away the taste of that," he said, and his thin lips tilted to one side in a sly smile.

"I didn't think you'd come back," I replied as I took the drink and swished it around my mouth.

"Eh, I guess we should call a truce on this one," he said with a shrug before he knocked back a gulp of caramel colored liquid in a shot glass.

"Southern Comfort?" I asked.

Adam nodded. "Smooth."

"Disgusting is more like it."

"Fruity drinks are for girls," he shot back.

We sat in silence as I finished my drink and he knocked back a few more shots from the bottle he brought with him.

"You sure you don't want some?" Adam asked, and I could tell he was on his way to wasteland from the glassy look in his eyes. I wanted to be there too— to stop thinking about the way I was punishing myself with a pointless relationship to forget him.

"Sure, why the hell not?"

Adam chuckled as he handed me the shot and watched me tip it back. The liquid burned down my throat, and I came up coughing. Adam patted my back until I stopped, but then his hand remained there, fingers running over my spine.

"You know what I wonder?" Adam broke the silence as my body heated from his touch, or the alcohol, or both.

I rested my chin on my shoulder and sighed at him. He swallowed as his gaze ran over my bare arms and up to my face.

"What?" I asked, biting my lip, so his eyes drifted to them.

His eyes remained there for a second before he answered.

"Why we keep choosing people we know we'll never be committed to."

It was more of a statement than a question, and I nodded for another shot. Adam's brow furrowed, but he poured me another and watched me drink it.

I didn't cough this time.

"Because we're masochists for watching each other with anyone but one another," I replied.

I looked down at the shot glass. Shit was like truth serum—dangerous.

Adam's fingers ran up my back before running down my arms. His eyes watched the goose bumps as they appeared beneath his touch.

"What about you and Bobby torturing each other, is that the same?" he asked in a low voice as he leaned his arms against his thighs.

I let my fingers trace the stars exposed on his forearm as the room became a hollow drone around us.

"Bobby doesn't torture me, and I don't mean to torture him," I replied.

The pounding of the bass in the background faded to a dull thud, and the voices of the others at the party muted to nothing against the pressure of my heart in my chest and Adam's breath lingering with mine as our gazes locked on one another.

"So why do you torture me, River?" Adam's voice was a coarse whisper, and it reminded me of his singing—all emotion and raw pain.

My breath locked in my throat as I tried to comprehend

the question, its meaning and how my heart suddenly felt as though it was shattering into a thousand pieces and being welded back together again.

"Hey you!" Monica broke our conversation as she slid into Adam's lap.

Adam's head snapped back, and he blinked several times at her as if he was trying to figure out who she was. I could feel the burn of alcohol instantly making its way up my throat as I glared at her, and I shattered again.

"Hi," he finally said.

She smiled at him as she moved her arms around his neck and shoved her chest into his face. My whole body felt too hot as I stared at them. Adam's words burned into me *why do you torture me?* What was this if it wasn't torture?

"I think we need to do some body shots, Boo," she said as she wiggled her body against him.

Adam's eyes darted from her to me before he nodded. "Sure."

I wanted to scream. Why? Why would you do that after what you just said? Instead, I sat back, and my eyes zoned in on the empty bottle of Southern Comfort. I wanted to chuck the thing across the room.

"Hey!" Tara's voice cracked into my skull as I tried to obliterate the glass bottle with my mind.

She hopped into my lap and stared down at me with puppy dog eyes.

"You look like you need more to drink," she said.

"I could use something that doesn't taste like acid," I

replied, and she pulled me up from the couch and towards a pink cooler.

"Here you are," she said as she handed me something the same color as the cooler.

It tasted like lemonade, which was fine with me. I combed the room for Adam, but couldn't find him. He was probably getting his brained screwed out by that bitch. I glared down at the bottle in my hand; being drunk sure made me a bitch.

"You look like you're ready to kill someone," Tara said, and I realized I hadn't said one thing to her.

"When did you get here?" I managed to ask.

She raised one eyebrow before answering, "About an hour ago—you invited me, remember? I saw you and Adam on the couch and figured I best leave you alone, though."

"Mhmm," I replied as I tipped more alcohol I didn't need down my throat. Maybe with enough of it, I would forget Adam's confession.

"Being drunk sure makes you bitchy, huh?" Tara asked.

I shook my head. "Adam having a girlfriend makes me a bitch."

"That reminds me, where's your boyfriend?" Tara asked.

"Where's yours?"

"Eh, I broke it off with him. He was kind of stupid," she admitted with a shrug.

"Andy's right up there, too," I said before tipping back the rest of my drink.

Tara and I stared at each other for a moment before bursting into ridiculous giggles.

"I'm going to find Bobby," Tara said, continuing to laugh as she walked away.

I shrugged, looking around the room before deciding I should probably find my vanishing boyfriend and end it with him. I wasn't so wasted I didn't have my wits about me, but I was gone enough to be truthful with myself.

I didn't like one thing about him.

The problem was, I couldn't find him anywhere, and there weren't many places to hide in Adam's apartment. I was starting to feel like Adam wasn't the only one who abandoned me. I made my way to the last room to check, Bobby's and opened the door half-heartedly only to hear a soft moan.

"Hey!" Andy shouted.

My head snapped around to see him naked on top of Monica.

"What the fuck!" I grabbed the nearest pillow on the ground. "What is wrong with you?"

I started beating him with it, yelling expletives. Before I could comprehend what I was doing, Adam's arms were around me, holding me from pounding the living daylights out of my cheating boyfriend. My brain was foggy. I was going to break it off with Andy anyway and why was I so surprised? Lemonade flavored bile rose up my throat and my eyelashes fluttered against my cheeks.

Oh, yeah...that.

"What's going on in here?" Adam shouted over my screeches. Then he saw Monica grabbing at sheets.

"*Kiki* over here decided Andy was more her taste," I spat.

I had no idea where the name had come from, but it seemed to fit her well.

"Is that supposed to be racist?" Monica hissed her eyes slits.

"No, it means you're a fucking *whore*," I said as Adam continued to hold me back.

Andy held the pillow he grabbed from my hands over his crotch saying, "Who could blame her? I mean I have at least three inches on this dude."

The reference he was making was not to height because he was at good eight inches taller than Adam. I could feel the bile rising again. Gross. Just gross.

Adam's muscles tighten around me. "You'd be surprised, dude."

"What about the fact *you* cheated on *me*?" I yelled, lunging at him again, only to be held back by Adam.

"He's not worth it. They're both pieces of shit," Adam said, breath warm on my shoulder, but his tone lacked the venom.

I wasn't sure he cared. I wasn't sure why I did, or if I did, or if I was just loaded on Southern Comfort and pink stuff.

"Hey!" Monica said.

"Really?" I mocked her, eyebrows arched.

"Get the hell out of my apartment, and never come back, got it?" Adam said, and before anyone could respond he was turning me away from them and guiding me out of the room.

Adam's hand stayed entwined in mine as he led me to

his bedroom to escape the overcrowded room. I closed the door behind me and leaned my head back against it.

"I should've known," I said as Adam reached over and locked his door.

There was nothing like a cheating boyfriend to sober someone up. Adam put his hands on either side of my head and lowered his face to mine.

"I'm sorry," he whispered.

I sighed, looking up at him with a smile. "It was bound to happen sooner or later."

"Mhmm," he said as his eyes searched my face. "The thing is I don't really give a shit."

I nodded and moved around him to drop onto the bed.

Adam crawled in beside me and pulled me into his arms. I closed my eyes as I leaned my head into his shoulder and let the feeling of his body heat wick into mine before taking a deep breath. His sweet scent swept over me, intoxicating me more than the liquor I'd consumed; despite the alcohol, he still smelled like Axe cologne and my fabric softener.

"You know something?" Adam said as his fingers traced imaginary lines over my bare arms and caused my skin to dance in pleasure.

I shook my head as I looked up at him. I wasn't sure if I was breathing anymore, or if I even cared if I was.

His free hand cupped my chin, thumb stroking my cheek as his lips hovered so close I could taste them against mine.

"You're the first girl I fantasized about, the first girl that made every part of me feel like it was on fire...and every time I see you I still feel it. It's like you're the only thing I ever really needed. You're my best friend, but every part of me wants you more and more every time I see you—hell, it's every time I think about you. That kiss...you can't tell me it didn't mean anything to you?"

"You were upset," I whispered, watching as he slowly shook his head.

"That kiss meant *everything* to me," he said.

"*You* are everything to me," I answered, and his lips crashed into mine.

I didn't need to breathe anymore. All I needed was him as my body filled with half panic and half intense yearning kept in too long. His lips raced across mine, then to the skin of my neck, and I knew he felt the same. I let out a soft moan, and Adam rolled his body over mine, his hands pressing mine into the pillows. His tongue swept over my collarbone before he paused for a breath, letting it wash over my skin in a way that made me want to scream. I freed my hands from his and pulled the weight of his body onto mine, biting at his neck as my fingers dug into the firm muscles of his shoulders.

"God, River, you're trying to kill me," he gasped in response.

I let my lips trail up to his ear before whispering, "Are you enjoying it?"

He chuckled before turning his lips back to mine, taking my breath away again as his fingers unbuttoned my shirt. His eyes watched mine as he pulled away, kisses trailing further and further down my abdomen as he worked each button free. I sat up as he pulled me into his arms, lips grazing my neck and bare shoulders as the material fell away.

I ran my hands up his shirt, pulling the soft cotton over his head and throwing it aside so I could kiss his chest and shoulders. Adam groaned as my hands worked their way down to his pants.

"Wait," he said as I began to slide them off his hips. Everything stopped for me; my breathing, my thoughts, and my heart.

I swallowed. "What?"

His chest heaved as he closed his eyes and pressed his forehead to mine. "Are you sure you really want this?"

I answered him with one slow kiss, letting his lip ring slide through my teeth.

"I'll take that as a yes," he gasped as he pulled my body to his own, his hands freeing my bra and tossing it aside.

He swallowed as he looked down at me.

"You're amazing," he whispered as he leaned in to kiss me softer than before. The panicked edge to the kiss was gone replaced with a passion that was just as irresistible.

Everything slowed from there into a fuzzy ecstasy I wasn't sure was a dream or not. His body fit perfectly into mine, and the heat of the pleasure was almost too much to take. It took minutes for my chest to stop heaving, and soon I drifted off to a sweet sleep with the rise of fall of his breathing beneath my head.

Chapter 23

When I woke the next morning, I was groggy, and my head had a dull thud in it. I shot up, taking in my surroundings. I knew where I was, and judging by my lack of clothes, I hadn't been dreaming. Adam came out of the bathroom, followed by a plume of steam with a towel wrapped around his waist.

"You might want one of these," he said with a light smile on his face as he handed me a glass of water and a Motrin™.

I sat up to take the glass without thinking, and the sheet covering me fell around my waist.

I watched as Adam took a deep breath. His eyes drifted over my naked upper body as our hands clasped over one another on the glass.

"Thanks," I said as I took the glass from him and tossed the pill in my mouth.

I set the glass down after chugging it and grabbed the nearest shirt to pull over my head. Adam stood watching as I yanked my jeans over my bare legs.

"Leaving already?" he finally spoke.

I looked up and smiled at him. "I don't think this would be the easiest thing to explain to Bobby."

He looked down at the floor where the rest of his sheets lay tangled, biting the lip ring into his mouth.

"Yeah, I suppose you're right."

I leaned up and kissed his neck. "We'll talk later, okay?"

His arm wrapped around me, pulling me to his skin.

I took a deep breath of his clean, comforting scent as he whispered in my ear, "I like the way you look in my t-shirt."

"Good, I'm keeping it," I said as I pulled away and looked up at him. Every part of my body tingled and ignited as we stared back at one another—I didn't want to leave, especially now that I knew the feeling was mutual.

"We'll talk later?" he repeated as his eyes studied my face.

I nodded before turning and sticking it out to check the coast was clear before scooting out. As I closed the door to Adam's room his eye's met mine, begging me not to leave.

We had so much to talk about, but I was already running away. I shut the door anyway, and when I turned a light yelp, I covered with my hand echoed from my mouth.

"Tara!" I said as quietly as I could in my surprise as I looked at my best girl-friend sneaking out of Bobby's room.

"River!" she said, just as shocked but she had a happy smirk on her face.

We both rushed to the front door trying to withhold the fit of laughter. She looked hilarious in Bobby's extra large shirt, literally now a dress on her, and I was quite sure my hair was sticking straight up in several places. When we got into my apartment, we fell on the couch in a fit of loud, happy giggles.

"Holy crap!" Tara said. "What happened last night?"

"Freaking heaven, that's what!" I replied through tears.

"You're telling me!" she answered, and we started laughing again.

After several seconds of trying to catch our breath, we turned to face one another, suddenly serious.

"Really, what happened?" I asked finally.

Tara shrugged. "After you and Adam ushered *Kiki* out," she dragged out the word, teasing my nastiness. "Jackie threw a temper tantrum, at which point Bobby went ballistic on her. So then that was over, and Bobby and I were talking on the balcony...I was pretty loaded, and for some reason I just happened to admit I had a crush on him since I met him...one thing led to another, and here we are—very satisfied, I might add."

I scrounged my nose at the last comment. "That good, huh?"

Tara took a deep breath, flopping back on the couch. "You have no idea."

"Eww, he's like a brother to me!" I said, grabbing a pillow from behind me and swinging it at her.

She sat up, grabbing the pillow, and eyed me. "Speaking of brothers, what happened with you and his?"

I looked down at Adam's t-shirt covering my body, and the butterflies rose up again, along with an unhealthy dose of doubt.

"We went into his bedroom to escape the madness the party had become, and then he admitted how long he had a crush on me...one thing led to another," I said, playing with the hem of his shirt.

"What's wrong?" Tara asked, leaning forward and taking my hands in hers. "You were so happy a second ago?"

I closed my eyes and took several breaths before opening them to see Tara's soft eyes pondering mine.

"I know Adam."

"No!" Tara stuck her index finger in my face. "Don't you dare start thinking like that! You do know Adam, and he wouldn't do that to you!"

I swallowed, trying to reassure myself, but my response came out weak, "I know."

Tara frowned at me. "Go take a shower; you smell like good sex and unnecessary regret."

"I need coffee," I groaned as I stood up.

Just then a hammer made itself known as my brain rattled in my skull.

"After we both shower, so hurry up so I can clean up, too!" Tara said, her sheet of thick brown hair falling in a tangled mess in her eyes.

When I came out of the shower covered in a towel Bobby and Tara were wrapped tightly around one another on my couch.

"Hello," I coughed and for the first time, when Bobby looked up at me he didn't look like he wanted me.

Relief washed over me. Maybe Adam and I could be together.

"Hey," Bobby said, smiling at me. "Sorry, I just couldn't wait to see her again."

"Eww," I said, making a mock sick face as I went to the bedroom.

When I came out dressed Bobby and Tara were nowhere in sight, but the shower was running. Great, now my two best friends were doing it in my bathroom. I rolled my eyes; it was much better than Andy being in there; that was for sure. I stood in my empty kitchen and wished Adam was there making me breakfast like he had a few weeks before. I leaned against the counter as I looked around the space, taking a shaky breath.

Everything felt different all of a sudden. I felt like I was being torn in two—I yearned to walk across the hall and fall into Adam's arms again, but the other half of me doubted it was real. The worst part was the internal battle raging that said everything could be destroyed now. This could result in the ultimate demise of a relationship I had for my whole life. Adam wasn't just the man I loved; he was my best friend, the person who knew me better than I knew myself—but now, what were we? I didn't have the guts to ask.

"I feel much better!" Bobby said as he walked out of the bathroom into my living room, toweling his hair.

I rolled my eyes at him, leaning over my kitchen island. "Usually, that's what happens when you finally get some."

Bobby chucked the towel at me. "Why didn't you ever tell me Tara was interested in me?"

I grabbed the towel out of the air and stared at him for a moment with my mouth open. "You never asked!"

"Well," Bobby replied, leaning forward as well. "You should've told me."

I narrowed my eyes at him. "This better not be another booty call, got it?"

Bobby lowered his head to mine, his lips in a stern line as he answered, "I like her, River. It's the first time...I've been able to forget about you."

Our gazes searched one another before Tara walked into the room.

"Why so serious?" she asked as she looked between the two of us.

"Hey, gorgeous," Bobby said, pulling her into his arms and kissing her lightly on the forehead.

My eyes drifted across the room to the door. I wondered what Adam was doing and if he was thinking about me as much as I was thinking about him. And most of all I wished this was reversed— that I was there in his arms with him kissing me and telling me how beautiful I was.

Chapter 24

I tried to slow my breathing as I closed the door to my apartment Monday morning. I'd only left the apartment with Bobby and Tara for coffee to save my head, but the rest of the time I sat looking through photo albums and questioning my actions on Friday night. The worst part was Adam hadn't made any attempt at talking to me.

I felt eyes on me, but when I turned Adam was already half way down the stairs. I watched his back fade and then listened for the sound of the door opening and closing. The tears were already coming heavily down my face, and although I wanted to turn back into my apartment and bury my head in my pillow, I didn't. I marched down the stairs and out to my car and went to work. I acted like nothing was wrong. When, in fact, everything was wrong.

"Hey," Jesse said from behind me as I stared at my computer screen without seeing.

He came around my desk and sat in one of the chairs, crossing his legs and propping his arms up.

"What's up?" I asked, my voice trembling.

Jesse frowned at me. "You okay there?"

I swallowed, pushing my bangs out of my eyes. "Yeah, why?"

Jesse shook his head at me. "I just wanted to check on the branding for the Marquee?"

"I'm running with this idea," I replied, opening a folder and spreading a few images out. "I like the abstract feel. It's modern, and here are the models I've called in for the shoot."

Jesse ran his eyes over the pictures. "Looks great—I'd like to see some bold colors surrounded by black and whites."

"Will do," I replied as I shuffled the papers and placed them back in their project folder. I couldn't help the flat tone in my voice. Normally, I'd be excited for a photo shoot and another branding project, but now everything felt so wrong. It felt like something inside of me had clicked and then fallen away when Adam ignored me.

"You sure you're okay?" Jesse asked, cocking his head at me.

"Positive."

"Does this have something to do with the brothers that are both head over heels for you?"

I found myself scoffing, and I had a feeling the look on my face wasn't all that attractive. I couldn't help it. I wanted to cry or punch a wall to stop the racing in my head, but I couldn't do either.

"So it does," Jesse replied.

I shook my head, and he pursed his lips at me in disbelief.

Change the subject.

"Bobby and Tara are dating," I finally replied.

"The big one, right?" Jesse acknowledged.

I nodded.

"You're in love with the other one anyway, so...?"

"I told you, I don't think he's in love with me!" I said before putting my head in my hands in shame. "Sorry, Jesse. It's just a bad topic right now."

I closed my eyes and pressed my hands against the desk, and when I opened them, Jesse leaned forward to place his hands over mine. He never touched anyone, and I was usually very fond of my personal space, but instead of pulling away I looked up and waited for his explanation.

I needed some explanation for Adam's actions.

"Listen, River, guys, are weird creatures. You've known Adam your whole life, right?" he asked, and I nodded. "Things change in a moment's time, and we can't control it. If he's been in denial as long as you've been head over heels for him, this is not going to be easy for him. He's a player—when you already are one, it's hard to think you can stop being one even for that perfect person."

I looked down at his wedding band. "You speak from experience?"

He stood, winking at me. "You know it!"

"Jesse?" I asked as I turned in my chair, facing him as he stood at the door.

He nodded, and I asked, "Should I trust him?"

Jesse smiled down at me, light eyes shining against the

dark suit he was wearing. "I think you already know the answer to that question."

"Then why hasn't he spoken to me since..."

"He's still stuck on the fact that it even happened," Jesse answered.

"So am I," I said to myself.

"He'll come around," Jesse said as he turned out and walked away. "Don't forget bold colors and black and whites!"

Chapter 25

Three more days and there was still no sign of Adam. I was frustrated, hurt and annoyed. I'd been blown off by guys before, but they never had mattered. Adam did, though, and now I feared Tara had been right when she initially said it could ruin our friendship.

I punched at the air as the thought repeated in my skull—the man I loved my whole life was suddenly out of the picture. I shook the thought from my head as sweat dripped down my face, back and neck. I was in the second hour of the kickboxing dance video.

I couldn't stop. If I did, I wouldn't be able to think about anything but Adam. My door opened, and I ignored it, huffing as I pushed myself to keep going.

I needed to keep going.

"That's just gross," Bobby said.

I ignored him, but darkness was beginning to vignette my vision. I'd pushed myself too hard. It wouldn't be the first time, and I was sure it wouldn't be the last. Instead of being able to stop and sit I found the blackness pitching in on me uncontrollably.

"Shit," I mumbled as my knees collapse, and I fell onto my face.

When I opened my eyes, the shower head was pounding water into my vision.

"What the fuck were you thinking River?" Adam asked. His face was obscured by the water, but his tone said it all – he was worried.

I blinked to clear the water from my sight and watched as Adam leaned forward to shut the water off. In my peripheral vision, I could see a worried Bobby taking up the whole doorway. My head tittered on my shoulders as I looked back at Adam.

"What are you talking about?" I asked, my words slurred.

"How long were you working out like that?" Adam pushed.

"It looked like she'd been doing it for hours," Bobby answered for me. "She was literally soaking wet in sweat, and her water wasn't even open."

"Why'd you do that?" Adam asked. His tone softened as he wrapped a towel around me and pulled me into his arms.

"I was frustrated," I said as I let my head fall to his chest. I couldn't have fought him even if I didn't want to be in his arms, which I did. God, I did.

His body rumbled with a laugh. "What could ever make you that frustrated?"

I didn't want to fight, and I didn't want to suffer in silence anymore. It wasn't like I could come up with a good excuse right now anyway, so I answered truthfully, "You."

He must have been holding his breath because it came out in a whoosh as he shut my bedroom door behind him.

"I think you need to go to the hospital," Adam said, and his voice cracked.

"Why?" I asked as he laid me on my bed.

He knelt down beside me and brushed a soppy piece of hair out of my face.

"You need your head checked if I made you that frustrated," he said as his Adam's apple rose and fell.

His warm eyes searched mine, and I wondered what he was looking for.

"I think you're dehydrated," he finally said.

"So get me some water," I replied, but it sounded silly in a whisper.

"You probably want to change out of that," Adam said as he stood with his fists clenched and white.

I looked down at my soaked clothes and attempted to stand, but ended up falling forward. Adam caught me in his arms once again.

My head felt so heavy that I couldn't even hold it up, and it was thudding. God, was it thudding.

"I think you might need to help me," I said, squeezing my eyes shut as my brain threatened to explode.

"Are you sure?"

"It's nothing you haven't seen before," I reminded him.

I felt the muscles of his arms tense around me at the comment.

"If you don't mind," I added.

Adam's chest rose against mine, and he tilted my chin up with his index finger. "I'm a guy, of course, I don't mind."

My pulse pounded in my ears from the intensity of the comment, and as Adam set me back down on the bed, I squeezed my eyes shut again. I tried to interpret the meaning of his answer, but I couldn't think straight.

Damn him. He was so difficult to understand right now.

"What do you want to wear?" he asked.

"I don't know," I answered, opening one eye; "just grab something comfortable."

"What's comfortable in the bra department?" Adam said as he opened my top drawer and turned bright red.

I burst out laughing. "See something you like?"

Adam blinked a few times before looking up at me. "Lace, lots of lace."

"I'll keep that in mind," I answered.

I put my head down on my pillow, lightheaded from the laughter and watched Adam frown at me.

"Nothing is comfortable in the bra department," I replied.

"Underwear?"

"I can live without it."

"Well, I'm not letting Bobby see you naked. That's for my eyes only," Adam said as he leaned up against my dresser, his chest rising as he glanced over at me.

"Grab me a baggy t-shirt and a pair of yoga pants," I said as a shiver went up my spine.

For my eyes only, I liked the way it sounded. I didn't like the mixed signals, though, especially when I was having trouble comprehending what a simple comment meant.

"Alright," Adam replied as he opened a few more drawers, turned red again, slammed it shut and then opened another.

"You couldn't warn me you have a sexy lingerie drawer?" he hissed.

"Suck it up," I said as I closed my eyes with a satisfied smile.

I was enjoying his reactions, and it made me think maybe Jesse was right.

"Does this work?" Adam asked, hovering over me with his shirt and a pair of hot pink yoga pants.

"Yes," I said as he helped me sit up and slid my sports bra over my head.

Adam paused for a second before lifting my arms and dropping his shirt over me. I stood, leaning against him for support and pulled my spandex workout shorts and underwear off in one swoop.

Adam looked straight ahead as I struggled with one pant leg and then the other.

"You going to be okay?" I asked.

"Yeah, sure," he muttered.

"I'm sorry I didn't tell you not to look in *that* drawer," I said as I sat back on my bed and grabbed the towel to dry my hair.

"Here, let me help you." Adam sat down behind me and took the towel from my hand. "You look lightheaded."

I sighed. "I am."

For more than one reason.

He pulled my head into his lap and gently rubbed my scalp with the towel. I closed my eyes, and when I woke I was wrapped in Adam's arms on the couch.

"Hey," Adam said as my eyes fluttered open.

"Hey," I repeated back to him.

"You scared the shit out of me," Bobby said from the armchair across the way.

I leaned up to look at him. "It's a good thing you came in when you did."

"I guess I should've known what to do, but when I saw you collapse, I called Adam over."

"It's fine," I said as I sat up, head still pounding. "Can I have some Motrin™?"

Bobby jolted up and went to the bathroom. He came back a moment later with a bottle, shaking his head with eyes wide. "Why do girls have that much stuff in their bathroom?"

"Because they're girls," Adam said, smirking at him.

"Thank God I live with you, bro!" Bobby said as he went to get me a glass of water.

"Yeah, because guys are just a bushel of roses to live with," I said with my eyelids half-shut in sarcasm.

Bobby handed me the pills, and I chased them down with the water.

"I don't think you should go to work tomorrow," Bobby suggested. "You still look like a ghost."

"I can work from home," I answered, nodding towards the laptop on the coffee table. "I'm big time now."

"Sure you are," Adam said, elbowing me in the ribs. "And it's all because of me. I saw the photographs in the salon the other day. They're amazing."

"You'd swear you two really were in love with each other," Bobby butted in, and we both turned to stare at him.

Bobby shrugged, but his eyes darted from Adam to mine in a telling fashion. He was fishing for information, and that meant one thing, Tara hadn't made it, so he was completely over me.

"I guess that's what happens when you've known someone for such a long time," I said after drinking the rest of the water. It was Adam's turn to sit and wonder what I meant. "I'm sure it'd have been the same if you were there instead of Adam."

Wrong answer. I knew it, but my wasted brain was too stupid to work in coordination with my mouth. I felt Adam's hand tighten on my waist, and I looked over at him. He was staring at the TV with his jaw clenched and neck red beneath the five o'clock shadow he developed over the week.

Bobby looked at us and coughed. "I'm ravished, anyone else want pizza?"

"Yeah, I'll get it," Adam answered as he stood.

"We can get it delivered," I reminded Adam, but he already had his keys out of his pocket and one hand on the door knob.

"I need to go for a drive," he replied before slipping out the door.

"Pepperoni!" Bobby called at him.

"That was weird," Bobby said as he came to sit down

next to me, pulling me into his big arms. "Actually, he's been weird all week—must be what happened with *Kiki*."

"Shut up!" I said with a disapproving shake of my head.

"You called her it, not me!"

"That whole night was a blur—speaking of which, how goes it with Tara?"

I needed to think about something other than Adam's strange actions. His caring for me was no different than our whole lives, but his open flirting had been, and then his reaction to my comment about Bobby—that had been out of character too.

Bobby shrugged. "It hasn't even been a week yet. We have a date Friday. Speaking of which, why don't you and Adam join us? You're both single so that you could use some time out with normal people like Tara and I. Maybe it'll inspire you guys to go out and find some normal people to date."

"Yeah, because you and Tara are the bane of normal," I said, glancing up at him.

"So are you in?" he asked.

"Yeah, if you can convince your brother to go—I think he's pissed at me."

"So what happened in the bedroom?"

"What?" I asked, my pulse rising at the thought that he might have heard something that night.

Had I been loud? I couldn't remember, but my body was tingling from the thought.

"A few hours ago?"

"Oh, that...nothing."

"Was there another bedroom incident I should know about?" Bobby asked, and his blue eyes bore into mine as they searched for an answer I couldn't give.

"No, not at all."

Bobby bit his cheek and looked away from me. "Alright."

I knew he didn't believe me. It was all over my face.

Chapter 26

Adam barely talked to me when he returned with the pizza, and he talked even less to Bobby. The next morning the two brothers came to check on me, and when Bobby rushed out to go to work, Adam soon followed. It was as if he was afraid to be alone with me, and the feeling was only confirmed by the fact he darted down the stairs the following day to avoid walking out to the cars with me. I was shocked when Bobby called me around midday and told me he convinced Adam to go to dinner with me, Tara and him.

Tara came over to get ready like she always did, but for the first time, I was a nervous mess.

"Help me!" I said as I flung another outfit on the bed and flopped down with my head in my hands. "I have no clue what to wear."

"Wow," Tara replied with her hands on her hips. "I've never seen you like this."

I looked up at her and huffed, throwing my hands up as I fought with the churning in my stomach.

"Alright, Alright!" she answered. Her laughter was evident in her tone as she turned to my closet. "What are we looking for here? Sexy, coy, irresistible?"

"Lace," I said, sitting straight up. "Find me something with lace!"

Tara's eyes widened. "Sexy and sophisticated it is!"

She dug into the back of my closet and pulled out a blush pink sheath dress, which was overlaid with soft lace. The shoulders and what there was for a back were completely sheer.

"So?" she asked, looking from the dress to me and back again.

I squealed as I grabbed it from her. "I don't remember buying it, but *hell* yes!"

"Nude lipstick, and cat eyeliner—irresistible!"

"You're the best," I said, pulling her into a tight hug before rushing into the bathroom to change.

When I came out dressed and dolled up, she was sitting on the couch in a sapphire number that pulled the blue from her ever changing eyes.

"Now," she sat up; "you have to help me do my hair!"

I went to the bathroom and grabbed the curling iron, waving it with a smile as I walked back into the room.

"Curls?" she asked as she tapped her fingers against her thigh.

"Yup," I said as I leaned over and plugged it before running my fingers through her already waving hair. "I'll just give it a little bit more than what's natural."

I was happy to style her hair. It kept my mind off of Adam and settled some of the anxiety that kept bubbling in my insides and making me dizzy.

"I'm good," I said as I came to the front of her and took

in the messy bun with light curls framing her heart-shaped face. "Go take a peek."

She squealed as she came out. "You 're incredible!"

I took a bow. "Told you so!"

"Hello! Hello!" Bobby said as he barged in the door without knocking.

"What if we weren't ready?" I asked as I crossed my arms and popped my hip out.

"Sure as hell looks like you're ready!" Bobby replied, a whistle coming out of his lips as he looked at Tara and me.

I smiled at Adam behind him. He was only looking at me, and it made me want to rush into his arms and kiss him—to feel his skin against mine again.

Amazing he mouthed, and I tried not to show the breath I had to take.

Tara nudged my back and whispered, "I think it's working."

"Ditto," I replied.

"So where are you boys taking us tonight?" Tara asked, linking her arm through Bobby's.

"Bella Noché," Bobby replied as he led the way out of the apartment.

Adam waited for me to lock the door, and we fell into step well behind them.

"They're good together, no?" I asked, nodding towards the laughing couple.

"Yeah," Adam said, but he wouldn't give me much else.

We walked in awkward silence to the car, which only continued in the car while Bobby and Tara chatted happily in the backseat. It made me painfully aware that Adam wasn't speaking to me at all. I was going insane. I wanted to smack Adam for the silence that suddenly engulfed our relationship.

"So how's work?" Adam finally asked as we stood outside the restaurant as we waited to be seated.

"Good, Jesse is giving me a lot more responsibility now. He seems to really trust me with the photography thing," I answered, trying not to grind my teeth.

Years of friendship had turned into this? *How's work?*

"He should; you do a fantastic job," Adam said with a stiff nod, his hands in his pockets.

"Yours?" I asked.

I'd play along with his game as long as I could hold it together, but I didn't feel like that would be much longer. My pulse was quickening, and I could feel the sweat dampening my body.

"Good," he answered with a shrug. "They make me take the lip ring out now. The kids think it's a bummer."

I looked up at the piercing and had to close my eyes as I remembered the cool feeling of it running across my skin.

"Yeah, it's quite the masterpiece," I managed to say.

"It's chilly out here," Tara said as she looked between the two of us.

The look in her eyes said it was more than the weather making her uncomfortable.

"There're two chairs inside," Bobby said, nodding to the only free space inside the waiting area. "You guys mind?"

I swallowed and shook my head. "No, go ahead. Let us know when our table's ready?"

"Of course!" Bobby smirked as he slung his arm around Tara's waist and ushered her in.

Tara mouthed *talk to him* over her shoulder at me, and I grimaced at her, tugging the hem of my dress. Great, now she was abandoning me because she thought we needed space to talk. I took a deep breath and glanced up at Adam.

He stood in front of me as I leaned against the brick wall, and his eyes darted from me to his feet. He stopped pacing, and looked up at me. In that moment I knew I had enough of the silence and games. I'd always been able to talk to Adam openly, why should this be any different?

"So now you're just going to act like nothing happened?" I asked as I crossed my arms more from annoyance than the cold.

He shook his head. "Come on Riv, you know it's not like that."

"I don't know what it's like. Have you already moved on from?" I asked, stepping towards him. I was angry, and I wasn't hiding it at all anymore.

I needed an explanation. He didn't move away. Instead, he rubbed his chin with his hand, his throat rising as he thought of what to say.

Finally he spoke, "I'm moving forward while standing still...I'm stuck on the way you feel—the sensation of your skin against mine, but it doesn't mean it's right. I shouldn't have—I'm sorry."

My insides twisted at his pained expression. That was

the problem with Adam, I couldn't be mad at him when he was honest with me. I shook my head and put my arms around his neck. I could feel the stubble on his chin against my forehead as he pressed it there with his hands resting lightly on my hips.

"I can't," his voice came in a crack.

The desperation in his voice was misplaced and as his eyes danced over my face I knew he was just as broken as I was. That kiss, those caresses—the feeling of his skin against mine had shattered our perfect friendship. There was no turning back now; having him was the only thing that would make me whole. Before he could continue I pressed my lips against his, but the resistance there was a slap in the face. I felt his hands grow stiff on my waist as he pushed me away.

"No!" he said, walking away and kicking the air. "We can't now. It was a mistake!"

I grabbed for his hand and pulled him back into me. I knew it wasn't, and I needed him to see he didn't really feel that way either. The heat of his hands hovered over my back as he hesitated in touching me back. His body was rigid as he pushed me against the wall and walked away again, his hands buried in the back of his hair. My body flushed with heat at his reaction, and I realized I wasn't getting anywhere. He made his decision and everything inside me felt shattered. Tears sprung to my eyes as I shook my trembling chin.

"Why did you do it then? Why?" The anger returned, coupled with the crippling pain of rejection. I loved him and in that moment I realized he didn't feel the same.

A painful, fake chuckle came from his lips as he turned and answered, "You know me. I'm an ass—a player."

The look in his eyes said it wasn't true, and I shook my head as tears fell to my cheeks. His eyes darkened.

"I was drunk out of my mind!" His hand went to his forehead as his breathing quickened and his eyes closed.

He had been. I had been, but that didn't change what I felt. His hand dropped and his lips twisted downward as he shook his head, the look in his eyes showing we didn't feel the same. He regretted every touch and word more than he regretted anything. The pain inside my chest rose, taking over my whole being as I realized he meant what he said.

Words tumbled out uncensored and untrue, only meant to hurt. "I hate you Adam! God, do I hate you! Out of every person in the world you were the last one I thought would do this to me. You're my best friend for God's sake, but still you treat me exactly like every other skank you drag in!" The tears were heavy as I yelled at him, "I never thought you'd do this to me. I never thought you'd enjoy breaking me like you've broken everyone else. You're such a piece of shit! You know I've loved you since we were kids! If this is who you really are...then...then there's nothing left."

I rushed past him, knocking my shoulders against his as he hung his own.

"I hate you!" I repeated, against an angry sob.

Then his hand snaked into mine, grabbing me and pulling me into a hard kiss. He pulled away as his eyes burned into mine, and he placed his hands on either side of my face.

"It's not because I don't want you," he said, voice cracking again. "I'm wrong for you. I'm an irresponsible player. I don't know how to be in love. I don't want to hurt you anymore than I have, but I can't lose you. Don't walk away from me."

His breathing came ragged as his lips crushed into me again, and I couldn't fight them. When he pulled away, his jaw was clenched as his eyes searched mine.

"Fix me, please. I want to be yours forever."

My breathing stopped as I stared back at him. He looked scared like I might say no. I shook my head, and his eyes fell.

"Adam," I said, and his eyes rose again. "I can't fix you. Only you can do that, but I'm yours despite it."

He scoffed as he moved away from me to face the wall. He turned back and threw his hands up in frustration.

"But for how long? How long can you love me when I'm such a fool?" I smiled and started to answer, but he stopped me. "It'll be different now—you'll have to deal with me as your boyfriend, not just an asshole you've known your whole life."

I pulled on the suit jacket he was wearing, so his hips were against mine.

"Say it again?"

"What?" he asked, and I could feel his heart racing underneath my palm pressed against his neck. It was strange to know I had this effect on him—that I may have had this effect on him for years.

"That you're my boyfriend."

"I'm yours, River. I'm yours," he whispered as his breath washed over my lips.

The world tilted on its axis then. Everything felt right for once in my life, and I didn't feel torn about the decision. I knew it was the right despite the way holding Adam's hand under the table while Bobby sat across from us bit at my conscience. The truth was, at that moment I was incandescently happy, and I knew telling Bobby about the new development in Adam and I's relationship would only ruin it. We'd have to tell him eventually, though I wasn't sure when that would be.

Chapter 27

The high from the previous night left me still smiling as I stared at my computer screen adjusting the colors for the Marquee's advertisements.

"Knock knock," Jesse said from the door.

I turned in my chair and smiled up at him. "Here to check on those bold colors and black and whites?"

"What? I can't just come in and say hi to one of my best employees?" Jesse asked as he pushed his shoulders up.

"Mhmm," I said with a roll of my eyes as I turned back to the computer screen and leaned to the side so he could see the files. "What do you think?"

"Epic," Jesse said, pointing to the name. "It's exactly what I was picturing. I love this font you chose for the name, it's edgy."

I spun back around to see his face plastered with an arrogant smirk. "You know me—I'm all up in the coolest things."

Jesse's gray eyebrows rose into his forehead as he repeated me. "All up in the coolest things?"

I nodded, wiggling my eyebrows at him.

I watched as he leaned back against my desk. "That statement says otherwise."

I let my eyes rise. "You're an old man; you wouldn't know!"

Jesse nodded, lips pursing. "Not the first time I've heard that this week. My ten year old told me I was *so not cool.*"

I laughed as I turned back to my screen, watching as he walked to the front of my desk. "Ten-year-olds are hard to please."

"You know it," he said as he sat and narrowed his eyes at me. "So, you're glowing?"

"Whatever do you mean?"

He tapped his finger against his lip before asking, "You and Adam?"

"Maybe," I answered, drawing out the words as the smile spread across my whole face.

"What did I tell you?" he said, crossing his arms, so his suit seams pulled.

"I guess I should've trusted the old man."

"Damn right!" Jesse said as he stood. "Don't forget it...Speaking of the devil!"

I turned in my chair just as Adam sauntered in past Jesse who clapped him on his back.

"Hey," he said as he sat down on the edge of my desk and leaned down to kiss me.

"What are you doing here?" I asked, and I felt the warmth travel up my cheeks as I watched the girl in the cubicle across from my office narrow her eyes at me.

"What? I can't visit my girlfriend at work and bring her out to dinner?" he asked as his eyes trailed down my body to my crossed legs.

I looked down at my watch to see it was five thirty. "I didn't even realize it was that late!"

Adam nodded over my shoulder at the files I showed Jesse. "Too hard at work, I see."

"Yeah, I just got them approved by Jesse, and I'm sending them off to get the files printed. The billboard is going to be right in Copley Square," I said.

My chest tightened at the thought of *my* advertisement being in the middle of Boston. It was a good thing Jesse trusted me.

"I'm assuming the guy that who just left was Jesse then?"

I nodded, and his lips twitched at their edges.

"What's wrong?" I asked.

"He's kind of good looking?"

I wasn't sure if it was a statement or a question, but the fact he was nervous about it was cute. I stood and put my hands on his shoulders. "Who? Old gray hair?"

"Yeah," Adam said, placing his hands on my hips. "The blue eyes and gray hair...broad chest—he's got a James Bond thing going on."

I bit the inside of my lip as I tilted my head. "First, he's not you, and second, he's very happily married with two kids," I said as I played with the buttons on his vest. "I much rather have the hot-rocker-teacher."

Adam's hands slid behind my back. "Really?"

"Yeah, it's super sweet he'd get me at work to bring me out to dinner."

Adam winked at me, and my heart began to race. "Let's get going then?" he asked.

"Where are we going?" I asked as I leaned over and shut off my computer.

"Huh? What?" Adam asked as I looked over my shoulder to see him staring at my ass in the air.

"Really?" I asked as I grabbed my purse from the desk.

"Sorry, it's distracting. Especially now that I don't have to hide I'm staring," Adam said as he pulled me into his arms, one hand on the small of my back and the other on my chin as he tilted my lips to his.

I pulled away, trying to catch my breath as I glanced over my shoulder with burning cheeks. "I'm still at work."

Adam shrugged, and his hand slid from my chin, down my arm, and into my hand, leaving my skin burning. "We won't be soon."

"Where are you bringing me?" I asked as we headed towards the exit.

"Where would you like to go?" he asked as he held the door for me.

"Sushi!"

Adam's nose and mouth moved upward. "I've never had that."

I slipped my hand back into his as we fell into step in the parking lot. "You're missing out!"

"If you say so," Adam replied, and his tone showed his doubt.

We stopped at our cars, and my eyes drifted from his to mine and back again. "Are we taking two cars or one?" I asked.

"Two, if Bobby catches us we can just say we ran into

each other," Adam said, his posture straightening at the mention of his brother. My chest tightened as I thought of what kind of blow up that could mean. It could go either of two ways; he could be okay with it and continue to pursue Tara, or he could flip shit. I was counting on the later.

"Right." I bit my lip before adding, "How long are we going to keep this from him?"

"Until we know this Tara thing is serious. Hopefully, he won't be so crushed then...but I'm not counting on it," Adam replied as he loosened his tie and unbuttoned the collar of his shirt.

Despite whatever Bobby's reaction might be I hated keeping something from him. It made this, which felt so right, feel wrong. I reached in my purse for my keys, and Adam's hand stopped me.

"Hey, why are you upset?"

"I'm not," I replied, giving him a fake smile. His slow blinking told me I wasn't fooling him.

"Really? I know you better than you know yourself, and your face says others," Adam said as he released my hands and leaned against his car with crossed arms. I watched as the cotton of the button-up stretched around his upper arms in a distracting fashion.

"I don't want to hurt Bobby," I finally replied.

Adam reached for my hands and entwined our fingers. "We fit perfectly, Riv. You think he didn't see this coming?"

"I didn't ever actually think it was going to happen, though," I said, looking at our hands perfectly molded together.

My eyes wandered upwards, and I watched as Adam licked his lips and then dragged his teeth over them. "Would you've settled for him?"

My head jerked back. "What?"

"Would you've settled for him eventually?" he repeated, and his eyes raced over my face, watching my expression.

"No," I answered, but my voice faltered.

I wouldn't have, would I?

"You don't sound convinced," he said.

Ten years hadn't softened me. Ten more wouldn't either.

I locked my eyes on his. "I wouldn't have."

He narrowed his eyes as he reached up and moved a hair out of my eyes. "I'm glad I got to you first. I would've never forgiven myself."

He didn't believe me.

"Let me try this again – no," I said.

Adam leaned in and brushed his lips against mine. "Let's say I'm glad we can't run that risk now."

Our lips parted slightly, and I leaned in again, running my hand through the back of his hair as I deepened the kiss. His hands worked their way down my back to my ass before he pulled away and pressed his forehead against mine.

"Very glad," he replied.

"Me too." I pulled away and turned to my car, looking over my shoulder as I asked, "Where to?"

"My bedroom?" he asked, a glint in his eyes.

So very tempting but my stomach growled, reminding me I hadn't eaten since eleven in the morning.

"You can sneak into mine after, but I'm hungry," I

replied. I had to admit the idea of skipping dinner was far more appetizing than raw fish.

"Is that a solid invitation?" Adam asked, leaning against his open driver's side door.

"Well, I like to have dessert with my dinner," I said with a wink before hopping in my car and revving the engine at him.

He shook his head and nodded for me to lead the way.

Chapter 28

I sat at my desk readying the camera gear for the photo shoot for a local bakery that was looking for a set of very tantalizing wedding cake advertisements. By tantalizing, I mean sexy, and the whole theme made me uncomfortable on so many levels. I didn't like the idea of the ad, let along having to be the photographer behind the lens taking the pictures for it. This was a major client, though, so when Jesse gave me the assignment I caved—but not without grumbling. I heard Tara's stilettos clicking against the tile floor before she made her way into my office with a huge huff. I turned to see her leaning against the doorframe with a pout.

"What you doing tonight?" she asked as she looked down at her new fingernails; bright red with Swarovski crystals encrusted on them. They were so Tara, and they made me smile.

Just like I was pretty sure what I was about to say would make her smile. "Doing a kinky cake shoot."

Her chin jerked back into her neck and her eyes widened. "I wasn't aware you did porno?"

I looked at the ceiling before I stood and stuffed the camera in its bag. "It's not a porno. It's just some chick in lingerie and a dude in boxers getting in a cake fight."

"That doesn't seem like an idea you'd come up with," she said.

"What the client wants, they must get," I replied, using Jesse's exact words when I balked at the idea.

"Right..." she said. She chewed on the inside of her lips before asking. "Do you think it's a good marketing idea?"

I shrugged. "It depends on the image you're going for. If it were my wedding cake, I wouldn't go for the cake advertisement with the naked people in it."

"Is there a ring on your finger I don't know about?" Tara asked with a squeak as I turned to face her.

She was standing straight now, hands over her mouth in excitement.

"We just started dating—"

"You what?" she asked, and she stepped forward, placing her hands on her hips as one eyebrow arched.

I felt my whole body flush with heat, my face becoming unbearably hot as I replied, "Yeah, we kissed and made up."

She clapped her hands. "Finally!"

I nodded and watched as her happy expression disappeared into a pout again. She sighed, her lips pursing.

"So what's wrong with you today?" I asked as I stood and slung my camera bag and purse over my shoulder.

"Did you forget?"

I furrowed my brow at her before walking past her. "I guess so?"

Tara kept pace with me and grabbed her purse off her

cubicle as we passed it. "Bobby's gone for a four-day week-end in New Hampshire with the hockey team?"

I stopped walking and turned to face her. "Huh?"

"He didn't tell you?"

I shrugged, and we kept walking. I was about as emo as she had been a second ago. The truth was Bobby pretty much stopped telling me anything since he started dating Tara. There was a tinge of jealousy as I thought of it, but I fought it down knowing I had Adam now. I never expected Bobby would no longer need me or confide in me about anything. I guess that wasn't true because he did confide in me...about Tara. It just happened to be a *little* too much information I didn't want to *know* about either of them. I hadn't noticed Tara continued to babble next to me.

"Right?" she asked.

I ran my hands through my hair as I nodded. "Sure."

"So I should worry about him going away?" Her voice softened and faded as she reflected on my response.

"I guess you should repeat the question?" I asked as I unlocked my car, and she jumped in the passenger seat.

I raised an eyebrow at her.

"You weren't listening. Now I have to come with you to explain!"

I chuckled to myself as I slipped my sunglasses over my eyes.

"Alright, start from the beginning," I said.

"So, Bobby and I are going great—"

"So I've heard."

She narrowed her eyes at me, and I signaled with my hand for her to continue.

"I know he goes on these trips a lot because you've told me about them, but you've never told me what happens when he goes on them," she began.

I shook my head failing to see her point. "He coaches his team on how to play hockey better? Yells at them when they mess up and cheers them on when they're doing well."

Tara huffed, crossed her arms and looked straight ahead.

"What point am I missing?" I asked.

"What happens *after* the games?"

"They sleep?" I answered, watching her out of the corner of my eye. Her expression was a nod and widened eyes. "Oh, who does he sleep *with*?"

Her head jerked up and down as her face turned red.

"A pillow?"

She blinked at me several times, and I kept my eyes on the road.

"Come on, Riv!"

"Okay, he's never told me about any sexual expiates during one of them before. They're stressful, and every once in a while his parents show up and take him and the team out to dinner for winning."

"So I have nothing to worry about?"

I reached over and squeezed her leg. "I know Bobby's got a brother who's a player, but Bobby's never cheated."

"Phew," she said, and was quiet before continuing, "Do you worry about Adam, you know, cheating?"

"Adam's never cheated on anyone. He just changes his mind about as often as he changes underwear."

"You didn't answer the question."

I kept my eyes straight ahead as my chest constricted. "We've been dating two weeks."

"Doesn't every girl worry?" she asked, and I could see her eyes set on me from the corner of my vision. She wasn't going to take that for an answer, and I doubted she would drop it unless I confided in her. I pulled into the parking lot and shifted the car to a stop before looking up at her. "I thought you were the one who told me not to worry?"

"I don't think you should worry..." Her voice drifted off before she continued, "I'm just curious why you haven't told Bobby yet? I mean, if you think it's going to last, why wouldn't you tell him? It's going to hurt him even more if you tell him after you guys have been together for a month or two."

I swallowed. I knew she was right.

"We'll tell him soon enough," I said.

"You think his freaking out is going to hurt me?" Tara asked as I grabbed my camera gear from the backseat.

"Wouldn't it?"

She shrugged. "I know he's going to freak out. It doesn't matter how much time you give him."

"Doesn't that bug you?"

I glanced over my shoulder and watched as she looked at her feet.

"It was kind of part of the package."

"You didn't answer my question."

"What do you think, River? Would it bug you if you knew Adam had feelings for someone else that you could do nothing about?"

I picked up my pace and turned to face her, stopping her in her tracks. "The reason I'm asking is because I spent my whole life practically feeling like that."

Our eyes met, and I watched as hers darkened to the turquoise color which meant she was upset. "I'll make him forget you."

I put my hands on her crossed arms. "We're giving you time to do that before we tell him."

"Fine," she replied with narrowed eyes before pulling away and walking around me. "Give me two more weeks."

"Two more weeks it is," I said with a smile as my mind drifted to a total of four days where Adam and I didn't have to watch our every move.

"Eww!" Tara said, slapping my arm.

"What?" I asked, snapping out of my day dream.

"You're totally thinking about how many places you and Adam can screw without worrying about getting caught!"

"That wasn't the whole thought," I replied.

But it certainly was a part of it.

"Well, if you're thinking of the apartment—Bobby and I have touched every surface except for Adam's bedroom and bathroom."

"You two are like bunny rabbits, I swear!" I said.

"I don't even want to think about how much action the back of the GLI has gotten," Tara said as I opened the door.

"The GLI is sacred ground, Tara. You should know Adam would never taint that," I replied.

She shrugged. "I'd make it so he couldn't wait to get home."

"Are you saying I can't?" I asked as we faced each other and I crossed my arms.

She mirrored my posture before asking, "Wouldn't you say Bobby's truck is pretty sacred to him?"

I narrowed my eyes at her. The Beckerson boys both loved their vehicles almost as much as they loved their guitars or hockey sticks. "You're sick."

"No, *I'm* just that good."

I choked at the comment just as the models came out of the dressing room. I closed my eyes as I looked at the male model in boxer briefs.

Tara turned slowly to see what I was looking at. "Mhmm...tasty... and I don't mean the cake."

"Oh, puke!" I said as I looked at the ceiling and counted to three. I could do this. "I thought Bobby was all you wanted."

She cocked her head at the model, and she wasn't looking at his face. "Bobby's bigger."

I crossed my eyes as I gagged. Or maybe I couldn't take it—not with the second most perverted person I ever met as my sidekick. Tara's dirty mind was only outdone by Bobby's.

"Both of you need to learn what information I don't mind hearing, and what information makes me want to burn my earlobes off."

"Oh, so you do know how good I am!"

184

I closed my eyes, and when I opened them, she was wiggling her eyebrows. "Unfortunately, yes," I replied.

She laughed to herself, and I shook my heads as I clapped minds and walked towards my models. "I suppose you're Mark, and Angela?"

Chapter 29

Thursday was boy's night out, so even though Tara invited herself to the photo shoot, I was glad she came and kept my mind occupied. I was even happier when she remembered she left some of her clothes the last time she came over. I wasn't used to spending the night alone anymore, and I knew Adam was too exhausted after whatever he did on Thursdays to come over. Tara took away my obsessive thoughts about where Adam was with "his boys". I trusted Adam, but it bugged me that we'd known each other almost our whole lives, and I'd never realized he did this almost every week. Plus, Tara's girl talk was growing on me.

"So what's the first thing you're going to do tomorrow with Bobby gone?" Tara asked, smirking over the top of the pillow she was hugging.

I looked up at the ceiling, pushing my tongue into the corner of my mouth. "Leave the apartment holding Adam's hand."

"Aww! You're too cute—you're blushing so much right now!" Tara said. "So...has the L word been mentioned at all?"

"You mean love?" I asked. She nodded, and I shrugged. "He hasn't said it."

"Does that bug you?" Tara asked, moving up the bed and resting her head in her hands.

"We haven't been dating that long."

Tara blinked at me a few times before she sat up and crossed her legs. "You've known each other since you were five!"

Her points were valid, but I wasn't sure. He did *just* admit his feelings for me recently. "Maybe he doesn't love me yet."

Her eyes widened, and they were green against her gray sweatshirt. "Oh! Bullshit!"

"What?" I asked as I picked at the frayed edge of my sweatshirt sleeve.

"You don't think he'd know if he loved you?"

I let the breath I was holding out slowly. "It doesn't mean he wants to say it."

"He *is* Adam," Tara said. "I doubt he's ever said the word before."

Our eyes locked on each other, and we both nodded in unison. I hadn't realized how tense my muscles became until that moment. I sank into the bed, relaxing.

"Probably not. Honestly, I don't think I've even heard him say it to his parents," I said.

"Really?" Tara was interested now.

"Nope, they have a rocky relationship."

"Speaking of which, I haven't seen your parents lately?" she asked.

I grabbed a pillow from next to me and put it over my stomach, playing with the edges of it. As sad as it was, I didn't really miss Mom. I did miss Dad, though.

"Eh, my mom is busy with her new job, and my dad, well...I think he's kind of upset I flipped out on the Beckersons'. He's very proper, you know?"

"I would've loved to see it," she said.

I shook my head. "You wouldn't have—I made Bobby super upset."

"I could've comforted him...and that would've sped up this whole process of us both getting the booty we wanted," Tara said, and her wiggling brows made me laugh.

"Yeah, it's all about the booty," I fired back as I leaned back against the headboard.

A pillow suddenly struck me in the head. "Stop thinking about it! I know you've done it in this bed, but God, keep those thoughts kosher while I'm sitting on it!"

Leave it to Tara to turn something, or anything, dirty.

I snatched the pillow up and chucked it at her head. "You're the one who told me all about tainting every surface in Adam's apartment!"

"It was a fair warning!" she said as she grabbed the pillow from the air and smacked me with it.

Then it was on. A full-blown pillow fight ensued only stopping when a whistle came from the doorway.

"I, honest to God, thought this sort of thing never happened in real life!" Adam said, and his tone was laced with amusement.

We both turned and dropped our pillows when we saw

him. At least we were both fully dressed, so it wasn't a full blown guy fantasy.

"I thought you'd come home and go to sleep," I said as I hopped down off the bed.

"I was going to, but then I heard some very distinct squealing and was wondering what my girlfriend was up to," Adam replied with a smirk. "I'm glad it wasn't what I thought it could be."

"Ha!" Tara jumped down as well. "River would never cheat on you! She hasn't stopped talking about what you guys are going to do with Bobby gone for a whole weekend."

Adam's eyebrows twitched, and his lip ring pulled ever so slightly in his mouth. "Really?" he asked.

Tara shrugged. "Something about holding hands where everyone can see."

"Oh," Adam said, and his eyes went down to his feet as he tipped onto his toes and back again.

"God! You two are such perverts!" Tara replied as she slipped past Adam into the living room.

Adam's eye rose to mine, and there were dark circles under them. His hair was still damp with sweat, curling out over his forehead. I wrapped my arms around his neck. "You look exhausted."

He nodded. "A bit."

"Tara's sleeping over," I said.

Adam's lips curled at the edges, dimples forming in his cheeks. "I got that picture."

"I can take the couch!" Tara said to us as she came out of the bathroom.

Adam leaned down and kissed me. "I had my boy's night so that you can have your girl's night."

"Are you sure?" I asked.

"We have all weekend to hold hands," he replied before winking and turning to leave.

"Behave!" he said to Tara, pointing a finger at her.

Tara stopped, put her hands on her hips and raised her eyebrows. "Really, Adam?"

Adam's shoulders rose and fell as he laughed. The smile on his face as he closed the door behind him left me breathless and wishing I could drag him back in.

"Where does he go?" Tara asked as she flopped on the couch with a bag of chips and a can of soda.

I sat down with her and took the bag, throwing some chips in my mouth before answering, "Not a clue."

She chugged her soda and burped before turning to me crinkling my nose. She smiled wide.

"We should so stalk him one Thursday and find out what his dirty little secret is...Oh! I forgot *you're* his dirty little secret!"

"Where's that pillow when I need to biff you with it?" I shot back.

Tara sat forward and pulled the throw pillow from her back and waved it in my face.

"Mine...all mine!" She taunted me, sticking her tongue out as she pulled it away from my grabbing hands.

"I figure he'll tell me what he's up to when he's ready to."

Tara narrowed her eyes before shrugging and grabbing the chips back. She was fixed on the TV now, and my thoughts drifted back to what Adam had been doing. There were only so many things you dressed semi-casual for and then still ended up sweating your ass off...There wasn't any I could think of at the moment I'd be okay with.

"What are you getting?" Tara asked as I stood.

"Ice cream."

I needed it now.

Chapter 30

When I woke up Tara was already awake, humming to herself in the kitchen and from the smell wafting over me, she was cooking.

I shot up in bed. Those were two things that were very unlike Tara. She never woke up earlier than eight, and she sure as hell didn't cook, especially not...my nose lifted...French toast. Then I heard another familiar voice, and the sound made a happy sigh come from my throat. I slipped out of bed and peeked into the living room to see Tara sitting at the island twirling around on a bar stool with Adam behind the stove.

He already had a button-up shirt and vest combo on that was making me drool. He hadn't put his tie on yet, and his shirt was just unbuttoned enough to show the shape of his chest. Tara spun around to see me and smirked, fluttering her hand over her face in his hotness. I mouthed the words *I know, right*, and she nodded in response.

I made my way into the kitchen and wrapped my arms around Adam, standing on my toes to tuck my chin in his collarbone and kiss his neck.

"That better be River," Adam said.

"You're *so* not my type," Tara shot back as Adam turned and kissed me.

We both looked over at her in disbelief.

"You were so drooling over there," Adam said, pointing to her with the spatula.

She shrugged with her eyes wide and innocent. "For the French toast!"

Adam blinked at her a few times, and she smiled widely back at him.

"Sure," Adam said, drawing out the word.

"Did you make—"

"Your cup's right there." Adam cut me off with a nod to the counter.

"Mhmm," I said as I let go of him and grabbed the cup with both hands and took a deep sip. "Perfect, as always."

Tara huffed behind me, and I turned slowly to face her. "What?"

She sat with her head in her chin, voluptuous lips pursed as she swayed her feet side to side.

"I know I'm not from around here, but I just don't get it...It's barely Fall, and Bobby's already away for something to do with hockey?"

"You really aren't from around here," Adam said as he divided out the food and handed each of us each a plate.

I went around to the other side of the island to sit next to Tara. This way we could both drool over Adam as he ate.

"Connecticut isn't *that* far away," Tara said as she shoved a piece of French toast in her mouth.

Adam raised an eyebrow at her before shaking his head.

"Whatever part you're from must be Alaska compared to here."

"Whatever! Just explain to me why they're freezing their asses off in a skating rink instead of basking in the remaining summer sun." Tara replied.

"You want to explain it?" Adam asked, tilting his head at me as he brought his coffee up to his lips.

"Hockey's a big sport around here. It's really like any other sport," I began to explain with a shrug. "The players prepare all year for the next season."

Tara huffed again before taking a sip of her orange juice. "Still sucks."

"Hockey is pretty much Bobby's life, so you'll have to get used to it," I said.

"I don't think I'm going to be able to get used to him going away for days on end. It's just...weird."

Adam and I looked at each other. We both agreed from the time we were kids that the hockey tournaments were a reprieve, usually not so much from Bobby as from their parents. The gushing over how amazing he did was plenty punishment when they got back for enjoying the fact they were gone.

"You get used to it," Adam said.

"Sure you two will." Tara pointed between us with her fork.

"Hey, he's still my best friend and brother," Adam reminded her as he took our plates from us and placed them in the sink.

"You have to admit right now," Tara pushed; "it's just what you two need."

Adam and I looked between one another.

"Despite whatever drama this creates, he's still the best part of my family—well, besides myself," Adam said as he popped his collar and leaned back against the countertop.

"Yeah, what's that about? I always got the idea from River that your parents were nuts...Bobby doesn't seem to share that view." Tara ignored his flaunting as I burst into a huge smile, which quickly vanished in response to her question.

Adam's smirk and air of arrogance disappeared as his eyes averted to his feet, and his fingers found the belt loops of his slacks. He tapped his foot before licking his lips.

"Bobby's kind of the exact opposite of me," he said.

"Duh?" Tara chimed in.

Adam took a deep breath as he looked up at us. "You can understand how they'd love one of us more than the other then."

Tara's forehead wrinkled at the comment, and she shook her head. "Not at all."

"Well," Adam sighed; "that's the way it is in the Beckerson family."

"I don't think Bobby would agree," she said with a shake of her head.

Adam's eyes found mine as he bit his lip. I knew how hard it was for him to explain, so instead, I did. "Bobby doesn't see it because he doesn't believe it to be true. Bobby doesn't see Adam any different than himself. Adam is just

Adam. I guess that's because he doesn't feel the way they do about him, and he's blinded by the love they show him. He just doesn't see it."

Tara looked at us. "It still doesn't make sense to me—I mean I have a brother, and I've never felt like my parents loved him any more than me."

"Lucky you," Adam said.

Tara was beginning to look uncomfortable, and I knew Adam was by his averted eyes and tapping foot.

"You'll see someday. They also despise me!" I said as I stood.

"Now that I definitely don't believe! Especially seeing both Beckerson boys adore you."

I looked over to see Adam smirking. "Exactly!"

"Your family makes about as much sense as hockey year round!" Tara finally said with a confused shake of her head.

"Get used to it," Adam replied as he came around the island and gave me a kiss.

"I guess I'll have to," Tara said, her eyebrows still scrounged in confusion. "Well, you two make out or whatever you do before work. I'm going to take a shower!"

When she left, Adam sat on the bar stool and pulled me into his arms. "She's not all that bad, huh?"

I knew he always had doubts about it, and for a while I did too, but she seemed different now that she and Bobby were dating. "No, and her and your brother are so similar, it's sickening. She really likes him."

"I bet she's as glad as I am that you decided I was the better brother," he said as he nipped at my neck.

I turned and pulled at the collar of his shirt. "I prefer Abercrombie and Fitch to Chippendales."

His head tilted back with a chuckle, and I kissed the stubble of his chin. "You liked that comment, huh?"

"It was kind of adorable. It's one of my favorite memories of us, despite the circumstances."

"Any other favorites?" Adam asked, his eyes running over my face and meeting mine.

I nodded. "I think they all are. You?"

"When your mom took away your nightlight, and I snuck into your bedroom with a jar of fireflies. You flipped out on me because you were afraid I was going to kill your beloved wish-granting-fairies!"

"You're never going to let me live that one down, will you?"

His eyes bore into mine as his hands ran over the bare skin of my arms. I took a deep breath as he kissed my chin.

"Are you still afraid of the dark?" His voice was thick as he asked the words, and every part of me yearned to rip the sexy teacher-getup he was wearing off.

"Not when you're here," I murmured back.

"Then I won't ever leave."

His lips hovered above mine, threatening to consume every part of me until I couldn't take it anymore and leaned into him. The kiss was soft and slow as his hands moved down my arms until our fingers entwined. The embrace was so light, and our hands stayed within one another, yet I yearned to let them wander; to show him how much I loved him.

That was it—I loved him desperately, completely, and he wasn't threatening to consume me anymore. He already had. Everything that was me was him. My heart, mind, and soul were all as much a part of him as they were me. His lips moved from mine, and our eyes met, staring into one another's souls. I couldn't separate what parts of me were because of him, and what parts of me were my own. Somehow over the years, they became one in the same. Only then did I see how utterly lost I'd become in him. There was no going back. I only hoped he'd never leave, because that was the darkness that truly scared me now.

Chapter 31

When I got home, Adam was sitting on the hood of his car in the parking spot next to mine with his eyes closed as his thumb tapped a beat against the metal. I knew he must hear my car idling there, but still he didn't move, so lost in his music he didn't care. I put the car in park and grabbed my camera to snap the shot before hopping back inside and pulling into the spot.

When I looked up to unlock the door, Adam was already standing there waiting for me.

"Writing a new song?" I asked as I slipped the camera strap over my head and grabbed my purse.

He shrugged as he pulled me into his arms and kissed me until I was lightheaded. "Thinking about doing that," he replied as we began to walk towards the apartment.

"Either way," I began as I took my camera and showed him what I'd taken; "made for a damn good shot."

He rolled his eyes as he opened the door for me. "That's because you like this tie-vest getup."

I leaned into him as we took the first step and kissed his chin below his ear. "You've got that right."

I felt the shiver pass through his body, and he stopped,

using his grip on my hand to push me against the stairwell wall.

"That's not fair," he growled at me.

"Life's not fair," I replied.

I tried hard to breathe, but his chest pressing into my own coupled with the way he was looking at me made me dizzy. All I could sense was his body against mine, and the intoxication of the feeling mingled with his comforting cologne.

"I used to think that." Adam let my hands drop, and his finger tilted my chin to his. "Then you let me kiss you."

It was over then; there was no holding back as I pulled on his vest until our lips crushed into one another.

"I," Adam gasped in between kisses; "can't walk...up the steps...and kiss you."

I pulled away laughing and raced up the stairs in front of him, daring him to catch me. At the top of the stairs, I stopped because I had no idea what apartment we were going in to. Adam reached the top and grabbed my arm, pulling me towards his.

"Bobby's not home," Adam said as he pushed the door open, and we slid in. "Might as well take advantage of it."

I closed the door, and Adam pulled me into his arms before we tripped over the couch and landed softly on it.

"Bedroom?" I suggested, remembering what Tara told me.

I didn't want to bless the same furniture they had. He continued kissing me as he pulled my legs around his waist and lifted me up. My jaw clenched at how strong he was without having to look like he worked out every day. That made me want him even more, but there was one thing standing in my way—his sexy teacher-getup. The number of buttons was damn frustrating. I got through one set, only to have to go through another.

"You alright there?" Adam asked as I let out a huff.

I looked up at him as I slipped the last button and let my lips hover over the area just above his belly button. "Really?"

He had a smirk on, and I stood from the bed. Two could play that game.

"Oh, no you don't!" Adam yelled as he pulled me back onto him.

"I'll wear a button-up next time," I snapped as my eyes wandered from his now bare chest up to his eyes.

He bit his lip. "As long as it comes with a pencil skirt like that I'm up for the challenge."

His hand cupped my chin and tilted it so he could nip at the soft flesh of my neck.

"Still mad?" he murmured as his lips traced a line up to my ear.

I sighed in response, and I could feel the smile on his lips as he continued until his mouth found my own.

Chapter 32

The weekend passed in a world wind of cuddling, kisses and pleasure without having to worry about Bobby walking in and getting, well, the right impression. Bobby returned exhausted, but still had another hockey game that Tuesday night. I bit my lip as I cocked my head at Adam, trying to keep the smile off my face. I missed Bobby, but I had to admit not having to worry about him was nice.

"How come you don't ever have that thing when Bobby is around?" Adam asked with a nod over my shoulder to the camera sitting on the window sill.

I sighed as I picked it up. "Bobby's kind of sensitive about it ever since he saw the pictures of you and me. It's like he blames the camera for the whole thing."

Adam smirked as he took a swig of beer.

"Blaming an inanimate object for us being in love with each other...he'll always find some excuse other than we were made for each other."

His comment was so matter of fact for mentioning the love, and I bit my inner cheek as I played over the words. It made me wonder why he hadn't just come out and said it directly to me. I pinched the plastic cover off the camera as a distraction and looked through the viewfinder.

It was one of those beautiful nights in Boston where the city lights reflected up into the dark sky and danced with the stars. The moon was low, partially hidden by a building two blocks away as it perfectly framed Adam. He stood there with his button-up half untucked, his tie nowhere to be seen, and his beer dangling from his fingers. At that moment, Adam reminded me of the type photography I preferred. Un-posed just felt so much easier, or maybe it was just taking pictures of him. In the studio, I often felt confined and lost as I took pictures I was ordered to take. Sometimes I just felt like I could never get *the* shot, the one I had in mind when I designed the shoot or started thinking of the advertisement. With Adam I never really had to plan anything—every picture just felt right. I didn't feel lost, and every picture seemed to play itself out with such ease. It reminded me that I actually could get *the* shot.

I set the shutter and aperture to handle the dim lighting before I began to click away. A smile crept onto his face as he rolled up his sleeves, placing the beer down before turning back to face the city. I could feel the smile entering my face as I watched his every move through the tiny glass frame.

Everything about his composure screamed flawed. He leaned his forearms against the cool metal of the rod iron balcony, his head tucking slightly between his shoulders as I clicked away.

Then he looked directly at the camera over his shoulder

and everything screamed perfection. He was caught by the lens with his eyes passionate, yet soft while his thin lips were set in a deep line. The whole picture was made even sexier by the lip ring that accented his face and the scar that traveled the entirety of his lip to the edge of his nose. It was a mark he'd been self-conscious about since the day a hockey puck to the face gave it to him; a mark girls drooled over as much as I was now.

"Give me that," his firm order knocked me out of my Nikon stupor.

"Huh?"

"Give. Me. That," he repeated. "It's my turn."

"No!" I said as I yanked the camera away from his outstretched hand.

"Yes!" he replied, a smirk covering his face as he planted his feet and used his body to block the only exit from the balcony.

I judged the distance carefully before dodging him and slipping through the window. His hands reached for me, but my shirt was short enough that instead of catching onto anything solid his hands moved against my skin. It caused a shiver to go up my spine, but I rushed forward with the camera in the air and put the couch between us.

"You really think you can outrun me?" Adam shouted at me.

"Of course, I can!" I said as he ran at me.

I scooted around the couch that created an island between us and stuck my tongue out. What I didn't expect was Adam to run and jump *over* it, quickly closing the gap.

"Not fair!" I squealed as I raced into the only room with an open door—his.

"Ah Ha!" Adam said as he ran at me, tackling me onto his bed. He pinned me down with the weight of his body and grabbed the camera from me, putting it just out of reach on the chair piled with his clothes. "Now I've got you where I want you!"

Our eyes were locked on one another, and his sadistic smile turned incredibly sexy. I took a deep breath as I was reminded he was finally mine—that he could lean over and kiss me, and that I knew for once that he wanted exactly what I wanted.

"Do I want to know what's going on in here?" Bobby's voice echoed from the doorway.

Adam shot off of me, his hands both stuck in his hair. "I was...err...trying to get umm...River's camera from her."

Bobby's oversized neck muscles twitched as his eyes followed me. I grabbed my camera from the chair and stood, my eyes moving from Bobby to Adam. I fought the smile on my face as I narrowed my eyes at Adam.

I couldn't help myself—I shot past him screaming, "I win!"

"Oh, no you don't!" Adam called after me, evidently forgetting his incredibly pissed off and jealous hulk of a brother.

He took off after me and caught me as I tried to unbolt the door.

"You know what the punishment for attempting to escape is?" Adam asked as he grabbed my camera and tossed it on the couch, pinning me to the door with one hand on my waist.

"You take a picture of me?" I asked, fluttering my eyelashes at him.

He turned to face me, and his brows shadowed his eyes as he moved closer to me. Bobby was still watching, but I was completely captivated by Adam's addictive presence.

"No," he answered with a slow shake of his head. His lips twitched as he tried to remain serious. "It's a crime punishable by tickling!"

"No!" I yelped as his fingers ran up my shirt and to my ribs. "Please, stop!"

He tilted his head back. "Muahahaha!"

"Adam!" I squealed as my knees began to cave with the laughter.

"Do you surrender?" he asked as I crumbled to the floor in his arms.

"Never!"

I was crying from the laughter half caused from the tickling; half caused from the insane amount of joy he brought me.

"Now?" Adam asked again.

"Fine! Fine! I give up!" I said, and he slowly withdrew his hands before helping me stand.

"Was it worth it?" he asked with his hands on his hips.

I narrowed my eyes at him.

"Are you done making me want to puke?" Bobby interrupted us.

I looked over Adam's shoulders at him.

"Are you done being a cry baby?" I fired back.

Bobby rolled his eyes. "I thought we were ordering Chinese?"

"You guys are getting Chinese?" Adam asked.

"Yes, *River and I* were," Bobby said.

Adam missed the point. "After chasing River around, I'm famished."

Bobby's eyebrows crushed over his eyes, causing angry wrinkles to form across his forehead. He was not happy. I peaked over Bobby's shoulder and smiled at Adam. "You want to join us?"

"Sure!" Adam replied.

I watched as Bobby ground his teeth at me. He'd have to deal with it, but I did feel a bit guilty. It was the first time we planned any time with one another since he started dating Tara, and I'd secretly started dating his brother.

"We'll do something some other time," I said to Bobby as I walked past him to get a menu.

"You know it's hard with the girlfriend around," he hissed back at me. "It's not like she's a fan of me hanging out with you alone."

I stopped and cocked my head at him. "Really? Don't try that on me."

"She knows," he said.

I widened my eyes at him. "Yeah, she does."

I watched as his eyes flickered back and forth over mine as he tried to formulate a response to what I said.

Finally, he swallowed and replied, "I don't know what's going on with you and Adam, but *I* wanted some time with you—it's like he's got a River timeshare, and he's not interested in ever leaving."

"You'll get some time with me," I replied as I glanced around his hulking frame. Adam was sitting on the couch pretending to watch the TV, but he was looking at me out of the corner of his eyes.

"When, River?" Bobby asked.

"Tomorrow?"

"No Adam?"

"No," I replied with a pat on his arm as I grabbed the menu and went to show it to Adam. I could still feel his eyes boring into my back as Adam, and I smiled at one another.

I wondered how obvious it had become.

Chapter 33

Despite whatever Bobby thought might be going on with Adam and me, he didn't mention anything when we went bowling the next day. He didn't even mention it when our date continued over pizza. We talked about work and hockey—about the competition he was going up against this season with his team, but never once did we talk about Adam, and for once I was glad about it. I knew he'd be suspicious, and I wasn't sure if I could lie to his face. What should have concerned me was his lack of talking about *his* girlfriend. In the past, I never found it unusual that he only mentioned them when they pissed him off, but I should have realized far before that there were other reasons he never brought them up. I smiled up at him as we stood at my apartment door after the night was over.

"This was fun," Bobby said into my ear as he lowered his body towards mine, and my arms went around his shoulders naturally.

"It really was," I said, and my face felt warm as I smiled into his shoulder. "I always miss you when hockey season gets into the swing of things."

"You could come with me," he said, his nose tucked into my hair.

I pulled away slowly, my hands falling onto his biceps. I was thrust into the reality of exactly why he never mentioned his girlfriends.

Me... it was always me.

"What about Tara?" I asked, and I could feel my throat thickening as I waited for his response. Somehow we were back at square one. My heart was pattering out of control because the hope that Adam and I might actually be able to be a couple in public was quickly drifting away.

Bobby looked down at me, and his chest rose as he let a deep breath out. "She's great..."

The warmth in my face turned from comfortable to flaming as I pushed myself out of his arms. "Oh, no you don't! Don't give me a *but* at the end of that sentence."

Bobby gave me one of those Beckerson Boy smiles; the one that made it so they could never do any wrong in any girl's eyes. Except mine— I'd known them long enough to know better. That smile meant one thing—trouble.

"Night, River." He ignored my question as he leaned down, taking my chin in his hand and kissing my cheek.

"Bobby!" I yelled at his back as he opened his apartment door in two steps.

He looked over his shoulder and winked, sending the pattering of my heart to a complete stand still as I swore at him in my head. Then I saw Adam sitting on the couch behind him. His jaw was in a tight line as he stared at the TV, which I knew he wasn't watching. He looked over at me, and his brown eyes accused me of betraying him. I shook my head at both of them as Bobby closed the door.

I stood there for a moment as I tried to collect my thoughts. Adam had apparently been watching and gotten the wrong impression of the situation. I'd never known him to be jealous, especially not of any one I hung out with, but his eyes showed something different now. The thing that bothered me the most was the lack of trust I saw there.

Chapter 34

I looked up at the brick school building Adam worked in and took a deep breath before stepping out of my car. The building was set in a suburb of Boston, one of those rich areas where all you saw were Lexus' and Infinitys. I knew Adam felt out of place when the kids had more expensive clothes than him, but the parents did treat him right. They respected him despite his somewhat rebellious appearance, and I guessed they expected that out of the music teacher. The kids loved him, and he loved them too. I smiled at the thought as I made my way up the cobblestone steps, past the rose garden and fountain to the front door. I grabbed its oversized handle and tugged it to find the secretary behind a wall of glass smiling at me.

"River?" she asked, and I nodded with a confused expression. "Adam has a few pictures of you on his desk."

"Ah," I said with a nod. "So would I be able to come in?"

"Sure thing, you just need to sign in here." She pointed at the clipboard that barely fit out the hole she passed it through.

I passed it back, and she slid me a badge.

"Keep this on your person at all times. You'll need to

return it before you leave," she said as she buzzed me in the door.

"Of course," I said as I slid the lanyard over my head. "What room?"

"212. Go up the stairs, third door on the right," she answered.

I nodded and headed in the direction she instructed. It was eerie how quiet it was, and I felt the whole school could hear my heels clicking against the marble floor. When I got to door 212 it was covered in musical notes and symbols I never bothered to learn. I only ever memorized the chords Adam taught me and never actually bothered to find out how to read the sheet music. I looked through the wired pane of glass to see Adam's back facing me. He was sitting on a chair with a keyboard in front of him as he moved his arms to whatever he was explaining. The children sat on various bean bags on the floor, chins in their hands as they listened in rapt attention. I wanted to stay there and watch him teach without him knowing I was there, but I knew eventually one of the children would notice. I raised my hand and tapped on the door—another loud noise against the silent hallway.

Adam looked over his shoulder with a surprised expression that instantly turned into a broad smile. He held up one finger to his class and headed towards me.

"What are you doing here?" he asked as he opened the door.

"What? A girl can't visit her boyfriend at work?" I asked, as I tilted my head and looked at him through my lashes.

"I just wasn't expecting you," he said as he looked passed me down the hall; anywhere to avoid staring at me.

I moved from foot to foot as I stared up at him. "I wanted to see you and make sure you were okay."

"Why wouldn't I be?" he asked, and his eyes went down to his feet.

"You gave me a death stare last night."

Finally, his gaze rose to mine. "I saw Bobby hugging you, and I know him...he wasn't being Friendly-Bobby he was being I-Love-River-Bobby."

He was correct about the way Bobby was acting, and it had pissed me off too. But just like I knew to expect it, Adam should too. The feelings weren't mutual, another thing Adam should know.

"And what was I being?" I asked.

"Best-Friend-River," he replied as he adjusted his vest buttons and his gaze drifted away from me again.

I sighed, and that brought his attention back up to my face. "And you were being Jealous-Boyfriend-Adam, who I didn't even know existed!"

A small smile twitched across his face. "I didn't know he did either," he answered.

I leaned up on my toes and planted a quick kiss on his lips. "So you're okay?"

He nodded. "You came all this way for that?"

I looked up at the too-high ceilings and pushed my lips to the side. "Maybe I could stay for a bit?"

Adam waited until my eyes drifted back down to him to

answer, "If you're going to be here you're going to have to help me teach these rascals."

A smile parted his lips. "I have no problem with that."

"Let's go then!" he ordered with raised eyebrows and a tilt of his chin back into his classroom. I followed him and closed the door as quietly as I could behind me; there was no need to make even more noise by accidentally slamming it.

"Alright, kids! We have a special guest today!" Adam clapped his hands, and the kids turned to him with attentive expressions. It was evident they admired him. "This is my friend, River."

"She's pretty," a little blond boy commented.

"You're very right about that," Adam answered. "She's going to teach you guys a song today."

Adam smirked at me, and I ran my tongue over my teeth. He thought he was smart. He'd taught me how to play the guitar when we were teenagers, and I had a good memory of it. I smiled at the kids and grabbed the old Yamaha acoustic off the wall, taking a stool next to Adam.

"Alright, kids—my mom used to sing me this song all the time when I was a child," I said as I took the pick Adam produced smugly from his pocket.

A little girl scooted closer to me, cupping her chubby cheeks in her hands. "What is it?"

"Yellow Submarine by the Beatles.' Has anyone heard of it?" I asked.

Adam chuckled to himself.

What he didn't realize was I knew how to play more than just one Beatles' song. I learned over thirty of them in the time that passed since he taught me to play. I began to strum the guitar and sing. The kids soon joined in when they learned the chorus. Adam sat with one foot on the floor tapping out the beat, the other foot on the brace of the chair, and his chin in his hand.

Adam clapped when the song ended.

He leaned over and whispered in my ear, "You've been hiding something from me, hmm?"

"Would anyone like to hear another?" I asked the kids, ignoring him.

By the time, I finished the hour's worth of Beatles' songs Adam was sitting on the chair shaking his head.

"Wow," Adam said as the kids ran outside to recess. "You've really been holding back on me."

I shrugged as I handed the guitar back to him. "I like this guitar. It's a lot easier to play than that bulky Fender you taught me on."

"That's because it's ancient," Adam said as he took it and placed it on the hook. "It's the school's."

"I figured as much—you're not much for acoustic."

"I still have that bulky Fender." Adam corrected me.

"Then I can show you what else I can play," I said, biting my lip and letting it slip through my teeth.

"The fact you knew those Beatles' songs was impressive—now you tell me you know more than just those?"

I nodded. "I know some Deftones and even some Tool."

"The secrets you've kept from me," Adam murmured with a shake of his head. His eyes narrowed, but the smile on his lips showed his amusement.

"Do you like that I can play guitar?"

He pulled me into his arms. "I like the fact my kids love you, and that *I* know *I* taught you to play that well."

I rolled my eyes. "Yes, it's all you!"

"Shows me I actually do know how to teach!"

My gaze fell back to his, narrowed to slits. "Hey! What's that suppose to mean?" I asked.

Adam sat down on the edge of his desk. "It means you didn't really take to it from what I remember."

"I was faking so you'd spend more time with me," I said as I placed my hands on his shoulders.

He shook his head. "Of course, you tricky, tricky woman."

"So...what are you doing tonight?" I asked as he put his hand on my hip and let his thumb drift under my shirt, finding the hidden tattoo there without even looking down.

"It's Thursday, so it's boy's night out, but after..." His voice drifted off as his eyes moved up the curves of my body to my face.

"I see how it is," I said as I let my hands slip down to his chest. "You're using me for my body."

Adam let his hands slide around my waist to my backside.

"Oh, that's just an added benefit," he whispered.

The intense look in his eyes made me want to do very bad things to him. I let my fingers run over his tie before wrapping it around them.

"Oh, what I could do to you if there weren't small children in the general vicinity," I replied.

Adam placed pressure on my backside, pulling me into him, so his lips were hovering over mine. His eyes lingered on them before meeting mine.

"That's very naughty." His voice was hoarse, and I knew he was thinking about it just the way I was.

"I have a desk in my bedroom," I suggested, and I knew my cheeks were pink from the heat I felt there.

His chest rose. "I can be at your place at ten?"

"Isn't that a little late for a school night?" I asked.

"I wasn't planning on sleeping tonight anyway."

My whole body flushed hot, but I didn't have much time to compose myself. Little feet were running through the hallway and I pulled away from him just as the kids flooded back into the room.

"Miss River—will you come back again sometime?" one of the small boys asked.

I looked over my shoulder at Adam, who was cracking his knuckles as he took a deep breath.

"Only if Mr. Beckerson wants me to," I replied.

"Mr. B, can your friend, Miss River, come and help you teach us again?" the boy asked with a huge grin as he slid his tiny hand into mine.

There was no way he could have said no if he wanted to.

"Of course, she can," Adam replied with a smile that set my heart racing.

The little boy looked up at me, beaming. "See Miss River, we all love you—Mr. B does, too!"

I looked over my shoulder at Adam with the boys hand clasped in mine. Adam's eyes were locked on me.

"Who couldn't love her?" he replied.

Chapter 35

I should have been used to Adam's boy's night out, but waiting for him was killing me. I wasn't much for TV, and there wasn't much on anyway. I ended up watching a rerun of *The Big Bang Theory* I had seen about three times already. It didn't matter because I really wasn't watching.

I let my mind rerun the moments of the day—the happiness of playing guitar with Adam, and the way he made me feel. I took a deep breath and looked down at my watch. It was 10:30, and Adam still wasn't here. I sighed and headed into my bedroom to change into my pajamas. Then the knock I had been waiting for came on the door, and Adam snuck in.

"Hey," he said as I came out from the bedroom. "I'm so sorry I'm late."

"You brought your guitar?" I asked with a nod to the hard case he was carrying. It was rather beaten up, and it wasn't one I ever recalled seeing before.

Adam smirked as he placed it on the couch and flicked open the bronze buckles. "Nope," he replied as he opened the lid.

The Yamaha guitar I played earlier in the day was nestled in soft red velvet.

"What's that?" I whispered as my pulse thrummed in my ears.

He lifted it out of the case and handed it to me. "I made a trade with the school. I took this one, and I bought them a brand new Fender. They thought it was a fair trade."

I looked down at it in wonder. "But it really isn't."

"To them it was, new versus old—new will always win. At least that was what I was figuring on when I asked," Adam said as I handed the guitar to him over the couch, and he placed it back in the case. "Do you like it?"

"Of course, I do," I said as I looked at him, breathless.

He was wearing dark wash jeans and a black button-up with the sleeves rolled up, but his hair looked like he had been sweating from the way it was matted down.

I couldn't keep in my curiosity anymore.

"What exactly do you do on your boy's night?" I asked.

Adam snapped the bronze buckles shut before looking up at me.

"It's a secret," he replied as he pulled his lip ring into his mouth with his upper lip.

"Is it something I'd approve of?" I asked, picking at the seams of the cushion underneath my hand.

Adam walked around the couch before tilting my chin, so our lips grazed one another. "I'd never do anything you didn't approve of."

I narrowed my eyes at him. "Then why aren't you telling me?"

His hand went to rub the back of his neck as he thought over his answer, and with each passing second, I felt my breath slowing until it felt as though I wasn't breathing at all.

"I'm in a band—I swore Bobby to secrecy a few years back," he finally admitted.

"Bobby knew, but you didn't tell *me*?"

"Yeah...it was a really heavy metal band at first—and I didn't want you to know about it because I didn't want you to be around that scene."

"But?"

"Now, it's more Five Finger Death Punch slash Of Mice and Men with a hint of 10 years, so it might be safe for you to come," he said, slipping his hands into his pockets and rocking on the balls of his feet.

I stepped back and leaned against my couch, arms crossed. "But you don't want me to come."

"You might hate it."

"I love your voice," I replied as I took his hands and ran my fingers over the calluses.

"Really? Cause I kind of hate it," he admitted.

"It's amazing—especially with that kind of music," I said.

When his loving eyes met mine, they were insecure, and it made me reach up to cup his face.

"When I hear you sing it's like the whole world fades away. If I'd heard you sing years ago I never would've been able to keep my feelings from you secret—it's like you're singing to only me...just me," I whispered.

He closed his eyes and smiled before resting his forehead

against mine. "That's because I am. I just think of you, and I lose myself in it."

I leaned on my toes and gave him one soft kiss, letting my lips hover over his as I pulled slightly away. Before I could move away from him, his hand found my chin and tilted our lips to touch again. I let my lips wander down to his neck, and he moaned softly.

"Every time you touch me," he murmured. "I feel like I'm going to light on fire."

I responded by nipping at his ear, and he pulled my legs up around his waist, lifting my bottom to the edge of the couch before tilting my head back and letting his mouth wander down my neck and to my chest. My breath came out in a gasp as he slipped my shirt off and continued to kiss my chest as his fingers unhooked my bra and it slid away. I tilted my head back as my hands buried in his hair.

A single knock came on the door before it swung open. I barely had enough time to pull my body into Adam to cover my naked upper half before we both turned to see Bobby standing in the doorway.

His mouth was stuck open in an O, and the veins in his neck were bulging as he looked at me wrapped around Adam half-naked.

"What. The. Fuck," he finally managed to choke out before turning and slamming the door so hard the wood cracked at the edges.

I closed my eyes and tilted my head back. "Shit."

"That was not the way I wanted him to find out." Adam swallowed, his arms still balancing me in the air.

"You should've locked the door," I said, but there was no anger in my tone. We both made the mistake of not thinking of it in our mad dash to rip one another's clothes off.

"Yeah, I can see that." Adam set my feet back on the ground. "What are we going to do now?"

I hooked my bra back and reached over to retrieve my shirt.

"Explain it to him?"

"Yeah...that sounds like a great way to end a night. I kind of like my face the way it is," Adam said, rubbing his neck as he gave a pained laugh.

"Me too." I heaved a sigh as Adam placed his hands on the edge of the couch and leaned forward, head bowed.

"This is so fucked up," he said.

We stood in silence for a moment. I stared at the top of Adam's head between his tensed shoulders as he thought about his decisions.

Mine weren't anything fabulous either.

"When were we going to tell him?" I finally asked.

"When we knew Tara had fixed the whole obsession with you thing," Adam said as he began to pace.

"Do you really think even if he didn't still have feelings for me he'd be okay with this? With us?" I asked as I sat down next to the guitar case.

Adam stopped pacing and locked eyes with me. "No, because everything is a competition with him, and you were the ultimate prize."

I crinkled my nose at the idea of being some sort of trophy, but I knew Bobby well enough to know Adam was right. It wouldn't matter if he were married to Tara; this would still drive him nuts.

"I don't think of you that way," Adam said, coming around the couch to sit next to me and placing his hands over mine.

"I know," I said, tipping my head back. "It just means there never really was going to be a good time, or way, to tell him."

Adam bit his knuckle before standing. "I guess I should talk to him."

"Let me grab a sweatshirt, and we can go together," I said.

Adam nodded, and I went to my room to grab one. When I came out Adam was standing in the same place staring at the door.

"Ready?" I asked as I slipped my hand in his.

"Can you stand in front of me, so my face doesn't get rearranged?" Adam said, but his voice was tense.

"Anything to keep you looking pretty," I said with a smile over my shoulder.

Adam leaned in to kiss my forehead before we headed across the hall.

I opened the door and stuck my head inside. "Bobby?"

There was no answer.

"Bobby?" I asked again as I walked in the door with Adam behind me.

I went to the balcony off of the kitchen and stuck my head out the open window. Bobby was leaning against the wall, one foot pressed against the bricks and a beer in his hand. He didn't look at me, but his body went rigid, and he took a deep swing of the beer before speaking.

"So how long has it been going on?" he asked.

I held my hand up to signal Adam to stay inside before I slid through the window.

"A few weeks," I said as I pressed my arms against my stomach and tilted my head, chewing the inside of my lip.

"I thought you'd never find out," Bobby said, chewing on his inner lip. "I never thought he'd have the balls to realize he loved you almost as much as I do."

"I'm not sure what balls have to do with anything..." I tried to ease the situation, but Bobby's icy eyes remained cold and straight ahead.

"Doesn't matter now." His voice was bitter. "He's got you wrapped around his finger."

"You might want to consider your words closely," Adam said as he climbed out the window to join us.

"Mhmm," Bobby replied, and his head jerked back. His eyes twitched but remained set on something in the distance.

"We're dating now. I didn't want you to find out like that—" Adam began.

Bobby finally reacted and started towards Adam. I stepped between them, hands on either ones' chest.

"You didn't want me to find out ever!" Bobby said, pointing at him over my shoulder.

"I wanted to wait until I knew you'd act like a normal fucking human being!" Adam fired back.

"What's that supposed to mean?"

"It means you treat River like some sort of prize, even though you have a girlfriend!"

Bobby's tone quieted, and his muscles slackened as he replied, "I never said River was a prize."

He backed away, and I knew he saw Adam was right.

"It's not what you said. It's what you did," Adam said.

Bobby shook his head. "I've been trying to compete with you for fifteen years for her."

"I'm not a competition!" I said as my composure broke. Hearing him admit I was some sort of pawn in his sick game was painful. I felt nauseous as I looked at him. Years as my best friend all boiled down to a petty competition over my heart.

Bobby's eyes met mine at the sound of hurt in my voice. "I know...I just." He heaved a sigh. "I don't fucking know anymore."

"We're dating now," I said. "So you need to suck it up."

Bobby's eyes looked dark as he nodded. "Sure."

I stared at him for a moment as he looked down at his hands and played with his leather bracelets. I took a deep breath before turning on my heel and nodding for Adam to lead the way out. He looked at Bobby over my shoulder with his lips in a thin, pissed line. His eyes darted over his brother's frame, and I could tell Adam believed Bobby about as much as I did.

This would not be the end of it.

Chapter 36

In the decade Bobby had been my best friend he never once made me feel like I was a prize or that my love was a competition. I suppose that was because he felt he was winning the game. He never really saw Adam as competition, because he was Bobby, and he always won. It didn't matter when I told him I was in love with his brother; he still tried to sway me to see he was the person I should be with. We went years dating other people, but never one another, and he still hung on to that notion. I never once looked at Bobby and felt the way I did when I looked at Adam. Still there was a level of guilt I couldn't explain associated with my actions. Maybe it was because things with Bobby didn't feel like they'd ever be the same. I was reminded of it as I watched Tara and Bobby walking to the car laughing with Bobby's arm slung tight around Tara's waist. I couldn't help but feel I somehow lost more than I thought I would when he started dating her.

"It's getting to you isn't it?" Adam asked as he climbed through the window out to the balcony with me.

I jumped at the sound of his voice. "What?"

Adam leaned on the rail and nodded towards the happy couple. "Them."

"Why do you think that?"

I watched Adam's knuckles go white as he gripped the metal. "The look in your eyes."

"You think I have a thing for Bobby?" I asked.

Adam pulled his lip ring into his mouth and let it out slowly. "I hope not."

"If I had a thing for Bobby I'd have been with him a long time before this," I replied, and I watched as Adam cringed. The look on his face said that wasn't the answer he was looking for. My eyes drifted to the mammoth truck driving away. "I don't have feelings for your brother," I said.

Adam turned to face me, leaning back against the rail, but his eyes stayed on his Nike™ Cortez shoes. "Why are you looking green then?"

I thought about it for a moment. I never felt this way when he was with any other girl. I always dealt with his explanations of his exploits and never batted an eye. This time was different.

I swallowed before answering. I knew it would sound petty. "I feel like I've been replaced."

"That still sounds like you're jealous," Adam said, his eyes finally finding mine.

I stepped forward and wrapped my arms around his neck. "Do I look at him the way I look at you?"

Adam's chest rose against mine. "I don't know."

"I've never looked at anyone the way I look at you," I said as my eyes closed.

Adam tilted my chin, and I opened my eyes as he asked, "Then why do you feel like you've been replaced? You were never with Bobby."

I inhaled slowly, biting my lip. "Bobby used to talk to me about everything..." my mind drifted to the things he told me about Tara and him. My mouth twitched. "Even things I didn't want to know— it feels like Tara's not just his girl-friend, but his best friend. *That's* how I feel replaced. I used to be the best friend."

Adam's eyes ran over my face, softening. "I get...but, I'm pretty sure he feels the same way about you and me."

"How? You were both always my best friends," I replied, shaking my head.

"It's different now, though, isn't it?" he asked, and his thumb traced calming circles over my neck."

He was right. Maybe Bobby was retaliating, or maybe he just found what I found in Adam in Tara. Adam's hands slid down from my face and over my hips before finding their way up the back of my shirt and setting my skin tingling.

"Yeah," I replied.

He leaned forward, trailing kisses down my neck. "So, I was thinking..."

"No, nothing kinky," I replied as my muscles melted at his touch.

Adam's lips vibrated against my skin as he laughed.

"No, but..." His voice drifted off, and I lightly pushed his shoulder. "Fine, I was thinking about our conversation about my band. I'd like you to see us play, plus you already know my band mates."

I pulled away and blinked rapidly at him. "I do?"

"My volleyball buddies...When I said Joe is a sick guitarist, it's because I capitalize on it. Mark's the drummer."

"A three piece?"

"Yeah, I do the bass and sing slash scream," Adam said.

Tingles spread across my cheeks and then raced down my body. "I'd like that."

I watched his expression turn nervous, and his foot started to tap sending a hollow pinging noise into the air. "We have a special gig tonight, are you up for it?" he asked with his eyes averted.

I wrapped my arms around his neck, and his gaze wandered up my body to meet mine. His hands slid over my hips to the small of my back, causing my body to warm. "I've been dying to hear you sing again."

His lips hovered near my ear as he sang to me in that beautiful gravel of a voice, "In my arms I hold the only thing that matters...in my arms, I hold the entire world...in my arms are my heart and soul."

"That's not fair," I said in response, my voice barely audible against the sound of blood pulsing in my ears.

"All's fair in love and war." He continued in the sing-song voice.

"We have to go to dinner with my parents in twenty minutes," I answered as I looked down at his watch. "So we need to leave, like now."

Adam smirked down at me. "Why? You want to rip my clothes off?"

I pushed my hips into his, and his head tipped back so I could kiss his neck.

"Don't you want me to?" I asked.

He moaned. "Mhmm...what punishment this voice is."

I pulled away from him and headed back inside.

"Hey," he said as he closed the pane behind him; "remember you can't do that at the concert tonight."

"Aww," I said, winking back at him. "Darn it."

Chapter 37

Two more weeks proved Bobby wasn't over Adam and me. He hadn't looked at me, let alone spoken two words to me. It was almost unbearable, but Jesse had me working late nearly every night as we pushed to get the advertising and branding done for a big client who just signed a contract with us. My lack of being home took away the constant feeling of bitterness from Bobby, because well, I just hadn't seen him that much.

Adam hadn't been so lucky. He hinted to Bobby's attitude without really talking about it. I wasn't sure how much longer they could take one another, especially with all the yelling that was going on. I could hear them hollering at one another over the TV, followed by the slam of a door and my door flying open before Adam closed it and came to sit beside me.

"Shits hit the fan with Bobby. He's a fucking asshole 24/7. I can barely stand to be around him," Adam said as he let his head roll loosely against his shoulders.

"He has Tara, what's he being such a big baby about?" I asked as I lay beside him and placed my head on his lap.

He looked down at me, chest rising with a deep breath. "Tara's not you, Riv."

I clenched my fists and sat up with my back facing Adam. I wasn't Tara, and that was exactly why Bobby shouldn't be acting like a total ass. He had *her*. He proved he didn't need me even before he found out about Adam and me. He stopped talking to me about everything and was obviously confiding in her. I'd come to terms with that now, but I couldn't come to terms with him ignoring me and treating Adam like shit because we were in love. I ran my hands through my hair before looking up at Adam, finally asking. "What was that about?"

"I threw out the sponge because it was gross, and apparently he needed to use it."

I furrowed my brow before asking, "Do you think I should talk to him?"

Adam rubbed my back. "He's livid with me—maybe with you, he'll be more understanding."

I looked over my shoulder at Adam's soft brown eyes and tussled hair. He was everything I ever wanted and needed. Adam was perfect for all his flaws, and Bobby was perfect as a friend, which was something he could never accept, but he needed to. We all needed him to, Adam, me and Tara.

"Your brother has known since we were sixteen how I felt about you," I said as I pulled my knees to my chest and hugged them.

Adam scoffed, head jerking back. "Asshole," he muttered under his breath.

"What?" I asked.

"Of course, he'd keep that from me," Adam replied with arms crossed and lips pursed.

I nudged him in the ribs with a smile."You still won, though, didn't you?"

Adam's eyes teased me as he tilted my chin, so our lips met. "Damn, right. He's won everything else, but all that mattered was you."

I narrowed my eyes at him as he moved away. "Really, I thought you said I wasn't a prize."

"You're not."

"So what am I the toy you both wanted for Christmas?"

Adam's eyebrows rose. "The only toy I'll ever need."

"You're so dirty!" I said as I stood to walk pass him, only to get yanked into his arms.

"We could get clean?" he suggested, lips trailing over my collarbone, making my stomach twist in happy circles.

"I thought you wanted me to talk Bobby off that cliff he's hanging off of?"

Adam heaved a sigh. "Yeah..."

"The things I do for you," I said as I stood again and headed towards the door.

"And for Tara," Adam added, and I nodded.

He was right. I wasn't going to let Bobby break my only girl friend's heart. I Bobby was different for Tara; with every other guy she was unbreakable, but she was head over heels for him.

I peeked my head in the door. "Bobby?"

"Hey," he answered, head in the refrigerator.

"Hungry?" I asked, walking in and glancing into the empty fridge with him.

"Yeah." Bobby leaned up and his stomach growled. "Kinda sick of pizza."

"You should come over and have dinner."

Bobby perked up. I should have known food would fix everything.

"Meatballs?" he asked, drool practically dribbling down his chin.

"Sure," I replied with the sweetest smile I could muster. I knew this was far too easy to be genuine and watched as his body stiffened.

He ran his tongue across the inside of his cheek. "Where's Adam?"

"Waiting for me to cook dinner," I answered, watching his reaction carefully.

Bobby turned his back to me. "No thanks," he muttered into the refrigerator.

"Come on Bobby!" I begged. "This has got to stop!"

Bobby whipped the door shut, and the appliance shook as he turned to look at me. "No!"

I stepped back, my chest tightening. "Why not?"

"It was always going to be one of us. I knew you made your decision long ago, but I didn't know it would hurt this much. You've abandoned me, and so has he," Bobby said as he braced himself with his hands on the island.

"It's not like that," I said, and I felt my throat thickening as my chin trembled.

"What's it like then? It was always him, wasn't it? I never

stood a chance...all these years and I was lying to myself. You were my forever River, and now I have nothing!" Bobby's voice cracked as his eyes washed over mine.

I knew my face held the answer.

"I still love you Bobby—you're as much a part of me as him. It's just not the same," I tried to explain, but his face showed I failed. I could feel the thickening of my throat as I saw his composure failing him. His words carved into my heart, and I knew no matter what my happiness would destroy at least one person I loved.

He clenched his jaw, a harsh breath hissing through his teeth as he looked at the hardwood floors.

"I wish I could've made you love me." His eyes rose, bitter, as he continued, "All he's ever going to cause you is pain."

I could feel the anger only adding to my urge to burst into tears. I turned away from him and rushed to the door. I knew he was following me.

I turned, a foot away from the door and thrust my finger into his chest. "He's still your brother!"

Bobby towered over me now, and I had to look up at him. He looked mean, meaner than I'd ever seen him.

"What," he hissed; "makes you think you're any different than any other girl *he's* fucked? Huh!"

I was trembling as I met his toxic stare. I went to reach for the door, but it burst open with a slam.

"You piece of shit!" Adam raced past me and nailed Bobby square in the face.

I heard the crack, and I knew either Bobby's nose or Adam's knuckles were broken—or both.

"I love her!" Adam yelled as he shook his swelling hand. His voice turned to a pained whisper as he stared his brother down, "I love her more than anything in this whole fucking world, including you!"

Chapter 38

Adam was always stubborn, even with his hand swollen to the size of a softball he wasn't going to the ER. Tara texted me she was bringing Bobby to make sure his nose didn't need to be set, but she never asked what led to the double black eyes she encountered when she came over later that night.

I guess she knew better.

Adam sat on the balcony with a blank stare on his face for three hours without saying one word to me. I sat on the couch with him in my line of vision as he drank the beer I gave him with the ice pack wrapped around his fist.

I didn't know what to say. Who was I to break up a friendship that was born into him? This was his brother he sucker punched, and it was all because of me. My phone beeped, breaking me out of my stupor, and I glanced down at my lap.

TEXT FROM TARA

Bobby's fine—just bruised, no broken nose. Adam should see the doctor, though.

I texted her back to let her know I'd try to convince him

and to thank her for letting me know. She didn't respond. I let it be.

When I looked up Adam had moved; his shoulders slumped and his head was in his hands. I stood and slipped out the window, running my fingers over his back.

"Hey," I said.

Adam didn't answer or respond to my touch. I felt nausea in my stomach as I wondered what he was thinking; if he was wondering if I was worth all of this.

"You okay?" I asked.

Adam's fingers gripped his hair before he let go and wrapped his arms around my waist, placing his head on my stomach. His back rose against my hands as he took a deep breath.

"You know I meant it, right?" he asked, looking up at me.

"What?" I asked, my voice soft.

"I do love you that much. I love you more than anything. It makes me irrational, apparently," he said as he let out a painful chuckle.

"Obviously, Bobby's a bit unreasonable, too," I replied as he stood, his hands running up my arms and causing chills to course through my skin.

Adam's hands reached my face, and his thumbs traced my cheeks as he lowered his lips to hover over mine. He cringed at the movement, and I pulled his injured hand on my own before placing a kiss there.

"You're not questioning how I feel, are you?" I asked finally.

My eyes drifted up to meet his. "You've never said it River."

"I love you, Adam Beckerson. I've loved you my whole, entire life—there's been no one else since the day I laid eyes on you," I answered.

His lips crushed into mine, stealing my breath away as his good hand tangled in my hair, and he tilted my head.

"I don't understand why I deserve you," he whispered as his lips drifted over mine.

"I complicate everything," I answered.

Adam's forehead moved against mine as he shook his head. "You make me a better person."

My eyes moved down as I swallowed. "You just clocked your brother because of me."

That wasn't my idea of a better person.

"Look at me...He had it coming. I should've done it a long time ago."

"Your mom is going to hate me even more now," I answered.

Adam burst out laughing, a smile cracking the sadness in his face. "I didn't think that was possible!"

"Oh, ha ha!" I shot at him as he led me back into the house. "You need to go to the ER."

"No, especially not after the fact I'm sure Bobby already went."

"We can go to the walk-in," I said, and my shoulders rose to my ears, palms pointed up.

Adam cleared his throat as he sat on the edge of my bed and unwrapped the ice pack from his fist.

"That does *not* look good," I said, and I could feel the blood rushing from my face. I had to sit to keep my knees from buckling.

His whole fist was black, and his fingers had turned an awful shade of nauseating blue-green. It looked painful, and I grimaced as I took it into my hands. I tried to move his fingers, and he moaned in pain.

"Maybe," he said as he sucked in a breath through his teeth.

"What?" I asked with narrowed eyes.

"I'm more concerned about how I'm going to teach guitar with this," he said, eyes glassy. "This will send them over the edge."

"I thought they didn't mind the lip ring?"

"Having the appearance of a bad ass is one thing; showing up with a broken fist is another thing." Adam tilted his head back and squeezed his eyes shut. "I'm fucking screwed."

"Let's go to the walk-in and see what they say. Okay?" I asked.

He nodded. "You're driving, though."

I smiled down at him, biting my lip and he rolled his eyes.

"You want to drive the GLI?" he asked.

I nodded, and he used his good hand to take the switchblade key out of his pocket.

I grabbed it and smiled at him. "Finally!"

"If you crash it, I'll kill you," Adam said, narrowing his eyes at me as he stood.

"You and your bum hand are going to take down this?" I replied, flexing my biceps at him.

"Twig," Adam said through a cough as he followed me out.

"Broken hand," I returned.

Chapter 39

Under some miracle of God Adam's hand wasn't broken; it was merely strained, but a good one at that. He wouldn't be able to play guitar for at least two weeks.

Two weeks where he couldn't teach.

I had to admit that his aura of worry was wearing on me, and I was starting to be concerned he might not have a job by the end of the day. I somehow managed to keep the sentiment of doubt off my face as I helped him to button up his shirt and put on his tie and vest.

"Looking spiffy," I said, palm against the faux silk of his tie.

His body rose against my hand, and he kissed my forehead. "You think they're going to believe you dropped a bowling ball on me?"

I looked at him through my eyelashes. "If they met me they'd believe it."

"They might need to meet you then," Adam said, his voice strained. "Especially when I'm teaching my students piano with one hand."

"You could also teach them vocals," I said as I grabbed my purse, and we headed out the door.

"Vocals? Me? I've never been formally trained," he replied.

"Didn't you teach yourself how to play all those instruments before you were ever formally taught?" I reminded him.

He rubbed his forehead with his good hand replying, "I never learned anything about vocals, though."

"Doesn't mean you're any less amazing," I said as I shifted the GLI into gear. The engine purred, and I couldn't help the smile on my face. It faltered as I remembered I wouldn't get to drive it on the highway.

"If you say so," he sighed.

"Fade Burn was amazing the other night, and did I forget to mention how much I love the name?" I said as I tried to cheer him up.

Adam remained hunched in the seat for the remainder of the short, but too long drive through Boston traffic. When we got to the school, Adam gave me a kiss before he wordlessly left the car. I watched him walk into the school with his shoulders bent as if he was walking into his death. I looked down at my watch. I was supposed to give at least two hours notice.

Oh, well.

I dialed the number.

"Hey, Jesse—it's River...I don't think I'm going to make it in today," I said.

I heard Jesse choke on the other end. "No way, really? You're calling out?"

"I'm so sorry—"

"Don't be. I don't care if you're sick or if you just don't want to get out of bed. You've *never* called out sick," he said, and I heard him flipping some pages. "Actually, you've never even taken a vacation."

"Yeah," I replied as I picked at the corners of my nail polish. I had no clue what I could do to fix the situation I created.

"So, curiosity killed the cat—what the hell happened that you would?"

"Let's put it this way—I've created the biggest family feud on the face of the planet."

"Mhmm...Adam's fist broken?" Jesse asked.

"Sprained."

"And what does he do?"

"Teaches musical instruments to kids at a private school."

I cringed as I heard his sharp intake of breath that said he knew just as much as I did that we were screwed.

"How are you going to fix this one?" Jesse asked.

"I have no clue, but I can play guitar—"

"You can play an instrument?" Jesse asked, his voice rising in surprise.

"It's not that surprising!"

"If you say so," Jesse said, and his voice held a hint of laughter.

"I'll be in tomorrow," I replied.

"Take your time, just don't miss the shoot on Wednesday," Jesse said. "Tell Adam to aim for the mouth next time."

"Whatever. I'll be there for the shoot," I said.

"I know you will. Oh, and River, don't make any decisions for him. He's a big boy. He knows what's best for him—don't try to fix this."

Then the line went silent. I shook my head and straightened my back before going to the school and grabbing my visitor's pass.

I watched as Adam came out of an office shaking his head as the door shut behind me. I rushed forward to comfort him and as I did I rammed right into the edge of a locker, sending myself sprawling to the floor. I heard feet on the tiles, and when I looked up, Adam was leaning down to help me up. A bald guy was standing next to him with a puzzled look on his face.

"Are you okay, Ma'am?" the man asked as Adam helped me up.

I blinked my eyes a few times as I tried to knock the rattling out of my head. "Marble sure is hard."

Adam let a breath out. "Principal Michaels, this is my girlfriend, River."

As I steadied myself against Adam, I held out my hand to him. "Nice to meet you."

"You really are a bit accident prone, huh?" he asked, looking between the two of us, and then down to Adam's wrapped fist.

"Yeah, you see what I managed to do to Adam's hand. He's never going to let me bowl ever again!" I laughed, awkward and hoping my lie worked.

"I suppose so," Principal Michaels frowned. "Adam, I

retract my previous statement. I'm not sure how you're going to teach like that, though."

"I came in to help with Monday's guitar lessons...and Adam is going to do some vocals in his regular mix," I said.

Adam looked a bit pale as I said the word *vocals*.

"You sing?" Principal Michaels asked, turning to face Adam.

Adam tilted his head shoulder to shoulder as he shrugged. "A bit."

"Excellent!" Principal Michaels slapped Adam on the back and headed back to his office.

"You saved me," Adam said.

"By bruising myself?" I asked as I rubbed my shoulder.

"He was firing me," Adam said.

"Over a broken fist?"

"He thought I was lying to him about the bowling ball!"

"You're a sucky liar," I said with a smirk.

"Whatever, you being a ditz saved me...and you're going to teach guitar today?" Adam asked as he walked with me to his classroom.

"I guess so!"

"One of the kids has the acoustic on loan. You think you can shred it on an electric?" Adam asked as he nodded to the wall of guitars.

"Only if I can play the blue Gibson," I answered.

Adam used his good hand to grab the guitar off the wall. "Your wish is my command."

I smirked as I watched him place the guitar on a stand, grab a small amplifier and hook up the cords. He sat down and laid the guitar across his lap before playing with the knobs and strumming with one hand. Even to me it sounded off.

Adam tilted his head and picked at each one until he found the one that was out of tune. He then used his one hand to move the tuner what seemed like a minuscule amount before plucking the string again. It sounded perfect this time. He looked up at me and gave me one of those crooked, sly, amazing smiles.

"You ready to teach some children?" he asked just as the bell rang, and a handful of children flooded through the door.

"I guess so," I said as I watched them fuss over Adam and his hand.

"Mr. B! What happened? Are you okay?" was repeated over and over again in the cutest tone of voices. It struck me again how much the children admired and respected him. It seemed to be something rare in today's world; I was used to the screaming and fussing children from the grocery store.

"Miss River!" They suddenly noticed me.

I smiled, and they piled a hug on each of my legs.

"We're so glad you're back!" they said in unison.

I looked up at Adam with the blue Gibson ready for me to play. His face now showed a soft smile, and his eyes crinkled in the corner as he admired his kids and me.

"Ready?" he mouthed.

I nodded.

"We're going to start the day with a song. River's going to play the guitar, and I'm going to sing!"

The kids let go of me in an instant and found their bean bags as I took my seat next to Adam, and he handed me the guitar.

I grabbed a pick from the pile on his desk and began to play. I had to take a deep breath as Adam's voice began, "Yesterday..."

Chapter 40

"The last volleyball game of the summer!" Adam said as he came into the bedroom, throwing the ball from hand to hand.

"Good thing the doctor cleared you to play," I said as I pulled yoga pants and a sweatshirt on over my bathing suit. "And let me remind you it's not summer anymore!"

"Eh." Adam slapped my ass. "It's going to be fine!"

"It's Columbus Day weekend! It's going to be freezing!" I shot back.

"It'll be fine. Plus, you'll be moving so you'll heat up quick enough."

"You better not put me anywhere near the water!"

"Really?" Adam looked at me with a pout. "The water takes longer to cool after the summer, so it's still quite warm."

"Then you go in!"

"Maybe I will!"

I put my hands on my hips, and he smiled before tossing the ball on the bed and pulling me into his arms.

"You ready?" he asked as he kissed my cheek.

I closed my eyes trying to think of anything but the way his lips trailed over my skin.

Beach. Sun. Tan. I opened my eyes and looked at my pale arms—the perfect distraction from his mouth.

"I need a better tan," I managed to mumble out.

"Well, you're not going to get it completely covered up like that!"

I heaved a heavy sigh. "I might have to freeze my ass off to lock in a nice tan."

Adam pushed down the shoulder of my shirt and let his lips drift with the cold metal of his lip ring down my collar-bone.

"You're perfect the way you are. I don't like Oompa Loompas."

"Ha ha," I laughed, but I couldn't help the shivers running under my skin as his lips trailed up to mine.

A knock interrupted us, and Adam pulled away with a pout. "Damn, I was hoping for a little action before we had to leave!"

He winked at me as he turned to answer the door, and I rolled my eyes. I knew very well he just liked to be a tease. I grabbed my beach bag and went to the living room where I almost dropped it on the floor.

"Look who's joining us," Adam said as he turned to face me from the door. His brows rose, and his eyes showed his horror at the situation.

Bobby stood in the doorway with his arms protectively wrapped around Tara, and what could only be called an evil grin plastered on his face. Tara looked uncomfortable as she mouthed the words *sorry* to me.

"Sounds good!" I said.

I tried to sound cheerful, but the whole idea mortified me. Bobby hadn't let up on his asshole tactics, and now he was bringing Tara even further into our mess. She was just too head over heels to care, and I hated Bobby for treating her as second best to me. The order was all wrong—I shouldn't have even been in the order anymore, but Bobby wasn't letting go. I couldn't wrap my head around what the strategy behind *this* move was.

"We all going to take one car?" Adam asked as he grabbed the cooler from the kitchen island. His voice was even, but I knew he was wondering what the hell was going on as much as I was.

"Sure, why waste gas?" Bobby answered, his voice layered with bitterness over the false cheer.

I followed Adam and Bobby down the stairs, and Tara hung back with me.

"I just happened to mention you guys were going to kick some butt today at the volleyball tournament, and Bobby decided he wanted to invite himself. Something about you never being good at any sports, so he had to see it for himself," Tara said in a hushed tone.

"More like he thinks he can beat Adam," I said.

"That too," Tara answered with a swallow. "This day is going to be awful."

"I'm sorry you somehow got dragged into this bitter circle," I said as I linked my arm into hers.

She placed her head on my shoulder. "It's really not your fault. You're in love with Adam—and he loves you, which is amazing. Bobby loves you, and I love Bobby. It's a mess, but I think Bobby has to get over it sometime."

"Tara," I groaned as we slid into the back of Adam's car; "you shouldn't be second best to anyone...let alone me!"

Tara shrugged with a wink. "Don't worry I'm rocking his world one solid bang at a time."

"Gross!" I said as she buckled herself in the middle seat so she could be closer to me, and we could talk without the boys hearing.

"Listen," she said as she placed her hand on my knee. "I'm not taking it as second best. I'm trying to make him realize I *am* the best for him."

"Well, I'm trying to keep him from killing my boyfriend!"

"I think Adam stands a chance if they ever do get in a fight again," Tara said. "Those two black eyes were quite interesting."

"Adam sprained his hand!" I said, and we both burst into laughter.

"What are you two going on about back there?" Adam asked with a smile in the rearview mirror.

"Talking about how pig-headed the both of you are!" Tara said through a hiccup.

"I'm not pig-headed," Bobby said.

"Yeah, right, grouchy pants!" Tara replied as she reached over and attempted to squeeze one of his head-sized arm muscles.

Bobby turned and growled with playful eyes as Adam, and I exchanged looks of horror.

"Keep it in your pants, man!" Adam said as he shifted the car, and we headed onto the highway.

We all laughed, and for a moment I thought this might be a good idea; after all, the sun was already high in the sky, making it unseasonably warm and everyone seemed to be getting along.

My momentary lapse of intelligence dissipated the second Tara, and I stripped down to our bathing suits and headed on to the sand volleyball court on opposite sides. Bobby was glaring at my tattoo, and Tara was trying to make him act like a normal human instead of a bear. It wasn't working, and it only got worse as the game went on. Adam and I were destroying their team.

"And," Adam jumped up as he spiked the ball back at Bobby before concluding; "that's it!" as Bobby dove and missed it.

"So you finally found a sport you're good at!" Bobby said as he stood, wiping the sand from his knees.

The look and tone showed he was not going to be a good sport about this win. Adam nodded at him but didn't respond. I squeezed his hand in mine, and he gave me a stressed half-smile. We knew Bobby was being an asshole, but Adam's friends didn't.

They didn't know him like we did.

"Unless you're talking about with women!" Mark said as he slapped Adam on his shoulder.

"Shut it," I hissed as Mark's brown eyes sparkled, and he

shrugged. He didn't get what was going on; otherwise, he wouldn't have been so careless.

"The tattoos crush us again!" Joe called as he came up behind Bobby and slapped him on the back.

"What's that all about?" Tara asked out of curiosity.

I cringed; I knew this was about to send Bobby over the edge.

Adam's arms wrapped around me from behind, and his chin went into my shoulder. He was playing with fire, and I was caught in between wanting to pull away to prevent Bobby's explosion and actually enjoying myself.

"When they stand like that," Mark began to explain; "their tattoos touch, giving them superpowers to kick all our asses at volleyball!"

Bobby's blond eyebrows twitched, and his neck became corded. "Magical tattoos? Come on!"

Mark laughed as he kicked back a beer. "Adam was good at volleyball before, but with River here, he destroys us 100% of the time."

Bobby's eyes narrowed. "I guess magical tattoos are more believable than either of them being good at anything besides strumming a guitar."

I didn't have time to respond as Adam let go of me to lunge at Bobby shouting, "You're such a piece of shit!"

Fortunately, Mark was able to step between them before Adam's fist could make contact with Bobby, but he still stumbled backward and knocked into Tara. She was sent flying backward into the volleyball pole net, and as I ran towards her, she crumbled to the ground into a sobbing heap.

"You're such a fucking ass!" I yelled at Bobby as I leaned down and pulled her into my arms.

"Adam made it happen! Why do you blame me for everything?" Bobby hollered back at me.

"Are you okay?" I asked Tara.

"I guess being second best to you does hurt," she said as she rubbed the back of her head.

"Look what you've done!" Bobby yelled at Adam, who was heading towards us with a bag of ice.

"Fuck you!" Adam said before kneeling down in front of Tara and I. "Let me see?"

She turned her head, and Adam felt the bump there. She winced but didn't move as Adam came to the front of her and looked at her face.

"Do you feel dizzy?" he asked.

She nodded.

"Tilt your head a little. I need to see if your pupils are dilated," Adam said, and Tara listened.

"How do you know so much?" Tara asked as he handed her the ice pack to apply to her injury.

"Taking care of kids all day teaches you a thing or two. I think we should bring you to the hospital—your eyes are a bit dilated, so it's possible you have a concussion," Adam said as Bobby finally cooled down and came over.

Tara smiled weakly at me.

"I think you got the better brother," she whispered as the Beckersons exchanged glances.

"We'll take a cab to the hospital," Bobby told us.

"Why?" I asked as I helped Tara up.

"Because Adam and I are bound to kill each other if we spend another second together," Bobby said, voice shaking with anger as he took Tara into his arms.

I stepped back at his disturbing revelation, shaking my head.

"I don't think Adam wants to fight over this anymore. You're the one who keeps it going," I said as I reached forward and rubbed Tara's arm.

"Of course, you'd choose his side," Bobby snapped as he swept Tara up, so she wouldn't have to walk.

"I really don't give a shit right now," I answered as I leaned up and kissed Tara on the cheek. "Let me know when you get out?"

Tara nodded before turning her head into Bobby's chest. She looked fragile as he carried her away, and I had to take a breath to calm myself.

Adam came up behind me.

"Please don't be mad at me," he said as he put his hand on my shoulder. I turned, shaking my head as the tears began to fall, and Adam wrapped his arms around me. He ran his fingers through my hair as he continued, "I'm so sorry for the mess I've made."

I looked up at him. "It's not your fault—it's mine. Maybe I led him on the past?"

Adam took my face in his hands, rubbing away the tears with his thumbs. "I think you only ever tried to be a good friend. He was always the one that wouldn't give up."

"Thank you," I said as Adam kissed my forehead.

"You still want to get lobster with the guys? We can go home if you want," he asked.

I smiled at him. "You were really looking forward to the last lobster roll of the season."

Adam shrugged. "It's just a crustacean on a roll."

I burst out laughing as his eyes wrinkled at the corners, and he stuck his tongue out as if it weren't the most delicious thing on the planet.

"No, Tara would want us too, especially since you were her knight in shining armor," I said.

Adam stepped back and let his hands refer to his sculpted body.

"This? Shining armor? I think not," he replied as I eyed him.

I tackled him into the sand, holding his arms above his head as I kissed him. "No, much better than a knight in shining armor—a half-naked knight."

A whistle echoed from across the beach, and Adam rolled on top of me before pulling me up.

"Save that for dessert, baby!" he said.

I smiled to myself knowing Tara would have found the whole thing quite amusing.

Chapter 41

A few hours after Adam and I arrived home Tara texted me she did indeed have a concussion. She hadn't said much else to me, and I wondered if she was as mad at me as I was. On Tuesday, two days after the disastrous volleyball game, she still hadn't spoken to me. I looked for her when I got into work, but she was nowhere in sight. I distracted myself in with my daily tasks as I worried about how she was feeling and why she was ignoring me.

I sat staring at the different font options I had up for the branding plan for yet another company when a knock came at the door.

"Can I come in?" Tara asked as I turned and looked over my shoulder at her.

"Sure," I replied as I took her in. She was dressed more casually than usual in black slacks, a white pinstripe button up, and ballet flats. The white of the shirt didn't help the pallor of her face. She sat down in the chair slowly.

"Saturday—" she began.

"Look, Tara, I'm so sorry that happened. Adam didn't mean for you to get hurt," I said.

She smiled as she sighed. "It's not Adam's fault. Bobby was being an ass, we all know that."

"Still, he feels awful, and so do I. I should've—"

"Warned me? I've known for years there was a feud between the two of them over you. It didn't stop me from sleeping with Bobby, or falling head over heels for him," she said, pausing to shake her head at my open mouth so I wouldn't interrupt. "I knew exactly what I was getting into, Riv. I'm stubborn—so is Bobby. I know he cares about me, and I can't pretend I know what's going on in his head about you, but I do know he cares about me. That's enough, River, whether or not you agree with it."

"I just want you to be happy," I replied, my eyes falling to my keyboard before they met hers. "I don't want Bobby to hurt you, especially not because of me."

"You took a risk with Adam, didn't you?" Tara asked, her eyes obstinate as she locked them on mine.

I smiled and nodded.

"I took a risk with Bobby. It's a risk staying with him, but I think it's worth it. I can't go back now, Riv. I really do love him. I've been in God knows how many relationships, and not one of them have been serious—you know that. You have to admit this one is different."

"Yeah," I said.

"I need you to tell me the truth when I ask you this. Do you think it's different for Bobby too?"

I sat back in my chair and took a deep breath. I knew it was. The way they looked at each other and tolerated one another's flaws showed they did love each other. There would be no other explanation for dealing with someone's shit than that. You love them all the more for it, even if they drive you crazy.

"I've never seen him so torn before," I said.

She got up and leaned over to squeeze my hands. "Then let's hope that means this is different. Maybe we can all be happy then."

Chapter 42

I stood on the balcony watching my breath come out in plumes as I thought over what the next few hours could be. I used to look forward to Thanksgiving; to the family gathering—eating too much, laughing and smiling until my face felt like it would crack. There was always the anticipation of what might happen, though, and this one was no different in that aspect. It was worse than usual, because now it wasn't just what Adam's parents might attack him with, or what Adam's mom might attack me with—it was the first time Adam and I were *us*. The fact we forgot to tell anyone but Bobby was lingering on my mind too. His reaction had been acidic enough on its own.

I wondered how it was possible in Bobby's irritation he hadn't told his mom. Tara confirmed he hadn't though. I kind of wished he had; it would have been easier that way. It was going to be hard to explain why we hadn't mentioned it when we'd been dating for over four months now. In my mind Thanksgiving was bound to be as much of a disaster as the volleyball tournament had been.

Except this time I was going to be the one coming back with a concussion—an emotional one.

"Hey," Adam said as he stuck his head out the window. "There you are...aren't you freezing?"

I laughed, and my breath froze in the air. "Yeah, maybe."

Adam smiled at me, and my insides warmed after the frigid thoughts I'd been having.

He held out his hand. "You ready?"

I shook my head before responding differently, "As ready as I'll ever be."

I climbed in the window, and Adam rubbed my arms. "It'll be alright."

"As long as Bobby doesn't throw another hissy fit."

"Good thing we're not driving together," he said with a smirk.

I nodded in agreement.

The drive out of Boston wasn't as bad as I feared it might be; most of its residents made their way to their destinations earlier in the day. Bobby and Tara had been one of them. Bobby always spent the entire day with his parents and Tara was more than willing to help our moms with preparing the meal. She admitted she was nervous as she dragged me into her apartment to try to pick out something that was cute, but not too revealing of her shapely body.

In the end, I convinced her to wear jeans and a cardigan set with rhinestones on the shoulders that I lent her. It was something she would never have bought in a million years, but she agreed it was perfect for the occasion.

"What are you thinking about?" Adam asked as he shifted the car and put the cruise control on.

My stomach churned as my mind drifted to exactly

where we were going. I sank deeper into the seat before answering, "Wondering how Tara is doing with the Moms. I texted her, but she hasn't responded."

"They'll love her—my mom tends to like everyone...well, except you."

I must have looked as green as I felt because Adam reached over and squeezed my knee. "It's going to be fine."

"She won't suspect anything is up from us driving in together, but she's going to die if you kiss me or something."

"That's the first thing I'm going to do...stick my tongue down your throat," he said, pulling his lip ring into his mouth. "Oh, baby!"

I tipped my head back against the seat before turning to look at him. My face flushed with heat as I stared at the shiny object wrapping around his lower lip.

"Whoa! What did you just think of?" Adam asked with a chuckle at my expression.

"That!" I pointed at his lip ring. "Does she know about that yet?"

He moved his lips back and forth as he pursed them. "Not exactly."

"Explain!"

"Well, I took it out the past couple of times I went over and saw them."

"You sissy!"

"Now she gets to see it *and* my tongue down your throat!"

"Are you trying to give her a heart attack?" I asked.

"I'm not really going to stick my tongue down your throat," he said, patting my thigh with a wink.

"Really? I think the effect of your arm around my waist will pretty much be the same," I said as I sunk into my seat.

"Come on, Riv. It *will* be fine—I promise."

"I hope Tara is ready to rein Bobby in," I said as I took a deep breath.

"River..."

"Adam..." I repeated, copying his tone.

He looked over at me, his light brown eyebrows rising over his matching eyes. I stuck my tongue out at him, and he squeezed my leg until I wriggled free.

"Ass," I hissed.

"You know you love me," he said, and his eyebrows rose and fell quickly over his warm chocolate colored eyes.

"Whatever," I mumbled as I reached for the radio and turned it up.

I relaxed into the racing seats and watched the rolling hills of New England as they spread out before we turned off the highway back into suburbia.

"Almost there," Adam said, and I watched as his thumb echoed him playing slap bass against the steering wheel.

"You're nervous, too?"

He glanced over at me with a raised eyebrow before looking back at the road. "No more nervous than I ever am when I see my parents."

I nodded and sat up as the familiar houses began to pass until we turned onto the dead end we grew up on. When

Adam parked in the driveway behind Bobby's behemoth of a truck, we both sat and stared at the front door.

"Ready?" I asked after a moment.

Adam looked at me, lips curled to one side, brow furrowed, and I knew he was thinking the same thing, *here we go.*

Adam met me at the front of the car and held his hand out for me. He squeezed it tightly over mine as we headed up the steps, and the front door began to open. Adam's mom greeted us with a huge smile that narrowed as her eyes darted down to our hands. I watched as her knuckles went white against the doorframe.

Yup, she was going to flip shit.

"Adam, love!" she said, pulling him into her arms and yanking his hand out of mine.

"Hi Mom," Adam's muffled response came before he pulled away and slid off his jacket.

"Hi Vickie," I said as she took his coat away from him and ignored me.

"Hello, River. Your parents are in the living room with Bobby and Tara. She's such a sweetheart!" her voice was sugar sweet, yet filled with venom.

I could never get used to the odd mix.

Adam went behind me to slide my jacket gently off my shoulders, which only made his mom's fake smile twitch more.

"Yeah, she's been one of my best friends for a few years now," I replied. "She's had a crush on Bobby the whole time. It's nice to see them together."

"I didn't realize," she began.

"Tara didn't tell you?" I asked, my fake smile becoming real as hers threatened to crumble. She probably thought she could form an alliance against me with her.

"I was just so thrilled to meet her..." Her voice trailed off.

"Riv!" Tara said as she came in the hallway and wrapped her arms around me. "What took you two so long? Your parents—both of them are great!"

I looked over Tara's shoulder at Vickie as Tara hugged me. Vickie looked like her eyeballs were going to pop out of her head, and I narrowed my eyes at her as she crossed her arms and looked away. We all headed into the living room, and Tara plopped back down with Bobby as my parents hugged Adam and me. When we sat, Adam put his arm around me and pulled me close to him, leaning over and kissing my head. Dad burst into the biggest smile ever, Mom looked confused, Vickie's nails dug into Alec's arm and Alec tilted his head in curiosity before wincing in pain and peeling her hand off his arm.

"Are you two?" Dad asked, pointing between the two of us.

"Yeah," I replied, looking up at Adam, who was smiling down at me. He was enjoying his parent's reaction almost as much as I was dreading it.

"How long?" Mom asked, and her tone of voice didn't seem surprised or upset. I let the breath I'd been holding out slowly. One set of approval was better than none.

"Four months," Bobby said, and his voice was as flat as his eyes when they met mine.

Tara looked up at him with her lips pursed and hissed something quietly to him. He turned red and sunk deeper into the couch.

"That long?" Vickie asked as her chin began to tremble. My muscles clenched as I glanced up at Adam.

"Probably closer to five," Adam answered, and his voice portrayed a bit of amusement as his mom swallowed and blinked quickly at him. He was handling this better than I was.

"So almost a half of a year?" Alec asked.

Adam nodded, running his fingers over my shoulder. "I guess you could say that."

"And," Vickie's voice pitched; "you couldn't have found time to tell us?"

"Yeah, why didn't you tell us?" Dad asked, looking slightly hurt.

I bit the inside of my lip as I squirmed. Adam squeezed my shoulder, and I replied, "It never came up."

"Same," Adam echoed.

"And you knew, Robert?" Vickie popped out the full name, and Bobby cringed.

"Not for a good bulk of it. *They* didn't tell me either," Bobby said.

"You *live* with him," Vickie said through clenched teeth.

Just then the doorbell rang again, and Vickie was pulled away. Bobby shot us a look of *how did I get in trouble for what you did*, and I shrugged innocently.

He deserved it for being such an ass.

The doorbell continued to ring until the room was

milling with all of our relatives and several neighbors. It was a welcome distraction from Vickie's dagger eyes as we made our way around the room greeting people who were all happy that we finally came to our senses about each other.

Dinner was spent in the same fashion, and there were too many voices talking and moving around for Vickie to throw more accusations. Dad pulled me aside in a hug as Mom, Tara and Vickie set the desserts out.

"Congrats, Duckie," he said as he hugged me. "How'd you finally wrangle him in?"

"He came to me," I replied with a smile as Adam came around the corner to join us.

Dad pulled him into a guy hug that involved a fist grab and clap on the back before reminding him, "You better be good to her."

"Have I ever not been?" Adam asked.

Dad pointed his beer at him. "Good point. Hey, did you see the pool table your parents put in the basement?"

Adam shook his head.

"Did someone say pool table?" Bobby shouted from across the room, and I felt my jaw stiffen. He made his way towards us with Tara.

"I think I hear a challenge in your voice," Adam said as he crossed his arms and leaned back. His lips were in a thin line that curved downwards.

Oh, God help us.

"You heard right, brother!" Bobby replied. "We'll see if

you and Riv here have the same talent for pool as volleyball...doubtful!"

"Sounds good to me," Adam answered.

My stomach flopped, threatening to make my overcooked turkey have a second appearance.

"Pool Challenge downstairs!" Bobby shouted as he headed towards the stairs.

"Lucky thing I taught you how to play a few weeks ago, huh?" Adam asked as we reached the bottom step.

"Yeah, I guess so," I replied as we walked up to the pool table.

"Hope you're not as sore a loser at this as you are volleyball!" Adam said as he grabbed a pool stick and handed one to me.

"Shove it!" Bobby said, and his voice was as venomous as the glow in his eyes.

I rubbed the blue chalk on my pool stock as I watched the entire family fill into the downstairs. This was going to be a disaster. Adam was just as good at pool as he was at volleyball, if not better. He played every week with the boys when it was too cold for volleyball—or when the weather wouldn't permit it.

I was right, because with each ball in, Bobby's face got redder until the final ball finished the game. Bobby's eyes narrowed at us hugging as he leaned on the stick until he placed it down on the table. Tara reached for his arm as his mouth opened loud enough for everyone to hear, "I guess the matching tattoos *do* have superpowers."

Adam and I stared at each other, mortified, as we stopped mid-celebration, and all talking in the room ceased.

"Matching what?" Mom's voice was high pitched and layered with volumes of pissed I never heard before.

"Tattoos," Bobby replied, and that evil smile was plastered on his face as all eyes zeroed in on Adam and me. I bit hard on the inside of my lip as I tried to prevent the already threatening tears.

"You fucking bastard," Adam said under his breath, and I grabbed his arm for both support and to prevent him from attacking Bobby.

Adam's eyes washed over mine as I began to tremble. "It's going to be okay," he said.

I shook my head. "No, it's not. My mother is never going to talk to me again."

"Speaking of," Adam said as he took a deep breath.

We turned to our red-faced mothers.

"You two—" Vickie began.

"Have matching *tattoos?*" Mom finished as her eyes darted between us.

"We didn't plan it," I began.

"So you didn't get them on the same day?" Vickie demanded.

"Not exactly," Adam tried to explain only to be cut off.

"It's a yes or no answer," Mom said.

There was no way around it.

"Yes," I replied.

"Yes, you got them on the same day?" she asked. I nodded, and she yanked hard on her sweater sleeves. "What were you thinking? That's the most sluttish thing I've ever heard of."

My fists clenched at my sides as I managed to say, "We didn't plan it."

Adam's arm tightened around my waist. "Your daughter is not a slut because she has a tattoo."

Mom's eyes, bluer than my gray ones, flicked to him, and I prayed she wouldn't say it. My prayers weren't answered.

"Yours is disgusting enough as it is!" she said.

"We're that similar, okay? We didn't plan on getting the same tattoos! We got them at different places on the same day by *coincidence*," Adam replied as he took a step forward, so he was positioned in front of me, protecting me.

"Great, you're both delinquents!" Vickie said, head shaking.

"You've never had an issue with my tattoo before," Adam replied.

"Not that I've told you, but now that you have the same one as *her*," Vickie answered, and I felt the tears begin to trickle down my cheeks. "Not to mention whatever the hell that thing in your face is."

Adam ignored the shot at his lip ring as he spoke, "*She's* perfect for me. Got it? Perfect, so you can hate her all you want, and be pissed because she chose me over your beloved *Bobby!*" Adam's composure snapped. "She doesn't care that I'm a teacher. She loves me more for it! She doesn't constantly compare me to Bobby—but lets me be me because she loves *me*."

"What's that suppose to mean?" Vickie's tone reflected her shock as much as her wide eyes.

I looked between our mothers acting like petty children, and I felt my composure breaking. My mouth opened before I knew what I was saying, "It means you've always had a favorite."

Mom's eyes turned on me. "Where is this *thing?*"

I shook my head at her, and she stepped forward. "Where is it?"

Adam's body blocking me from them wasn't enough. It couldn't protect me from the hatred in their cold eyes, and despite the fact I felt it my whole life I knew it now. This over reaction showed it was never just in my imagination. The hate was palatable now—real and disturbing. I grabbed Adam's arm and launched myself across the room to the stairs past Bobby who was suddenly looking panicked and like he cared what he had just done. He knew before he said it what it would do. Mom was still harping on Adam's tattoo after he had it for six years. She was still saying how disgusting and awful it was, and Bobby put me directly in the line of fire to hurt Adam not realizing how much his mom's words would hurt me as well.

When I reached Adam's car, I was sobbing as I bent over against it. The cold November air sent even more daggers into my chest as my breath came out in soft, yet unforgiving plumes.

Adam pulled my trembling body into his arms. "I'm never going to forgive him," he whispered into my hair.

"He's a bad person...I never realized how bad of a person he is," I said with my head buried in his shoulder.

Adam's body shuttered against mine, and I knew he was crying too. It was only confirmed when I felt a tear drop hit my bare shoulder where his chin was resting.

"He's my best friend—my brother. I can't believe he'd do this. I thought he'd want us to be happy," he said, and his was thick with emotions.

"Am I really worth it?" I asked as I pulled away to face him.

Adam held my face in his hands. "You're worth the world to me, River, but am I worth it to you?"

"Bobby was right. I made my decision long ago—I just didn't realize he'd use it to hurt me—us, this much," I replied.

"Do you regret it?" Adam asked, his throat moving up and down.

"I could never regret anything with you," I replied before kissing him. His lips sunk into mine, riding over the emotions bogging me down and sending love into my heart to replace the sickening hate. The kiss deepened as if he felt that something light wasn't enough.

He pulled away only slightly, his lips grazing over mine as he said, "God, I love you River. I'm so glad I finally realized it."

"Me too," I replied before he kissed me again.

The kissed reached the deepest parts of me, confirming everything they felt was wrong and that this was right.

He was all I ever needed.

Chapter 43

The drive back to Boston was spent in silence. I leaned my head against the cold pane of glass and watched the signs as they passed by knowing nothing would ever be the same. I knew some things were almost impossible to fix. The relationship I had with Mom was one of those things. In truth, it had never been that great. I always just agreed, held my tongue and was respectful to her attitude and opinions.

I closed my eyes.

As a child and even now as an adult, I wondered if she could love me for who I was, and now— now I knew. No. My chest tightened with the thought, and then my mind went to Bobby. The thought strangled me, and I had to take a deep breath. Bobby knew. He knew how it was! Yet his anger at his multiple losses had driven him to say something he'd regret forever.

Something I'd regret forever.

I looked over at Adam as he parked and placed his hands firmly on the steering wheel. His fingers paled with the pressure as his lips moved, air whishing out, but the words seemed to escape him. He squeezed his eyes as he released the steering wheel and scratched his chin.

Finally, he spoke, "How do you feel about me living with you?"

Adam continued to look ahead, his eyes flashing over something in the distance.

For the first time in hours, the pressure in my chest released. "You basically already do."

He turned to look at me, and his neck flushed up to his ears. "I don't want to push you when enough shit has happened."

I reached out, taking his chin in my hand and smiled. "Yes, Adam, I'd love it if you moved in with me."

"Are you sure?" he asked, and his eyes closed again, his muscles relaxing against my touch.

"Look at me," I said, "Yes."

"I promise Bobby's the pig."

I rolled my eyes as I opened the car door. "I know," I replied. "I've smelled his room."

Adam chuckled as he came around the car and put his arm around my shoulders. "You might hate living with me."

I looked up at him, my body warming as I laughed. "You've never lived with a chick before. As far as I'm concerned, it's more of an experiment for you than me."

Adam opened the door for me, cocking his head. "Did I miss a whole portion of *your* life where you lived with a guy?"

I narrowed my eyes at him before heading in.

"Guys don't hide their disgusting habits, girls do," I said, laughing as Adam froze mid-step.

"Disgusting habits?" he repeated his face blank.

I winked at him and kept walking.

"Should I be worried?" Adam asked.

I shrugged. Adam shook his head as he opend his apartment door.

"You wouldn't risk losing me to disgusting habits," Adam said as he went to the CD shelf and began to drag it across the floor.

The CDs rattled, threatening to topple off the shelf, and I reached forward as one did.

"Mest?" I asked as I looked at the signed case.

"What? I had a punk rock phase," he answered with a smile.

Despite the intensity of the situation, we could still be happy with it being just us. I replaced the CD and grabbed the other end of the shelf.

"No point in ruining the hardwoods," I said as Adam smirked.

"Don't hurt yourself," he joked.

"I'm not that weak," I shot back. "You've seen my guns."

Adam blinked at me as we made our way across the hall shuffling the shelf with us. We placed it down, and I unlocked the door before picking up the shelf again.

"None of these are Bobby's?" I asked as Adam nodded to the wall next to the bedroom door.

"Nah," Adam breathed as we placed it down. "Bobby is more about hockey than music."

We both stared at each other for a moment at the thought of Bobby.

"You want to grab the dresser next?" Adam broke the silence with his hand stuck in his hair.

I nodded and followed him out. Within forty minutes there was literally nothing left in Bobby's apartment to indicate Adam ever lived there. He even grabbed his acidic-green-poor-taste-in-soda stockpile.

"This is it," Adam said as he placed the last guitar on its rack. His hand lingered on the neck of the Ibanez™ before he picked it back up and slipped the strap over his shoulder.

I sat on the edge of the bed as he began to play without an amplifier. The noise was tinny without the electronic part hooked up, but that didn't matter. Adam's fingers moved effortlessly from fret to fret as he strummed the guitar. His head nodded ever so slightly to the beat and his bare foot tapped the floor as he closed his eyes and a smile formed on his lips.

I stood and placed my hands around his neck, yet he continued to play, nod his head and tap his foot with eyes closed. The only change was on his lips as they crept into the seductive grin. I leaned into him, letting my hands comb through the hair on the back of his head as my breath washed over his lips.

Still nothing. The guitar continued to hum with his talent.

I let my lips hover over his, then let them wander over the soft skin of his neck and up the stubble of his chin. The beat remained smooth, undisturbed as the strings squealed and he deepened the riff.

I paused as my lips reached his again, lingering at the

corner of his mouth where the cold metal of his lip ring teased me just as much as his fingers on the guitar. I let my mouth run over the metal until it caught in my teeth and I sucked it in.

Finally, his body reacted, tensing as he groaned—but his playing didn't cease, didn't change. He still resisted, hand strumming a tease over the strings next to the skin of my belly.

His mouth responded to mine as I let the ring and his lip slowly slip away from me. That was it— the guitar spun to his back, and he yanked my hips to his own.

"I need you to play me like that guitar," I said, gasping as his hand tilted my head, and his tongue ran over my trembling neck.

His other hand drifted down my body.

"Good, because I wasn't done with my song," he growled into my ear.

Chapter 44

One week...two weeks...three weeks...and still nothing—nothing from Bobby or Tara and nothing from Adam's parents. Dad tried to call and speak to me, but when Mom stole the phone away from him, I hung up. I couldn't stand the thought of her, let alone the sound of her voice chastising me for a part of me I loved.

My fingers began to slam on the keyboard at the thought of Mom, and the vile things she said. In my mind, she suddenly became as bad as Vickie. I never thought of her like that before, but now it made sense to me. She was best friends with the woman, after all. I knew it was judgmental and immature, but I couldn't stop rerunning the words *most sluttish thing ever* in my mind.

"Whoa, there killer!" Tara's voice echoed through my office.

I shot back in my seat and turned. Even at work Tara managed to avoid me, not that I made an effort to speak to her, but there was leaning against my door frame. My jaw dropped and then I shut it, narrowing my eyes at her.

"Don't look so surprised," she said as she walked in the room, around my desk and took a seat.

I turned slowly, so I was facing her. "Hi."

"Hello to you, too," she replied, fluttering her eyelashes at me with a sarcastic grin on her face.

I took a deep breath and placed my hands on my lap. I wasn't in any mood to be civil with someone who apparently took sides.

"Yes?" I managed to say in a somewhat sweet voice.

"Come on, Riv. You're mad at me for something Bobby did?"

"You haven't talked to me in weeks, Tara! What was I supposed to think?" I said, keeping my eyes locked on hers.

Her shoulders caved as she began, "Listen, Bobby played dirty –"

"Dirty doesn't even cover it," I said as I clasped my shaking hands together in my lap. "I have *zero* relationship with my parents right now, and Adam doesn't either."

"Right, so we," she said, signaling a circle with her index finger; "should all make amends. It's almost Christmas after all."

"Yeah, okay," I said, but the mention of Christmas...Alone—with no family, only made my stomach feel sick and empty.

"When was the last time you went to one of Bobby's hockey games?"

"The last time he played hockey on a team," I fired back, defensive.

"You know what I meant, River."

"A long time, okay? But when was the last time Bobby went to see Adam play?"

"Adam play?"

"Apparently all through high school he and Bobby kept the fact he was in a rather popular metal band a secret from me. They've been playing every now and again."

"That makes sense...but they kept a secret from *you*?" she asked, momentarily sidetracked in her shock.

I nodded.

"Fine, how about this—you convince Adam to come to one of Bobby's hockey games, and I'll convince Bobby to go to one of the band's shows."

I narrowed my eyes at her. "Why are you doing this?"

Tara locked eyes on me. "I know how much you and Adam mean to Bobby—and you mean a lot to *me* too. This whole thing sucks, and it especially sucks that it's all because Bobby can't stand that you and Adam are perfect for each other," Tara paused, shaking her head before she continued; "You know what he hates the most? That you make Adam a better person, and that makes him a worse person. He's doing that to himself, though; he's making the decision to be an asshole."

I looked back up at her and shook my head. "I'm still trying to understand why you deal with it."

"Despite all this we *are* perfect for each other...*we're* happy together. He just needs to get over the fifteen-year war he's lost to Adam."

"I feel like we're just going in circles," I said with a small nod.

Tara's red lips tilted with her head. "Bobby can hold a grudge."

"That's for sure," I said as she stood.

She squeezed my shoulder as she walked past.

"I miss you," she said. "Tell me when the next show is, and I'll get Bobby there one way or another. Then you hold up your end of the bargain and drag Adam to a hockey game."

"It's next Friday at The Tavern at 8:00. The band is Fade Burn," I answered.

"We'll be there."

Chapter 45

Fade Burn was growing in popularity, so much so that venues now were paying the band to play instead of it being the other way around. I'd become somewhat of a groupie as I watched in quiet wonder as they took flat air and made it into a symphony of drums, bass, voice, and guitar. The band was even beginning to build a fan base, selling out shows at the local venues as more and more people began to notice them, and I was starting to see that Adam was becoming addicted to it.

I couldn't blame him; the surprise on the faces of new-comers and the awe in the eyes of diehard fans was hard to ignore. I also couldn't blame him for not pursuing it as a full-time career. After one show he was exhausted as if the energy from the crowd pulled directly through him.

Tonight was no different, and half-way through the set I knew he was getting tired. It was showing in his eyes, but not in his flawless voice. My heart was pounding with the beat, and I had a smile plastered on my face despite the nerves that were coursing through me as I wondered if Tara was going to keep up her end of the bargain. I didn't know how Adam was going to react to the situation, and I didn't know if he would be mad at me.

I saw the change in Adam's face immediately, and I knew Bobby had walked in. The band had just finished a song, and I watched as Adam adjusted his bass guitar strap—something I'd not seen him do all night. He called something to his band mates, and they nodded.

I didn't have time to wonder what they were talking about because I felt Bobby's hand on my shoulder, and my eyes drifted to the floor as he leaned down.

"My girlfriend is a tricky one, but I think you had something to do with this too?" he asked before he slid into the chair next to me.

Tara took the seat on the other side of me, and her hand found mine under the table. She squeezed, and I squeezed back, neither of us willing to let go.

"I'm still mad at you," I replied.

He leaned over and kissed my cheek. "I'm sorry, River. I was irrational. I was mad. I've never lost a sport, especially not to Adam."

"It wasn't about that," I said, finally turning to look into those blue eyes. They darkened with his mood and were a dark sapphire against the dimly lit room.

His jaw tightened, and he nodded.

"No, it wasn't," he said.

"Was it worth it?" I asked.

He shook his head. "Nothing could be worth losing you and Adam."

I swallowed and turned back to face the stage as Adam's

bass echoed through the room. The beat was familiar, and I knew the song he was about to sing. It was the same song he sang when he first kissed me.

When Adam's voice hit the air, and the words began to sink in, I heard Bobby let out a surprised breath. I looked over my shoulder at Tara, who was staring at Adam wide-eyed.

"Holy shit," she mouthed.

"Right?" I answered with a smile.

I glanced over my shoulder at Bobby to see his face averted. He no longer looked shocked as he stared down at his hands in his lap. His eyes paced as he listened, unblinking to the words of the song. I gave in then, seeing how much they upset him and put my hand over his.

His eyes slowly rose to mine, and he blinked quickly as if to keep tears away before saying, "I've been a shitty brother."

I shook my head, and his eyebrows rose.

"Yeah, I have."

I heaved a sigh and nodded. "I think it'd help if he knew you felt that way."

He swallowed and looked away from me. "You'll have to convince him to listen to me."

"I might be able to do that," I replied with another squeeze.

"If anyone could it'd be you." Bobby sighed as he looked back up to the stage as the song ended.

"If anyone could it'd be you," he repeated.

We were silent again as Adam and Fade Burn continued

their set. When the show was over, we went outside, away from the crowd, to wait for the band to pack up. It was cold, but it wasn't as bad as the feeling of bodies milling around us inside.

Finally, Bobby broke the silence. "Thank you," he said, looking down at his feet.

"For what?" I asked.

He looked away to Tara, and then out into the distance as she squeezed his arm.

"Tara, can you get me a water?" he finally asked.

Tara looked at us with pursed lips before taking a deep breath. "Just say it, Bobby. I'm sure it's nothing that's going to surprise me."

Bobby's eyes went back to me, and I could still see the indecision there. Whatever he was about to say would be hurtful to Tara.

"Every moment I spent jealous that you'd chosen him—God," his voice trailed off as he ran his hand through his hair; "I didn't even realize how talented he was...or how much I'd hurt him just by being me. Jealous for a few months seems pretty petty compared to the way he's felt since we were kids. I've always seen the way he looks at you...I've just tried to convince myself *I* was the one, but I'm not. I realize that now—there is someone else better for you... and he's my opposite in every single way."

I raised an eyebrow. "And there's someone better for you."

Bobby pulled me into his arms and kissed my head before holding me out at arm's length.

"I think you always knew that." He sighed before continuing, "You're both my best friends...I can't deny how happy you make one another. I'm a jealous son of a bitch, but only because I've always seen it, and I've been afraid to admit it to myself. I still don't like it but hell, I have no choice in the matter, so I better suck it up."

"I love you, Bobby—I mean it," I replied with a smile, and I knew for once with the returned glance he understood exactly what I meant whether or not he liked it.

He nodded but froze as he looked over my shoulder.

"Adam," Bobby called.

I looked over my shoulder to see Adam in the doorway holding his guitar case. His eyes were unmoving as he stared at the three of us, his movement frozen in shock, or anger, or both.

I stepped towards him, and his head jerked back.

"River," he growled, and a plume of mist came from his mouth as his hot breath hit the frigid December air.

I stopped and crossed my arms at him. "Don't give me that tone of voice Adam Beckerson."

His eyes narrowed on me, and he began to turn on his heel but not before I caught his elbow in my hand.

"Adam," I begged. "Please, this can't go on."

He turned to face me. "How can you forgive him for the pain he's caused?"

"He acted out of jealousy—"

"No," Adam cut me off; "he acted out of malice."

"He's never understood the way your parents treat you," I began.

"That might be true, but he sure as hell knows the way your parents treat *you*. He knew what he was saying when he said it, and he knew what it would do to your relationship with them," he finished.

"It wasn't about me."

"Really?"

"It was *over* me, but about *you*."

Adam's jaw tightened as his eyes searched mine. "I don't get why you want me to forgive him."

"Because he's the only family you really have— the only family that has ever treated you with love for who you are—the only family that would never try to change you."

"He's mocked me for who I am."

"And you've mocked him for who he is. Just hear him out—I think he understands now."

"Think?"

"Adam!"

"Fine," he said, his chin bobbing with a small nod. "I'm doing this for you, though."

I slid my hand into Adam's free one, and we headed towards Bobby and Tara.

"Adam..."Bobby began, but his voice trailed off with the look of venom Adam returned. He stopped, put his hand through his hair and then started again, "Look, man, I can't take back what I did."

"No, you can't."

"Or what it did, but I am sorry. I know I've been an ass, and I've never really understood your dynamic with Mom and Dad...but I kind of get it now."

"And why is that?" Adam crossed his arms.

Bobby flinched. "That song."

Adam's stone stare dropped. "What about it?"

"You meant it to hurt me."

The Beckerson boy's eyes met.

The contrast between them was so vast, brown eyes and a slim swimmer frame facing blue eyes and a hockey player mammoth of a build. Their personalities, though—that was what made them Beckersons'. They were passionate, obstinate, arrogant, yet loving, kind and amazing all at once.

"No," Adam said. "I only wanted you to understand."

Bobby stepped forward. "I do."

Adam shook his head. "I don't think you can."

His brother nodded with downcast eyes before he let them rise again. "Maybe I can't actually understand what you've felt, but I get it—and I'm sorry for it—for whatever pain I've caused you over the years. I love you, and I need you in my life..."

"Is that an apology?" Adam asked as he ran his tongue over his teeth.

"It's as damn close as you'll ever get to one," Bobby said, a smile spreading across his face.

Adam returned the smile, and Bobby pulled Adam into a hug.

"I love you, man," Bobby said.

"Damn, you really are a big ass teddy bear, huh?" Adam asked as he pulled away, but there was a tinge of bitterness in his voice. I knew he was still mad at him.

I nudged him.

"Yeah, yeah...I love you too, big whoop," Adam said with a roll of his eyes—because no matter what he did love his brother.

Tara narrowed her eyes at me. "No fair! You totally got the better end of the bargain."

"Eh," I replied with a shrug and a smile as I looked between the two of them. I wondered how much of their truce had to do with me, and how much had to do with real forgiveness. The words they spoke weren't false, but they were strained. I knew them both too well to be fooled.

"What's this about a deal?" Bobby asked.

"Tara and I agreed she'd get you here, and I'd get Adam to a hockey game," I said.

"I would never have gone to a hockey game," Adam said.

"I would never have come here if I'd known I was coming to a Fade Burn concert," Bobby replied, running his hands through his hair.

"How'd you do it?" I asked Tara.

She puffed her chest out. "I can be persuasive."

"She told me I was going to get nachos," Bobby said.

"You're still going to get nachos," Tara replied as she looked at the sky. "Thinks with his stomach."

"That's a change," Adam said, and his eyebrows rose in a suggestive way.

Bobby smirked and nodded at Adam. "No, that's you, man."

Adam's arm snaked around my waist, and he kissed my neck. "Maybe you're right."

"Stop it the two of you!" I laughed as I pushed Adam away playfully.

"On second thought," Adam said as his stomach growled. "I could go for some nachos, too."

"Alright, let's go," I said, smiling and looking between the two of them.

"Share a car?" Bobby asked.

"As long as you two don't get in a dog fight again," Tara reminded them. "I don't want to get another concussion."

"Agreed," Adam answered.

"Seconded," Bobby added.

"I'm glad we're all on the same page now," I said.

I watched Adam narrow his eyes at Bobby. His lips were set in a thin line that showed he wasn't ready to let go of his anger. He wrapped his free arm tightly around my waist and slipped a finger through a belt loop with a single nod at his brother.

Bobby's lips gathered, and he pushed them out with his tongue before shaking his head.

It wasn't done in Bobby's mind either.

Chapter 46

Tara convinced us to go to the new theater in town that offered a "home-like" setting to watch movies in. It had the comforts of home, like reclining chairs, but with Butler like services, including fancy alcoholic drinks. Bobby and Adam had been tolerating one another, but it seemed they had more to say to each other than they were letting on. I'd sat in the backseat of the car and watched as they silently eyed one another. I texted Tara to ask her again why she needed to work late and meet us there; it would've been a lot less awkward if she was there to distract Bobby. When we arrived, Tara still wasn't there, and I asked where the bathroom was. I didn't want to leave them alone, but by this point, I didn't have a choice.

As I cracked open the door to return to the boys, I heard Adam talking, and I stopped in my tracks.

"I just want to get something clear." Adam's voice was hushed and threatening as he continued, "I'm never going to be able to forgive you entirely for trying to destroy my relationship with River. I'm making amends for her and no other reason."

"Don't flatter yourself," Bobby's said, voice bitter. "I won't ever forgive you for what you did."

"And what is that?"

"You made it impossible for her to love me," he said.

"I had nothing to do with that," Adam replied.

"Doesn't matter, does it? It won't change where we are now."

"You can't blame me because she chose me over you."

"And you shouldn't blame me for trying to keep her to myself."

Adam didn't respond immediately, and I wondered if I should make my presence known—if another fight was about to start.

Finally, Adam spoke with a level voice that surprised me, "I don't blame you for trying to keep her to yourself. We both played that game. I blame you for trying to destroy our relationship after we were together—for telling her she was like every other girl. You know damned well that River could never be like *any* girl."

"Don't hurt her, Adam. I'll pick up the pieces quicker than you can realize you made a mistake," Bobby finished.

I stepped out of the bathroom before Adam could respond.

"What took you so long?" Adam asked. His face reddened as he looked at Bobby.

"I had to make sure my makeup looked okay. Did Tara get here yet?"

Bobby glanced down at his cell phone. "Crap, I didn't even realize she texted me."

I wanted to say something about their bickering, and smack Bobby for involving Tara, but I kept my mouth shut and smiled. "She's here?"

Bobby nodded. "She's already at our seats."

"Sounds good!" I replied. I was trying to be cheerful, but it bugged me to know they hadn't made amends. Bobby shot me a smile that made my stomach turn before lengthening his strides and moving to the front of us. I watched as he swept Tara into an unrestrained kiss. My teeth clenched as the guilt of how she was wrapped up in this mess washed over me. I wondered if Tara could get out of the sick game only Bobby was playing before he broke her heart.

I shook my head before glancing over at Adam. "You couldn't just leave it be?"

Adam cocked his head at me as he slipped his hand into mine. "What?"

I felt my face twitch as I fought the happiness his hand in mine brought. My voice was low as I answered, "I heard your conversation."

Adam paled. "You weren't supposed to."

My eyes widened as I stopped walking and dropped his hand replying, "No shit!"

"River, come on."

"No, he's your brother. Suck it up!"

Adam looked at me as he crossed his arms with lips pursed. "Have you forgiven him?"

"That's different," I replied, looking away from him and down at my nails.

"How?"

"He's not *my* brother."

Adam narrowed his eyes at me as his voice lowered. "You should understand where I'm coming from. You're doing this for me, and I'm doing this for you."

I sighed, rubbing my temples. "I do understand...I just don't know why you had to confront him about it."

"You're not going to confront him about being with Tara while he's still thinking about how he can pick up the pieces if I fuck up?"

"Are you going to fuck up?" I asked.

Adam's brow furrowed as he looked back at me with scrutinizing eyes. "No."

"Then I don't have anything to confront him about."

Adam's lips curled into a half smile, and his hands reached for my hips. "What if I fuck up?"

I let my arms rest on his shoulders. "I'll just have to punish you."

"Mhmm..." Adam leaned his head down to mine. "What if I don't?"

"Then I guess you're stuck with me forever."

His lips hovered over mine, eyes fixed on my own. "Forever it is."

Chapter 47

I realized Adam's accusation that I hadn't forgiven Bobby was correct; after all, I hadn't made an effort to make things like they used to be. I was only just tolerating him, and I knew the only way to make Adam forgive his brother was to do it myself. I made up my mind, and as I turned from locking the apartment door, I saw Bobby's hunkering frame closing his door.

"You!" I yelled from across the hall at Bobby's back.

He turned and threw his hands up. "What?"

"We need to go out," I said, walking up to him and pressing my finger into his chest.

"Why?"

"Because we haven't since you and Adam decided to be big boys and get over yourselves," I said as he looked down at my finger with a raised eyebrow.

He flicked my hand away. "Bossy Boss is back."

"That's right!" I replied. "So dinner?"

"I'm at your disposal, as always," he said as he moved the hair that had fallen in his face back with a gentle smile. He hadn't cut it in quite some time, but the way it fell now worked for him. It accentuated his eyes and chiseled jaw line.

"Adam has band rehearsal tonight, so I say we go to that new Italian place downtown?"

Bobby looked down at his watch. "You think there'll be any reservations left?"

I raised my eyebrows, pulling my lower lip into my mouth as I tried to keep from smiling. "Know those killer advertisements that made it, so everyone was talking about it?"

He chuckled as he slung his arm over my shoulders. "I can only guess who came up with those."

"That's right," I replied with a smile as we made our way downstairs.

"Did Adam leave for work early this morning?"

"Parent-teacher conferences," I said, and Bobby nodded.

"Dealing with parents is a giant pain in the ass!"

I nudged him the ribs. "See you and Adam do have something in common...besides me!"

"Ha ha," Bobby answered. "I get the parents that want to beat the crap out of each other...usually moms."

"Speaking of parents, how are yours doing?" I asked as we headed towards the cars.

"It's a bit rocky lately. They don't really understand what's going on with Adam, and you know Mom is bent on hating you."

"How is *that* any different than the last ten years that I've had boobs?" I said.

"True," Bobby smiled down at me as we reached his towering truck. "Hey, why don't I drive you in? Then I can pick you up, and we can go straight to dinner?"

"I'd like that," I said with a smile.

"You need me to help you in?" he teased.

"I can handle myself, thank you!"

"Sure you can," he laughed under his breath.

Once the truck roared to life and we were on the road Bobby glanced over at me with a more serious look. The natural happiness that sunk in from my informal greeting seemed to have drifted away.

"Have you forgiven me yet?" he asked.

I felt my jaw clench as I looked at him. In order to, I needed to confront him about everything.

"For what?" I asked, and the words were more severe than my tone. I was trying to be honest, not an asshole. "Trying to rip Adam and me apart? Or annihilating my relationship with my parents? Or using my best friend as a pawn in your sick game?"

Bobby's lips dipped into a deep frown, and his lips twitched. "All of the above?"

I inhaled slowly. "I'm working on it."

Bobby's eyes darted to mine and then back to the road. His hands tightened on the steering wheel as he replied, "That's not really reassuring."

"You were jealous. I forgive you for that...as for my parents; you don't control them. They could have tried to make amends, but they haven't," I answered, but couldn't contain the way my body tensed at the mention of them. I looked down at my hands as my chest tightened. Parents weren't supposed to be like this, but mine—*ours*— were.

Bobby reached over and squeezed my leg. "Please know I didn't mean for that to happen. It was an instinct, a cheap shot—I swear I didn't expect your parents to practically dis-own you. I mean, Jesus, it's a freaking tattoo."

"Dad has tried, but Mom won't have it." My voice cracked, and I had to take a deep breath.

"You miss them?" he asked.

"Yeah, Dad the most. I'd never admit that to Mom, but she's put this rift here...and I'm having a tough time getting over that. You're right, it's just a tattoo, and honestly, I love the thing."

"I know you do," Bobby smiled over at me. "It'd be super hot if it wasn't the same as Adam's."

I rolled my eyes. "It's not the same. Mine's purple!"

"Ha! Big difference," Bobby shot back.

"I missed this," I said as I looked over at him, my body warming as our eyes locked on one another.

"Me too. So that boyfriend of yours—is he treating you right?"

I laughed. "That boyfriend?"

"It's easier to refer to him that way...so this conversation seems like any other we'd be having."

"He's amazing, and I love him a lot."

I thought Bobby's face might crack, but the soft smile that appeared was real.

"I'm glad to hear that. How's living with him?"

"I figured out which one of you is the pig," I answered.

"Hey!"

"How do you know I was referring to you?" I asked in a teasing voice.

"Your apartment is still spotless as always," he answered.

"You caught me!"

"Oink, Oink," Bobby said before winking.

"How's living with Tara?"

Bobby's face twitched. "You noticed that?"

"Kind of hard to miss that she has her parking spot now, which brings us to that other point of concern. The part about her being a pawn," I said, and I looked over at him with the sternest face I could muster.

Bobby's chin rose with his chest. "I know it seems like she's just a pawn, but she's not."

"She sure as hell better not be."

Bobby nodded once, and I reached over and squeezed his monster bicep. "So how's living with her?"

"Living with a chick is a lot different than living with another dude, especially my brother."

"How's that?" I asked, genuinely curious. Adam hadn't said anything about living with me.

"She bitches when I leave stuff dirty, or don't do the dishes...or forget to shower because I've been watching hockey for six hours straight," he said.

"Must be rough!"

He sighed heavily. "You know it. Bitches be crazy."

"Hey! That's my best friend!"

Bobby scowled at me. "I thought I was your best friend, besides Adam that is."

"You all are, in different capacities," I answered leaning over and kissing his cheek. "Thanks for driving me."

He cupped my cheek, and my heartbeat picked up. I hoped he wasn't going to try anything, but I couldn't trust that he wouldn't.

"Thanks for letting me back in, Riv. Life wasn't the same without you...or Adam."

I held in the sigh of relief as my muscles relaxed. "See you at five?"

His hand dropped as he nodded. "My stomach is already looking forward to it. You calling for seats?"

"Already did a few days ago," I said as I slid out the door.

"Tricky, tricky," he answered as he shook his head at me.

I winked and shut the door. He honked as I walked away, and I showed him my middle finger before smiling back at him. I knew what that honk meant, and I didn't appreciate the compliment.

Chapter 48

Bobby and Tara's presence in my life again partially filled the gap that opened, but left empty was the part where my parents would be. That part of me ached hollowly. I wished I could be like Adam and ignore the feeling, but it wasn't something I was accustomed to. Adam grew up always knowing the evil of his parent's ways, always knowing he would never be enough—but me? I was always able to hide my imperfections from them. I was always on the same page as them—even if I didn't agree with them—or more likely, Mom. We never really saw eye to eye on the Beckerson boys. Maybe it was because Vickie was her best friend, and she didn't want her to explode about either one of her sons and me. I think Mom always silently favored Bobby, too. He was the golden boy after all. Adam was always more the rebel, despite a 4.0, he always had a guitar or some musical instrument in his hand. God only knew where that talent came from.

I glanced over at him as he drove up the abandoned parking garage. Boston just past midnight was amazing—the usually bustling city streets died until it was so quiet you could hear the buzz of the light poles. It was the perfect time to lose yourself in thought, and when we couldn't sleep we sped off into the night to enjoy the serene silence. Tonight was one of those nights, and we knew each other well enough that we hadn't spoken a word to one another. Adam slid out of bed and grabbed the keys from the dresser, looking over at me with the soft smile that made everything bad disappear.

He parked on the top level of the garage before leaning into the back seat and grabbing two large down blankets. It was unseasonably warm for December in New England at fifty-five degrees, but the down would make it feel like it was summer again.

I got out of the car as he laid the thick quilted one down and sat, pulling me into his arms and wrapping us in the other.

"What are you thinking about?" he asked, kissing my head.

I looked up at him. "Right now?"

He nodded.

"How happy I am with you."

"You didn't seem too happy in the car," Adam said as his eyes raced over my face.

I leaned my elbows on either side of his body and looked down at him. His hand slid up my arm to cup my face as his thumb traced my jaw.

"I'm happy now...this is perfect, even if it is a bit flawed," I said.

He leaned up on his forearms, so our faces were only inches apart.

"Are you trying to say I'm flawed?" he whispered as he cocked his head at me.

I smiled and let my fingers run over his scar and to his lips where he cupped his hands over mine and kissed them.

"Beautifully flawed," I replied as my heartbeat slowed.

His eyes continued to search mine as he leaned forward and let his lips grazed mine. "You torment me with your perfection," Adam whispered into my mouth.

"I'm not perfect," I replied as his mouth trailed down my neck, and he tilted my head.

"Every time I look at you I think to myself that I've found perfection," Adam said as he shifted his weight over me.

I looked up at him and smiled. "Now that's flawed perfection."

He shook his head and slid my shirt off my shoulder so he could kiss it.

"Never," was his reply as his hands moved to my hips and his thumb traced the skin of my belly.

My back arched at the pleasure of his soft caress, and I could feel him smile as his face buried in my neck. His arms slid around my back to hold me tightly against him as I sighed.

I let my hands slip under his shirt and pull it over his head before I buried my fingers in the muscles of his shoulders. His kisses burned, leaving a trail over my skin and down my chest. I could feel the goose bumps rise over his skin under my kisses.

"Are you cold?" I asked as I pulled the blanket that slipped down to his waist over our heads.

"Not at all," he answered as he pushed my arms over my head and let his fingers glide down them again as he lifted my shirt over my head.

"Are you cold?" he repeated into my ear as my skin had the same reaction to him.

I shook my head as his hands found my inner thigh, and my back arched again. My hands slid to his pajama bottoms, and I pulled them off as he hovered over me, my lips stroking his bulging arm muscles as he held his weight.

He lowered himself to me, and his mouth found mine, breathing life into me as he stole my breath away.

The hollow ache slowly dissipated as he held me to him—every moment with him slowly healed the pain.

"All I've ever wanted is you," he sighed, his breath hot in my ear.

"You'll always have me," I replied, breathless as his hands entwined in mine.

His answer was a soft moan into my hair as I wrapped my legs around his and pulled him tighter into me.

Chapter 49

I woke the next morning barely knowing how we'd gotten from the garage back to the apartment. I figured at some point I fell asleep in Adam's arms, and he carried me to the car and then up the stairs without waking me. I blinked my eyes against the bright sunlight that streamed through the curtains and let out a contented breath. I couldn't help the smile on my face as I heard the sound of Adam in the kitchen, along with Bobby and Tara's laughter as he told them something funny.

I rolled out of bed and was glad Adam closed the bedroom door because all I had on was the blanket we'd been wrapped in. I slipped on a pair of yoga pants and one of Adam's comfy sweatshirts before joining them.

Tara was the first one to turn, eyes narrowed with a smile. "You never sleep in—something must have tired you out!"

Adam chuckled softly in front of the stove, and Bobby gagged.

"Come on, seriously?" Bobby asked.

Adam looked over his shoulder at me with a wink, and

I couldn't help but giggle to myself. Bobby's upper lip twitched, and he shook his head.

"Don't act so innocent," Tara said, spinning to face Bobby and wrap her arms around his bulky shoulders.

Bobby raised his eyebrows and pulled her into his arms, kissing her brazenly in front of us.

I averted my eyes as I walked past them and kissed Adam's cheek.

"And I thought you were a freak," I teased him.

"Hey, you're the one that seduced me on a rooftop," he fired back so only I could hear.

"I'd do it again," I said as I bumped my hip against his, looking down at the French toast. "Especially if it means you make breakfast."

"We'll need to burn it off later," Adam said as he pointed the spatula at me with one eye closed.

"Mhmm," I said as I wrapped my arms around a cup of coffee, one eyebrow raised as I thought of what I could do to him. The sound of Bobby sucking off Tara's face stopped me mid-thought.

"Are you guys going to stop?" I asked over Adam's shoulder. "Or do you need to go back home? It is right across the way."

Bobby came up for air.

"Sorry, French toast makes me horny."

We all burst into a fit of laughter at the awkward comment.

"I'm not making it for Christmas then...and I was going to make Eggnog style toast," Adam said.

"Speaking of Christmas...what are we going to do?" Bobby asked before taking a big bite of his food.

Adam and I looked at each other.

"Neither of us has been invited anywhere," I replied.

Tara looked down at her food. "Why don't we just do something here? Then Bobby and I can do New Year's with the parents?"

"Mom will probably blow a gasket if you guys don't show for Christmas," Adam answered. "Plus, you can't change your plans when it's next week."

He handed me my plate with a sad smile as we leaned on the opposite side of the island from Tara and Bobby.

The room was silent for a moment before Bobby spoke, "Screw it! I'm not letting you spend Christmas alone."

"Don't worry about it," Adam said. "Riv and I have each other."

"No," Bobby pushed. "We're a family. We're spending it together."

"Good luck getting Mom and Dad here," Adam chuckled, but it was pained.

I watched as Bobby's lips curled downward and he shook his head. "No, I mean us four. *We're* a family. We got over our issues with each other because that's what family does."

I let a deep breath out and smiled. Adam locked eyes with his brother.

"Thanks," Adam said.

Bobby nodded before cramming another whole piece of gooey toast into his face.

"So..." Bobby continued through his mouthful, "Eggnog toast? Sounds fabulous."

Adam leaned over and whispered in my ear, "Hide the mistletoe, K, babe?"

I nodded as his lips grazed my earlobe.

Chapter 50

I sat on the couch staring at the boxes of ornaments and the scattered pieces of a Christmas tree, but I couldn't bring myself to do it. I sighed and stood, ramming into Adam, who was standing with his arms crossed at the edge of the couch.

"I know it sucks," he said, his hands clasping my upper arms as he looked down at me. His thin lips were partially open as if he had more to say, but didn't know how to put it into words. Adam's mouth closed and his lips twitched. "I'm kind of glad, though."

"Why is that?" I asked as his hands slipped up to my neck, and I placed my own on his wrists.

He took a deep breath and looked away before his eyes came back to mine. "It's just us...it's kind of nice, right?"

"Christmas is for family," I whispered as I tried to keep in the tears welling in my eyes.

"Oh, Riv...I'm sorry," he said as he pulled me into his arms. "I know you miss your dad."

"What about Mom?"

Adam pulled away slightly and looked down at me with his brow risen, crinkling his forehead. "Really?"

I heaved a sigh. "I was trying to be fair."

"You know your dad would be here, or at least have you there if your mom didn't wear the pants," Adam reminded me.

I nodded as I looked over my shoulder at the boxes.

"I knew Bobby couldn't get away from your parents to be with us," I said.

"What's that?" Bobby's voice boomed into the room as the door flung open.

"Bobby!" I yelled as I raced into his arms.

He picked me up and spun me around before setting me on the ground. His lips pursed in amusement as he said, "If you always greeted me like that you wouldn't be with the skinny-mini-me."

I narrowed my eyes at him. "You totally just ruined it."

He pulled me into a bear hug. "Did I? I don't think I did!"

I couldn't help but smile into his warm chest covered by a plum-colored cotton Henley.

I pulled away, crossing my arms as I looked up at him squinting. "Purple?"

Tara moved her head around his arm, appearing around his large mass.

"I've got him wrapped around my little finger," she said as she stepped around him and slapped his ass. "Right, honey buns?"

He looked down at her and raised and lowered his eyebrows quickly. "Mhmm...*honey*."

My chin tucked into my neck as I looked at them to

Adam, who was standing with his lip ring in his mouth as he chuckled at my disgusted expression.

"Grossness aside," I replied as I brought Tara into a hug. "I'm so happy to see you two!"

"I know it's kind of late, but can we still have eggnog toast?" Bobby asked as his stomach growled.

"Didn't you eat at Mom's?" Adam asked as he looked at our spent Chinese food containers in the trash.

"Yeah, but I saved room for dessert," he replied with a shrug.

"You didn't eat dessert?" I asked as Adam went to look in the fridge.

"I saved room for *more* dessert," Bobby said with a wink.

"What about you, Tara?" I asked.

She looked at me and burst into a huge smile. "Like I could eat like I normally do while I'm trying to impress his mother!"

"You up for them, Riv?" Adam asked as he held up the carton of eggnog.

"I'm always up for your cooking!" I said as I bounced over to help him.

"You hid the mistletoe, right?" Adam whispered into my ear as I grabbed a bowl from the cabinets.

I nodded as he wrapped his arms around me to place the ingredients on the counter. His chin tucked into my shoulder as I replied, "In the bed."

"You've been a naughty girl," Adam said as he nipped at my neck.

I turned to face him and wrapped my arms around him.

"I guess you'll just have to punish me later," I said as he pulled my hips to his.

"I thought eggnog toast was supposed to make *me* horny," Bobby called from the living room as he laid back on the couch with Tara cuddled in his arms.

"Yeah!" Tara added.

"Yes, but Adam cooking makes me horny!" I shot back.

"The imagery," Bobby said as he gagged. "Adam only in an apron..."

"Hell, yeah!" I called back.

"Just make the food, God-damn it!" Bobby said as he turned on *A Christmas Story*.

"Hey!" Adam's head shot back around. "You turn that off—that's for when we're putting up the tree!"

"Right, I totally forgot..." Bobby began as he changed it to the hockey on-demand channel I special ordered for him ages ago; "not."

"That's better," Adam said as he began to break eggs into the bowl.

"What can I do?" I asked as I hopped onto the counter next to him.

Adam looked up at me with one of those looks that took my breath away— all chocolate eyes with thin lips in a dangerous smile—happiness and love.

"Sit there and be my River," he answered.

I smiled back at him...*my* River. I would never get used to how perfect it sounded coming from him.

We ate at the couch, screaming at the hockey players on the television before Adam and Bobby did their victory dance when the Bruins won. It wasn't like they hadn't seen the game already, but it was always just as good the second time.

"Alright!" Bobby clapped his hands together. "Tree time?"

Adam flicked the channel to *A Christmas Story* and Tara, and I watched as Bobby and Adam struggled to figure out the pieces to the tree.

"I know Bobby is all hockey hands, but you think with Adam's musical genius they could figure out how to put a tree together," she said as we watched them argue over what limbs went where.

"Should we help them?" I asked.

She cocked her head. "It's so cute watching them sweat, though."

"True," I replied, glancing over at her as she raised her eyebrows up and down. I laughed to myself as I settled deeper into the couch.

"Are you guys having fun?" Adam called over his shoulder at me with a suspicious glance.

"Are you asking for help?" I shot back.

Adam narrowed his eyes at me before Bobby turned and full out pouted.

"P-P-Please?" Bobby said.

Tara shot up. "I can't say no to that face!"

I rolled my eyes as I stood with her. In a matter of minutes, the tree was fully up, and we began decorating it.

"Why didn't you help us earlier if you knew how it went

together?" Adam asked as I handed him another plastic icicle.

"Your puzzled expressions were just too cute to interrupt," I answered with a tilt of my head.

"Thanks," he said, drawing out the word.

"Anytime," I replied as I stepped back to take in our work.

"One last thing," Bobby said as he took the star out of the box. He reached up to the top and placed it there. I grinned—only he could reach up there without the assistance of a ladder.

"Now!" Bobby clapped his hands together. "It's time for presents!"

"Someone can't wait to spoil me!" Tara said as she plopped back down on the couch.

"Sit, River," Bobby said as he took two small packages out of the bag he came in the door with.

I sat down next to Tara, and he handed us our gifts before sitting down in the recliner diagonal from us.

We both pulled the wrapping paper off at the same time to reveal matching blue boxes with a silver swan etched on them. Tara and I glanced at each other quickly before we opened our boxes together. We each had a matching Swarovski encrusted angel wing necklace.

We looked up at Bobby, and he smiled at us both.

"Angel wings for my two angels," he said as his face flushed.

I could feel my throat thickening as I looked back down at the glistening wing. Bobby stood and took Tara's box. He took the necklace and placed it around her neck before taking mine and doing the same for me.

I looked up at Adam, who was sitting on the edge of the couch with a blank expression on his face. He was tolerating it, but I knew his mind was unsettled by the way his eyes flashed across the TV screen.

"That was so sweet!" Tara whispered into my ear, taking my hands in hers. "Ugh!"

I smirked as I stood and went to Adam. I put my hands on his shoulders, and he looked up at me. "You okay?" I asked.

He lowered his eyes, putting his hands on my arms. He nodded and looked back up, eyes settling on me. "I guess I can't be mad at him for doing something that's true."

"Thank you," I replied.

He nodded again. "You want your present? I'm not sure I can top that."

"Sure."

I turned and sat back down on the empty couch as Adam disappeared into our bedroom. Tara moved onto the recliner and curled up in Bobby's arms. I could feel my breathing quicken as I anticipated what Adam could be getting from our bedroom. I was so organized that I wasn't sure if he hid something I wouldn't have found it. When he came back out my breath caught in my throat.

He had his red guitar with him, the one with the chip out of the bottom of it because I dropped it on the floor when he was teaching me how to play. He placed his miniature amplifier on the floor beside him as he sat on the edge of the couch before strumming the guitar. My breath came out in a whoosh as I closed my eyes at the sound of his voice as he began to sing, his foot tapping to the beat with each strum. Each vibration settled into my chest causing it to tighten with happiness.

Take me to the River
The River where I'll find my heart
Let me peer into the water
Let me see my reflection in your eyes
And I'll know after all this time
You were always the one I was meant to find
Take me to the River
The River where I'll find my heart
I've always been lost
Now as I drift on the waves of your love
I've never been so sure
That I'm where I'm meant to be
Take me to the River
The River where I'll find my heart
Let me stare into the depths
Where I'll see your soul stare back into mine
Take me to the River
The River where I'll find my heart and soul
Take me to the River
And I'll finally be whole

I opened my eyes and let the breath I'd been holding out. Adam sat staring down at me with his jaw tight, and his hand rested over the guitar strings as he waited for my response.

"You just destroyed me, man," Bobby said as I continued to stare into Adam's glossy eyes.

I shook my head as I took another deep breath, trying to settle the pace of my heart that seemed to have sped up to the point where I was lightheaded.

"I...I don't even know what to say," I said as I pressed my hand against my chest.

Adam bit his lip. "In a good way?"

I stood and placed my forehead to his, closing my eyes as our noses touched.

"In a very good way," I said as the breath he'd been holding washed over me.

I held his face before kissing him and letting my lips hover over his.

"I love you, River—words will never be enough, so I thought if I sang them they'd sound better," he said.

I let one singular laugh out as I shook my head, opening my eyes to stare back into his.

How could I explain to him that his voice pulled me in whether he was singing or not—that waking up to the sound of his whisper in my ear made my heart stop? There were no words to voice the emotion he pulled from me with every touch, every glance, and every moment.

"Every day I wake up thinking I couldn't love anyone any more than I love you...and every night I go to bed knowing everything you do makes me love you more...as impossible as that is," I finally said.

"Even when I do something stupid?" Adam asked with a smirk that made me want to rip off the black plaid button-up he had on.

"Even when you do something stupid."

Adam glanced over my shoulder. "Too bad you two are here."

I followed his glance and saw Bobby's eyelids fluttering in annoyance.

"You're still getting some tonight, so shove it!" Bobby shot back. "Now, where are my presents at? And please don't serenade me."

Chapter 51

Sometimes moments in life are so perfect you want to freeze frame them; capture them within your soul forever, so they never fade away—they burn themselves into your being until they're a part of who you are. Waking up in Adam's arms was always one of those things, but another one was waking up to hear Bobby's snores in the next room over. I smiled to myself as I moved slowly out of the bed and opened our bedroom door to see Bobby hanging off the couch with Tara cuddled over him with a blanket that could only cover her. Bobby's face was nuzzled into Tara's curls, which as always, were frizzing out of her messy bun.

"They do make a cute couple," Adam said as he tucked his chin into my collarbone.

"Yeah, they do," I replied, leaning my head back into him. "This is nice."

"It's about to get even nicer," Adam said as he let go of me and went to the couch.

"Don't!" I hissed as he knelt down. "He'll kick you in the face!"

Adam looked over at me and winked.

"Something you don't know that I do..." he said as he began to tickle the ball of Bobby's foot.

"Mommy...no...I wanna sleep more," Bobby mumbled as his foot twitched.

I couldn't help but burst out laughing at Adam's self-satisfied grin.

"I wanna sleep," Bobby repeated as Adam tickled him once more. "Mommy...Cut the shit, Adam!"

Bobby shot up, jostling Tara, who whined in reaction, but somehow stayed asleep.

"What did you have to do that for?" Bobby asked.

Adam was rolling on the floor laughing, and I was tearing up because I was laughing so much.

"Mommy—" Adam mimicked; "I wanna sleep!"

"Shove it, cowlick!" Bobby shot back, using Adam's pet name from the hair issue he'd cleverly turned into his hair just being tousled.

"Not everyone can have flowing golden locks," Adam said as he finally calmed his laughing and stood.

Bobby rolled his eyes and flopped back down.

I came to the edge of the couch and peered down at him. "Explain the tickling?"

Bobby cracked one eye open and looked up at me. "Mom used to wake me up every morning by tickling my feet."

"Aww!" I said, reaching down and pinching his cheeks. "You're such a Momma's boy!"

"You still have a night light?" Bobby asked with narrow eyes.

"No," Adam called from the kitchen. "She's not afraid of the dark anymore. She has me to protect her!"

"Gag," Tara mumbled into Bobby's chest as she pulled her eyes open.

"You're telling me," Bobby said.

"Speaking of Mom, how did you get her to let you off early enough to come back home anyway?" Adam asked as he came back in the living room and pulled me onto the recliner with him.

"You're done cooking already?" Bobby frowned, avoiding the question.

"Cinnamon Buns. Now answer the question," he replied.

"Lied."

"You lied to *Mom?*" Adam repeated.

"Said we had to go to Tara's parents...when we'd already gone on Christmas Eve." Bobby turned his palms up, readjusting himself in the chair as Tara snuggled into his arms.

"Tricky!" I said as Adam pulled a blanket over us.

"Too bad you can't use that excuse for New Year's," Adam said.

Bobby frowned. "Yeah, I'll never get out of *that* unless I get disowned."

I felt Adam's hands turn into fists on my stomach at the last word; after all, that's what happened to us. Bobby's eyes darted across my face.

"Riv," he began, and I shook my head. He sighed and looked down at the rug beneath the coffee table.

"The cinnamon buns aren't the crappy ones in the tube,

either. Adam made them by hand yesterday and let them settle overnight." I changed the subject to something I knew we could all agree on—Adam's cooking.

"I'm going to need to work out every day for the rest of my life after this week," Bobby said, but his stomach gurgled, and he smirked.

"You already do, Babe," Tara reminded him.

"Not today," Bobby said with a yawn. "Your couch sucks, no offense."

"Gee, there wasn't a bed only twenty feet away custom made for your jolly green giant frame?" I asked.

Bobby looked down at Tara. "I didn't want to wake Tara."

Tara and I both looked at each other before giving Bobby an incredulous look.

"She could sleep through a hurricane!" I burst out.

"It's true," Tara agreed.

"I was loaded down with eggnog toast," Bobby found another excuse that only resulted in more eye rolls.

The truth was it didn't matter what made them stay. It was amazing to wake up to all the people I cared about most there—even if one was snoring loud enough to wake up the whole building.

Chapter 52

I sat at my desk fiddling with the contrast on the photograph I was looking at using a local designer who was all about the "vintage" look. I'd taken the pictures on a rooftop littered with old couches; beat up with holes in them and wine casks as tables. I even convinced Adam to come and figure out how to string up a chandelier on one of my spotlights. I didn't know how he managed to, but the picture was almost perfect without any altering.

"No, that's too much," Jesse said as he came in my office. "Go back a bit, increase the brightness...there!"

I smirked up at him. "I'm so glad you think I can do this by myself."

"You took the pic," he said with a wag of his finger. "And I like how you took most of the color out of the photograph and started to play with the contrast. I'm sure you would have come to the same conclusion I just did."

"Mhmm," I replied as he sat down and stuck his feet on my desk.

"My question is why the hell you're still here at," he looked down at his watch; "eight on New Year's Eve. You're young, shouldn't you be partying it up?"

"Adam had a school function...staff only," I replied, my chest tightening at the thought.

"That's stupid!" Jesse said as he leaned forward and tapped on my desk. "I always let you invite a plus one."

"It's a school...I guess they can't afford it. Plus, it's the faculty party. I think it'd be awkward."

"On New Year's Eve, though?"

I leaned back in my chair as I inhaled before answering, "It was that or do it on New Year's day, and who wants to do that?"

Jesse rolled his eyes as he stood and clapped his hands. "Look who it is!"

I turned to see Adam in a black suit with a black button-up and green tie that pulled the flecks of the same color from his eyes.

"Why are you all dressed up?" I asked, blinking at him.

"You really thought the school was having a faculty party on New Year's Eve?"

"I guess so," I answered, pressing my hand to my chest as I took a breath.

Adam pursed his lips, his brows furrowing at me as he shook his head. "Not at all."

"I look like a slob compared to you—where are we going?" I asked.

Jesse came around my desk and moved my office door just enough, so I could see the dress bag hanging there.

"I think there's something here for you to wear," Jesse said before sliding out the door, patting Adam on the shoulder on his way out.

I sat further back in my chair and gazed at him suspiciously. Jesse definitely knew what was going on, and I was at a loss.

Adam nodded over his shoulder. "Go on, take it and put it on."

I narrowed my eyes at him before standing and taking the bag to the bathroom across the hall. I closed the door and stood to look at the bag in my hand. What could be so important we both had to dress up? I lifted the plastic off the dress and stood back to look at it.

It was a rose gold three quarter's sleeve sheath dress covered in what appeared to Swarovski crystals. I undressed and slipped it over my head. The neckline plunged in the front almost as much as in the back, but it fit me like a glove. I took a deep breath as I looked at the dress before slipping into my sapphire blue heels that fit it perfectly by accident. I stuck my head out of the door to see Adam leaning against my doorframe facing me.

He stood up when he heard the door.

"You like it?" he asked, and his face flushed as though he was nervous.

I stepped completely out, and his jaw went slack.

"Tara has good taste," he said to himself as his eyes went up and down my body, then back up until his eyes met mine.

"So Tara picked it?" I asked.

"You think I could've?" he replied as he stepped forward, pulling me into his arms.

"You seem like a metrosexual," I said as I tried to catch my breath from the way he was looking at me.

He ignored my comment and pulled me tighter to him, leaning forward and kissing me. I let my hands run up the lapel of his suit to the back of his head.

"You're still at work!" Jesse hollered from his office.

I pulled away from Adam slowly. He had the devil in his eyes now as he looked at me as if he'd devour me.

"Let's go." Adam's arm slid around my waist, and he guided me to the door.

"Drive safe out there. It's looking like freezing rain," Jesse called as we walked by.

"You too," Adam said, but I was too enamored in trying to figure out what was going on to respond before we were out of hearing range.

"You're up to something," I finally said.

"What makes you think that?" Adam's voice conveyed his laughter, and I couldn't help but smile.

"Nothing, nothing at all. You normally pick me up in a suit and hand me a crystal encrusted dress that probably cost a week's salary."

Adam held the door open for me.

"It matched this," Adam replied, fingering the angel wing around my neck. "I figured you might as well look like the angel you are."

"You two are going to be the death of me," I said as his arm found its way around my waist again, but this time, he swung me up into his arms.

"I don't have a jacket to lay on the ground, so I might as well pick you up," Adam said as I gasped.

"The death of me," I repeated as he carried me to his car. He set me on the ground only after opening the door for me.

We drove in silence, me casting him suspicious glances and him looking happy in his guilt. We took it slow because the temperature had plummeted and freezing rain was coming down heavily, but Adam didn't seem to be in a rush. I wasn't either. We parked in the lot of a gallery just as my phone rang.

"Who is it?" Adam asked as I dug my phone out my purse.

I looked down at the number and shrugged. "I don't know. I've never seen it before...Hello?"

"River Ahlers?" the voice on the other end asked.

"Yes?"

"This is the Mass General Hospital. We're looking for an Adam Beckerson?"

"He's with me now—is everything okay?"

The person on the other end swallowed. "There's been an accident."

"An accident?" I whispered back as Adam's eyes raced over my face.

"Robert Beckerson—"

"Bobby?"

"He's in critical condition," the woman explained. "You and Adam are listed as his emergency contacts."

"Critical condition?"

"You need to come immediately," she continued.

"This can't be... he and Tara were supposed to be at the

Beckerson's house for New Year's," I gasped out the words as I struggled to breathe.

"They were both in an accident heading north on the Mass Pike from Framingham. We aren't sure of the cause yet, but we aren't sure how long he has," the woman said.

The phone slipped from my hand into my lap as my eyes widened with tears.

"How long he has?" I repeated as my breath clogged in my throat.

Adam grabbed the phone from my lap with shaky hands and asked, "Where is he?" His eyes darted at the space in front of us as she answered. "What floor?"

He placed the phone down and looked straight ahead as the tears began to stream down his cheeks. His chest began to rise rapidly as his nostrils flared.

"We should go," I said, my voice a whimper against the driving rain that undoubtedly caused the accident.

Adam's motions were slow as he placed the car softly into gear and began to back out of the parking lot.

All the happiness the week brought slowly came out of me with each creeping mile towards the hospital. We drove in silence in as an urgent a pace as we could in the weather. The rain slapped against the windows, but I was already blinded by the tears as the words played over and over in my mind, *we don't know how long he has.*

"We should call your parents?" I finally spoke as we took the exit from the highway.

Adam didn't answer. He kept looking straight ahead.

I took a deep breath as I dialed the number, tears still streaming down my face.

"Hello?" Alec's voice was strained at the other end as if he had been yelling.

"Alec, it's River."

"River?"

"Bobby's at Mass General with Tara. They're both in critical condition. We all need to get there as quick as possible," I said in as steady a voice as I could.

"What?"

"Mass General, Adam and I just got here."

I hung up the phone before he could respond.

Adam stuck the car in park and looked over at me.

"This can't be happening...not to Bobby." Adam's voice broke as the tears interrupted his speech.

I took a shaky breath, closing my eyes before our gazes met and we both burst out of the car, racing hand in hand into the hospital.

Chapter 53

I'd never seen the man that stood in front of me, but I knew that look. My skin crawled with it as he looked back at Adam and me. He opened his mouth to speak, and all I could see was the movement; all I could hear was white noise. I felt Adam's hand go slack in mine, and the world spiraled back at me. The force of the realization knocked the breath I had been holding out of my body. I struggled to breathe as the words pounded into my brain and shattered my soul.

"There's nothing we could do for him."

Him. Bobby. Gone.

My head jerked in slow motion as I heard Adam's knees hit the floor. The hospital droned, but all I could hear was Adam's sobbing at my feet with his fists pounding into the ground. I realized I was still staring at the doctor unblinking as my brain struggled to catch up—as I struggled to get air.

In my mind I was trembling, screaming Bobby's name, ripping at my hair. In my head, I lost it. In real life, I was standing doing nothing. Not even breathing.

The doctor's eyes trailed down to Adam and mine followed.

Realty jolted into me and everything suddenly was going too fast; adrenaline rushed through me as I pulled Adam into my arms—a broken shell—something I desperately wanted to be but couldn't. The noises bore down on me now, pulsating into my skull as I tried to grasp on to Adam as the beehive that was the hospital exploded in my brain.

"Tara?" I finally asked.

I looked at Adam in my arms to the doctor. He swallowed.

More bad news, but it wasn't *that* news.

"We aren't sure yet. She's comatose."

I nodded as I pulled Adam to the chairs where he continued to shudder. I closed my eyes as I tried to block out the noises around me. My senses burned with the imagined stench of death, the sound of sobbing and the buzzing of machines as the person on the other end struggled to live...or died. The worst part was the emptiness I felt growing within me; a black hole that fought to consume me, one that already devastated Adam.

Then I heard it—the running—a heaved breath as two sets of feet stopped in front of me.

"Oh. God. No," Vickie's voice hit an unbearable pitch.

"River!" she screamed in my face. "Where's my son?"

I pried open my eyes, and the look on my tear-stained face told her what happened.

"No!" she screeched as I tucked my head into Adam's shoulder against the sound. "*No!*"

Her wails softened against the fabric of a shirt, and I knew Alec pulled her into his arms.

So we crumbled. A broken family even further broken by the lack of the one thing that held it together. Bobby.

Adam's sobs finally softened, but I felt the silent tears still continuing to stain my shirt. His, or mine—I couldn't tell.

It didn't really matter.

Once Tara's parents arrived, I managed to pull Adam with me to go home. There was no point in standing around anymore. There wasn't anything we could do. Adam's parents had to handle the final things.

I realized walking up the stairs to our apartment was the worst part of it all. With each step, it felt as though a thousand pounds of bricks was piled, slowly, agonizingly, on my chest until I reached the top.

Adam and I stood and stared at Bobby's apartment for a period that didn't seem it would end. We were glued to the spot, and I wondered if he were praying somehow Bobby would open the door and beg me to make dinner. I was praying for it, but there was no movement.

I finally dragged Adam into our apartment where he collapsed on the couch. His impeccable black suit was wrinkled now, and his tie was barely hanging on because he'd loosened it so much.

"You should change," I said, and my voice sounded strange against the silence that came over us in the car. The words seemed to echo, and Adam sat up.

"You should too," he replied as he rubbed his face but didn't look at me.

I nodded and went into the bedroom. I closed the door

behind me and pressed the back of my head against the wood, wishing I could mold into it. I took a deep breath before looking down at the gorgeous dress I was wearing, and for the first time that night—morning now—I remembered Adam planned something special enough to wear this dress.

I turned to face the mirror, taking in my pale face framed by dripping mascara lines. In something so beautiful I looked like the hell my life had suddenly become. I fought the urge to rip the thing to shreds and instead slowly released the zipper on the side and slipped out of it.

I turned away from the mirror and grabbed yoga pants and one of Adam's old band tees before cracking the door open. I watched as Adam slipped a box back into his pants before standing and kicking the air.

What was that?

The thought disappeared as Adam's red eyes met mine. My chest hollowed as I said, "You'll be more comfortable if you change."

Adam turned and nodded before slipping past me. I went to wash my face, and when I came back into the living room Adam was sitting on the couch, leaning his forearms against his knees as he stared at his cell phone on the coffee table. His arms and back muscles were visibly tensed in his shirtless state.

I sat down beside him and ran my fingers over his bare skin as I tried to make him relax, but instead, he flinched. His muscles stayed tense, and his eyes remained fixated on the cell phone. I pulled away, curling my legs into my chest and tucking my head on top of my knees as I tried to comprehend why he reacted that way to my touch. Every part of me ached from my heart and soul to my physical limbs. My head felt as though it might explode in the stillness that ensued because inside my skull the words kept screaming:

Gone. *Gone.* GONE. *GONE.*

Yet I couldn't produce a sound or a comforting touch. Instead, I sat there for hours, nothing changing. I silently begged the cell phone to ring and tell us the doctor lied—that there was no reason for the war that was raging in my head as I tried to find a reason for why this happened to us. To Bobby.

Adam's head sunk into his hands, and I blinked my eyes to clear the dryness that set in. His body shuddered, and I leaned forward by instinct, but I didn't touch him, afraid my touch may irritate him more.

"You'll never forgive me," he said, his voice flat as it echoed. The sound sent a shock to my system after such a long period of absolute silence.

He looked over his shoulder at me, his hands still cupping his head, and his lips pursed painfully tight as his eyes searched mine.

I shook my head, but my voice didn't seem to work. His hand sent the cell phone grating against the wood top as it slid towards me.

I grabbed it before it could hit the ground and the screen responded to my touch. There—on the screen was the answer for Adam's empty stare.

BOBBY- *You were right. Our parents are assholes. I won't let them do this to you anymore. You're the family that matters to me. Coming home. See you soon.*

I swallowed as my throat thickened at the words. My eyes raced over them again and again as I tried to comprehend the meaning. I looked up at Adam, and his eyes were fixed on me, just like they had been on the cell phone.

"It's not your fault, Adam," I finally whispered.

"They fought over me. He got in that car pissed and determined to get home to us and now...now...he's dead."

"It's *not* your fault, Adam."

The vacant look in his eyes let me know he wasn't listening anymore. He stood and went into the bedroom, his movements robotic as he grabbed his guitar off the wall. He flicked the amp on and began to play a slow wailing song I'd never heard.

All the pain in the world seemed to be drawn into our bedroom as he stood there by the window with his head pressed to the freezing pane. Each staggered breath sent a mist across the glass and as the tendrils began to retract his hand rose to glide harshly against the strings of his guitar.

His shoulders curled, and his hand gripped the neck of the guitar so hard his knuckles turned white. I knew what was going to happen.

I ran into the room to grab the guitar just as he turned to slam it into the ground.

His eyes locked on mine as we stood hovering with our knees crouched, the guitar inches from meeting its fate. I watched as his breath began to come rapidly before he let the guitar slip into my hands, and he hit his knees. I set the guitar on the ground before pulling him into my arms.

So we break.

Faded Perfection (Beautifully Flawed, #2)

48 HOURS LATER

I sat there with Adam's head in my lap, running my fingers through his hair until the tears stopped, and his breathing slowed. He was asleep, and I didn't know how to feel anymore. He flinched at my touch when he thought I'd blame him, but now it seemed to be the only thing holding him together...semi-together. He still blamed himself, and I didn't know how to fix it. I'd always been able to help Adam, and now I didn't know how to because I was just as broken. Sighing, I moved his head onto a pillow and stood to go to the door. Once outside the apartment I sunk to the floor with my back against the wood separating myself and Adam.

I was so close to losing everything I loved. Bobby was dead; Tara was lingering on the edge of darkness, and Adam...I didn't know what would happen to him. His grief was overpowering. It felt like all the air has been sucked out of the earth, and I was suffocating from it while drowning in my ocean of pain.

I struggled to feel as my eyes bore into the faded wood door across from me. I might never see two of my best friends walk through that door again. I'd certainly never see Bobby walk through it again. Finally, I bowed my head to my knees and sobbed. There was no one there to comfort me, but I wasn't sure that was what I needed. Adam needed me to be strong, so I would be—at least when he was watching.

My phone vibrating in my pocket pulled me out of my sadness. The number I feared wasn't on the screen; the number I wished I had never seen.

"Hello?" I answered.

"Duckie?" Dad's voice was a shock to my system, and I had to take a deep breath.

"Daddy...Daddy," my voice cracked as a fresh set of tears streamed down my face. "Bobby—"

"I know—don't say it."

"What do I do?" I asked through hiccups. "I don't know what to do."

"Where's Adam?"

"Asleep."

"You need me, Duckie?"

"Yes," I replied, my voice as weak as I felt. "But Mom will kill you."

"Nothing is worth your pain—especially not a stupid tattoo. How's Adam handling things?"

"He's screwed up," I replied. I thought back to the hospital. He hadn't said a word, not one. He handed me the keys to the GLI and curled up on the back seat. Then when we got home he stared at his cell phone until he admitted his guilt—that he thought the whole thing was his fault.

"We all are. None of us saw this coming...none of us could imagine..."

"I don't know if I can fix him...it's like he's not even there. He sobs, but doesn't speak—he holds me, but only to hang on."

"I know this won't make things better, but it's only been a few days—eventually everything will settle."

My head dipped back against the door, and I closed my eyes. "I don't think you're right."

I heard his car start. "I'll be there as soon as traffic allows. I love you, Duckie."

"I love you, too."

I hung up the phone and stared at Bobby's door again before standing and going to it. I placed my hand on the knob and pressed my face against the wood. Bobby's hands touched these surfaces. It was the only thing left, pieces of him, scattered memories. Our childhood. Twenty years of happiness and he molded himself into a part of who I was. Now I was torn in two. I needed to stay strong for Adam, but I wanted to crawl in the same hole Bobby would be buried in. The overwhelming pain of loving Bobby washed over me again, and every touch remembered sliced a part of me away. Each laugh that echoed through my skull was a memory of intense happiness suddenly overruled by intense pain.

"River?" a groggy Adam asked from behind me.

I looked over my shoulder to see him standing in the

doorway with his eyes wet, but the tears had stopped. I wondered if it was because there were none left.

"Hey," I replied as I let go of the knob.

"I heard you talking?"

I held my cell phone up. "It was Dad."

"Your dad?"

I nodded.

"He heard?"

"He's coming," I said.

"Now?"

I nodded.

"We need one good parent here," Adam said as he stepped forward and closed the gap between us.

He pulled me into his arms and buried his face in my hair, muffling his words. "I don't think I'll ever be the same again."

It was the one thing that pained me as much as the loss of Bobby—what if Adam couldn't ever be Adam again?

What if I could never be River again?

Ready for more? You can buy Faded Perfection from
any of these retailers:
Amazon – Kobo

Acknowledgements

I don't ever know where to start. I guess I should start with where it started—thank you Mom and Dad for supporting my writing since I was a toddler with an imagination and a stubbornness that's never left. Then there's that musician who stole my heart and healed my soul—Jeff, you'll always be my Adam (and my favorite cover model!). Of course, I can't forget those that helped this book become what it is. Special thanks go to my editor, Faith, who is always there to bounce ideas off. You're seriously awesome! In addition, I'd like to thank the bloggers and readers who have helped spread the word and continue to support my passion/addiction for writing.

About the Author

Cassandra doesn't remember a time when she wasn't writing. In fact, the first time she was published was when she was seven years old and won a contest to be published in an American Girl Doll novel. Since then Cassandra has written more novels than she can count and put just as many in the circular bin. Her personal goal with her writing is to show the reader the character's stories through their dialogue and actions instead of just telling the reader what is happening. She writes various genres but is most well known for her New Adult novels in various sub-genres including contemporary romance, and speculative fiction. In addition to being a published author, Cassandra is a full-time successful financial marketer and part-time photographer. When she's not making the characters in her head come to life she either has her bow and arrows or long board skateboard in hand. She's happily married to the man of her dreams and they live in the rolling hills of New England with their dogs, Bubski and Kanga. You can find her on twitter @cgiovanniauthor, Facebook/cassiegiovanni and Goodreads. Check out her website for more information about upcoming books www.cgiovanniauthor.com.

Other Novels by the Author

Adult

Love Exactly – Contemporary Romance

Finding the Cure – Contemporary Romance

In Between Seasons – Post-Apocalyptic Romance

Young Adult

Walking in the Shadows – Romantic Suspense

Children's

The Adventures of Skippy Von Flippy

Mystic Mayhem (Finding Freckles, #1)

Bermuda Bounce (Finding Freckles, #2)

COMING SOON

City on Fire – Adult Fantasy

Faded Perfection (Beautifully Flawed, #2) – Adult Contemporary Romance